Love
Dad and Mom

Dec 2017

# A White Stone

*A*

*prophetic novel*

*that addresses heart preparation*

*and  godly solutions*

*that allow*

*Jesus Christ to live His passionate life*

*through you as the only proper response*

*to His life, death, and resurrection*

By

## Jim and Merry Corbett

Published by
Covenant Support Network

# Acknowledgments

To our Lord and Savior Jesus Christ; we are forever grateful.

To Mom and Dad, who never give up

To Jenny and Jubilee, our daughters, who always love and also lived
through the "what ifs"

To Marianne S., Mack and Debbie K., Ron P. and all of the other
spiritual and financial participants, for their belief in this project and
their willingness to follow through
Thank you for your friendship through extreme times.

To Dr. Kathy B., Marti F., Cia M., and Paula R. for wisdom,
counsel, encouragement, patience, and kindness through all of the
writes, rewrites, and more rewrites.

To all of the readers of the first printings of this book
May you understand the need to revise this book so that it is
pertinent to the times in which we live.

To you, the reader, may you have mercy as you read this.
May this effort draw you closer to Jesus Christ
and His desires for your life.

## AUTHOR'S NOTE

The Bible refers to a time and season that will usher in the final days of life as we know it. It states that there will be wars, rumors of wars, and great upheaval in all nations as a purifying of the church, and as a call to many who do not know God or do not believe that He is an integral part of everything that happens, and that what is evident in our daily lives corresponds to what is happening in the unseen world of the heavenlies.

The book, <u>A White Stone</u>, has been written to display the transformation that must take place in the church so that she might become a true representation of how God wants everyday people to live as passionately as Christ did in a world looking for honest answers to life's questions. It demonstrates the power of God at work when He has surrendered vessels for His use, and the true freedom an individual can have when he or she has entered into the peace of living under the absolute Lordship of Jesus Christ, which results in the ability to live above the entanglements of surrounding circumstances. It is a fictional account of probable coming events, divided into sections that flow into one another with no definitive time boundaries.

The characters are a composite of people Merry and I have known and some others that we would like to know. Their lives are intended to relay to the reader that the Spirit, the power, and the quality of the life that Jesus lived as our example are available to each of us as we surrender fully to Him. In a time when fanatics with dead hearts claim that they are representing God in their murderous actions, God is raising up a standard of integrity and love that overcomes any despicable action - disarming an enemy and presenting the Lord's real life of love through His people to nullify the grim death of hate.

Since its debut in 1997, A White Stone has been greatly revised in this fifth printing to better address the issues arising in our rapidly changing world as Christ would. In our own nation, we have gone from functioning as a carefree society not very familiar with the need to exercise caution as we travel, work, and play to a people who must ponder and prepare for drastic life changes as part of our daily routine. Suddenly, we realize that we live in a world in which peril will most likely invade our lives at any unpredictable moment and we have no clue as to how to deal with it in a Christ-like manner.

Merry and I realize that these circumstances do not necessarily mean that we are living in Biblical end times. During many seasons in history, people have felt that they were living near the end; and in looking for the immediate return of Jesus, produced confusion and regrettable actions because of their misguided zeal. There is a need to be careful.

In these days, however, it does appear as if the Lord is exponentially accelerating the pace at which predicted events are coming to pass. So we must take note.

During these very important and very perilous times, we are convinced that our Father in heaven is bringing us to Himself by making us aware of our need of Him. We believe He is challenging each one of us to allow Him to make us His holy people and sense that He is willing to impart Himself, His peace, and His kind of freedom from fear to anyone who desires it.

Although A White Stone does take the reader into an end-time scenario, I am convinced that our Lord would have each of us live the kind of life portrayed in this story on a daily basis, so that we might truly prosper through perilous times. Living passionately for Jesus and for the best interests of others is our directive as followers of Christ, no matter where we are in the times and seasons of the Biblical calendar.

Jim Corbett

Printed in the United States of America

ISBN: 0-9772313-0-5

For information, write:
Jim Corbett
Web site: www.awhitestone.com
e-mail: jim@awhitestone.com

Original printing 1997
Second printing with revisions July 1999
Third printing January 2000
Fourth printing with revisions October 2001
Fifth printing with revisions June 2004
Sixth printing with revisions August 2005

## Remember Your Friends

People who read <u>A White Stone</u> find the Holy Spirit naming their friends who need to read <u>A White Stone</u> also. For your convenience, we have provided spaces below for you to list specific people He may bring to your mind as you read.

Write down the names when they are fresh on your heart, so that you don't forget someone whose life might be changed because you are obedient to the Lord.

1) ...............................................................
2) ...............................................................
3) ...............................................................
4) ...............................................................
5) ...............................................................
6) ...............................................................
7) ...............................................................
8) ...............................................................
9) ...............................................................
10) ..............................................................
11) ..............................................................
12) ..............................................................

# "A White Stone"

by

Jim and Merry Corbett

Revelation 2:17 (amp.) "He who is able to hear, let him listen to and heed what the Spirit says to the assemblies (churches). To him who overcomes (conquers), I will give to eat of the manna that is hidden, and I will give him <u>a white stone</u> with a new name engraved on the stone, which no one knows or understands except he who receives it."

*From Our Father's Heart*

How many people have seen My Son in your life?
How many have chosen to serve Me through My Son
because they have seen Him in you?
How many have turned from their ways to My
ways because of your ways?
Does your neighbor know that you are My
tabernacle?
Does your enemy know that you are told to lay
your life down for him and have agreed to do so?
Do you know that I love the abortionist, the
pornographer, the homosexual?
Do you know that I have sent you to them that
they might see My Son through you, so that they might
accept Him?
Do you have the eternity of your every contact in
mind when you address them?
If not, why not?

# CHAPTER ONE

*"...Go out into the highways and hedges and urge and constrain [them] to yield and come in, so that my house may be filled." Luke 14:23 (amp.)*

*"Behold, I am sending you out like sheep in the midst of wolves; be wary and wise as serpents, and be innocent (harmless, guileless, and without falsity) as doves. ...do not be anxious about how or what you are to speak; for what you are to say will be given you in that very hour and moment." Matthew 10:16,19 Amp*

"O.K., God, what in the world am I doing in a neighborhood like this?" Tom Bracken silently asked as he walked along the neglected, decaying sidewalk, trying to remain in the lighted areas of his surroundings. "I must have been nuts to come here all by myself."

Tom had been told by his boss to determine the amount of damage that had been inflicted on the hospital, which was given to the firm "to do with as they pleased." No one wanted it because it was located in an extremely dangerous neighborhood and because the building appeared far too antiquated to renovate although it had been in moderate use until a recent bombing blew out the front door and some of the windows.

Now that he saw the damage and overall condition of the building, he made up his mind to hand this job over to Jimmy, his apprentice, as soon as he got back to the office. The moment he stepped in the door he knew he wanted no part of this project. In fact, he couldn't understand why his boss would even consider it in the first place.

Almost fleeing the building, Tom traveled at a fast pace, as his assessment of the neighborhood barraged his thoughts. The pace and his constant vigilance sent him tripping over a small chunk of concrete, which had separated itself from the overused and abused sidewalk. A nearby, rusty lamppost stopped his fall as he lunged and held it tightly until he could regain his footing.

"Boy, I'm sure glad I don't live anywhere near this place."

As he leaned against the post, he raised his leg across his knee to look at the scuff inflicted by the concrete. Wetting his finger and rubbing the damage to his shoe, he mumbled, wishing the posted signs had allowed him to park closer. Traffic had been minimized in the area of the hospital since several bombings had taken place in a short period of time.

"Once I'm out of here, I'm gone for good," he vowed in his heart as he zeroed in on the location of his car and hurried toward it.

Tom's vehicle was now only four blocks away in a well-lit parking lot. He minimized his fear of being alone on the city streets in this kind of neighborhood as each step he took brought him closer to his destination – his getaway car. Once he made it around the corner, he would be able to see the lot. That thought made him feel a little better.

Unfortunately, the darkened block right in front of him caused him to imagine that unthinkable peril lurked behind every bush, down every stairwell and in every yard, especially those that imprisoned vicious-sounding dogs that ran aggressively to the chain link fence as he passed by. He found himself walking cautiously on the road near the curb just in case one of the fences broke loose as an agitated dog bounded against it, protecting its worthless domain.

Forcing himself to concentrate on the neighborhood architecture – what else would an architect do in this situation?- he avoided escalating his state of mind from fear to panic. Tom marveled as he walked past houses long past their prime. They seemed like silent tombs staring at the dirtied street. Numb from years of neglect, their outward appearance seemed to indicate the dying inside of them.

Totally unfamiliar with this kind of neighborhood, and unaware of any potential for happiness or life of any kind behind the dingy, brown-stained shades, Tom was confused about his feelings. On the one hand, he hated what poverty had done to the people who were living there. Righteous indignation rose up within him. How could this happen? On the other hand, a compassion stronger than he had ever felt began to stir in his heart. Imagine the children, the broken, the hurting, who must live behind the peeled paint of every front door and eventually become a counterpart to the decaying exterior of every residence.

"Did year after year of bad decisions or bad luck, or just plain bad everything bring the residents of the dilapidated structures to this point?" he questioned. "Was there ever a time when someone was able to leave this kind of life?"

Tom felt a different kind of sadness, one that embodied hopelessness and helplessness at the same time. "This must be how some of these people feel all of the time."

Then he noticed the little American flags in almost all of the windows, symbolizing the owners' love for their country and the freedoms that they possess. Somehow those tiny flags transformed impersonal dwellings into homes with people very much alive in them; thinking, feeling people with dreams and hopes just like he had.

"How different can we be?" Tom thought. "Maybe some day I should take the time to really get to know someone who lives like this. Maybe..." Reason put an end to those thoughts.    Tom knew that a lot more than distance separated him from anyone who lived in this neighborhood.

Passing a hedgerow of dried lilac bushes, Tom was startled as a young boy of eight or nine years of age ran into him while pursuing a basketball down the nearby driveway.  In reflex action, Tom caught the ragged object and automatically flipped it back to its owner.

"Nice ball," was all he could muster as the boy and his playing partner instantly overcame their surprise at his intrusion into their lives and spat foul words of disdain in his direction.

"What you doin' here, rich man?" they tried to intimidate Tom as he walked a little faster past them toward his mobile refuge.  Much to his relief, the presence of two men sitting on a bench at the end of the block stopped the two boys from following him.  Their helpless fish was off the hook and by the looks of his clothes, a well-to-do one at that.

As Tom neared the bench sitters, something rose up within his heart that took his mind off his fear.  Both men were disabled.  One had a leg missing and the other had lost his right arm and shoulder.  His face was visibly disfigured, too. Assuming that they had been hurt in some of the past terrorist activities or possibly in Vietnam, his heart of compassion reached out to them.  He wanted to do something to help them.

"Maybe I could tell them about the love of Jesus."  The thought took him by surprise - even though he did have his little pocket Bible with him, having gotten into the habit of carrying it around ever since he became youth minister at his church.  It was really more for show, a way of making a statement to the kids more than anything.  He hadn't opened it for quite some time.  In fact, he couldn't remember where it was in his briefcase.

" I'm sure these guys have no desire to hear about Jesus or anything else from someone like me," he rationalized.

Anyway, it had been quite some time since he last told anyone about Jesus. He slowed his pace long enough to deliver a simple, wordless acknowledgment and half-hearted smile, and then continued quickly on his way.

Tom didn't want to wait for the light to change at the intersection, but there was enough traffic to cause him to stop, stand and pray like crazy. With his back to the two men, he could hear their jibes and laughter at his expense as a seeming eternity of seconds passed. Just as he was about to step off the curb, one of the men stopped laughing long enough to address him.

"Hey, stranger," the man called to him. Tom turned around. "What you doin' in this neighborhood?" he said with a knowing grin. "You a little outta place, ain't you?" he continued, giving his buddy a little elbow jab to show he was about to have some fun with the "outsider." "But them are some pretty nice shoes," he said, looking at Tom's shiny, maroon-colored penny loafers.

Tom looked down for a moment at his very out-of-place shoes and then at the one-legged man.

"I could use that right shoe," the legless man teased as he leaned forward on the bench. The man put his hand to his chin and furrowed his brow as if making a decision on whether or not he should buy the shoe. The comment made both men laugh uproariously. One of them laughed so aggressively that he began to choke, which loosed some phlegm from his throat and sent it flying right next to Tom's foot.

"You must have some kinda story to tell us po' city folk," the second man spoke, becoming suddenly solemn, "so get on with it."

Tom, startled at the seemingly open invitation and an opportunity to follow through on his thoughts of a little while ago, began telling them that he had just finished an inspection of the hospital down the street and then somehow found

19

himself flowing into a presentation of the gospel as the two men sat stupified by the stark transition. For a time, they seemed mesmerized and simply stared and listened. As near as Tom could determine, they appeared to be held silent, almost captive, by some unknown force. Then as if released from unseen restraints, both men became visibly agitated, almost angry.

"Look, we got no need for God or Jesus, or any of that religious stuff."

"We got everything we need right here," the legless man reaffirmed. "Unless you give me your right shoe," he continued, looking into Tom's eyes with a dead serious intensity.

"Yeah, or unless you got some extra money in them fine pockets," the other man said.

Tom knew that it was time to go. These guys were interested in only one thing from him and it wasn't Jesus. He knew that if he stayed any longer they would find a way to get it, even in their impaired physical condition. He turned and walked across the road without saying anything. If he hadn't been frightened out of his wits by the blaring horn that erupted from the car that he had stepped in front of in his haste to get away, he would have been privy to some foul cursings from the two hapless men. When he did reach the other side of the road, he momentarily turned back in time to receive a physical, one-fingered statement of their displeasure.

Actually, Tom was somewhat relieved that the men cut his story short. He still had several blocks to go and the early evening light gave way to an eerie, darkened atmosphere. He couldn't wait to get inside his car. It was getting late now and growing frightfully darker by the minute. Shadows turned threatening and the somewhat unfamiliar became totally foreign.

Tom began to walk even faster after glancing at his Rolex. Fear rose up in him. He had to consciously repress it or it would easily turn to panic as he heard his own footsteps echoing on the pavement. Almost at jogging speed, Tom turned the corner to Beecher Street when something caught his eye.

"Nice rags, man!" Tom heard from one of the darker doorways.

Tom stopped so fast he almost fell as his leather-soled shoes slipped against the concrete pavement. His eyes, wide with fear, focused on the figure emerging from the shadows.

"Yeah! Hey, look at the Bible Man!" came a second voice from the side of the building, referring to the small Bible that Tom had taken from his briefcase during his conversation with the two men on the bench. Now how he wished he were still a few blocks away, even with them.

The men had been watching Tom for some time, waiting for the right moment to approach him. In fact, they had targeted him the minute they saw his car pull into the parking lot earlier that day. They had considered making their move when he was on his way into the hospital, but decided that it would be easier and safer to do it later - the later the better. All afternoon they plotted their strategy, even practicing their attack while waiting for him to emerge from the hospital's makeshift yet secured front door. In catlike fashion, the three tracked him all the way back from the hospital, just waiting for the perfect time to act.

Tom spun in reaction to the second voice, then turned back in the direction he had been heading. For an instant, he thought of running toward his car, which was now only two, but seemingly fifty-two blocks away.

"You a preacher man?" came a third voice that belonged to a steely-eyed person who moved in front of him, blocking his only escape. "Preacher Man, you shouldn't be walking all alone in this part of town," he continued.

"Yeah," the first voice said as he moved directly to Tom's right. "Someone might see those fine clothes and think you might have a lot of money or somethin'," he continued.

"Do you have a lot of money, Preacher Man?" the third man said as he pulled something from his pocket. Tom heard a definite click. The light from the lone street lamp danced off the shiny metal switchblade knife and as it did, Tom's heart sank. He could actually feel the blood drain from his face and he knew there was way more to this than money.

As each man became more visible, it struck Tom that even though their faces and clothes were different, they all looked the same. Their baseball caps were all cocked at precisely the same angle; and their eyes, facial expressions and movements all gave the situation the feel and appearance of a well-rehearsed play. It was as though "tough" had been practiced and the next choreographed move could almost be anticipated. It seemed to him that the young men were actually reveling in making him afraid. He sensed that they aimed to draw out this event, giving them more time to instill fear into their prey. They were definitely experts.

Consequently, a sense of fear, anxiety, dread and helplessness greater than Tom had ever felt before swept over him. Unfortunately, an involuntary, nervous smile formed on Tom's face. This only aggravated his captors. His initial assailant gave him a slap across the face in violent reaction to what looked like a smirk. The second grabbed him by the arm and spun him around, forcing him deeper into the shadows.

Tom literally saw his life flash in front of his eyes as the third man, who now proudly displayed his knife, strutted toward him. The man in the shadows held Tom, twisting his arm behind him and secured him by grabbing his hair and jerking his head back. As the man with the knife feathered the side of his neck with the blade, Tom experienced his warm, foul breath against his face and up his nostrils. Playtime was over. Gripping anger and hatred zeroed in on Tom as the man's face inched closer.

"You think this is funny, Preacher Man?" the man said slowly. "You think you're gonna live to tell your pretty wife about this? I think we need to show you how funny it's gonna be to die slowly, right here, right now."

The man pressed the edge of the knife to Tom's throat, poised to finish what he'd started. Tom held his breath.

*Do not worry, for I have My hand on you. You shall not lack. Do not look to the things that are said by man. My hand directs the stars, My voice commands the rivers to flow. They would stop if I desired it. My desire is for you to serve Me. Nothing will stop that. Draw close.*

*I notice the terrors of Satan that bluff and talk as if they know what they are saying. They do not know what I have in store other than what I have told them. You shall go forth for I am your God. Not the God that can be changed by the whims of people, but the God that is moved by faith in Me being able to perform what I promise. Have I not promised you?*

*When will you realize the magnitude of My power? When will you begin to truly trust Me? Seek Me for Me; not for what I can do for you, but for who I am as God.*

*You have no idea what I have in store for you, but I am excited by what I see. I am pleased by My people who have said "Yes." When I am praised, all creation knows that I am God.*

# CHAPTER TWO

*"All whom My Father gives (entrusts) to Me will come to Me; and the one who comes to Me I will most certainly not cast out [I will never, no never, reject one of them who comes to Me]."*

*John 6:37 Amp*

"Oh Lord, help me!" Tom silently pleaded as he waited for the man to cut his throat. Off to his left, he could hear nervous, excited laughter and knew the one "unoccupied" aggressor was ecstatic over the prospect of taking a life. He encouraged the steely-eyed man gleefully, "Poke him a couple of times for me before you finish him off."

How could this be? All of his life, Tom had taken the safe path, a path with the least potential for harm or misfortune. But now, here he was, moments from death in the hands of three men on a dark street - men that simply seemed to want to vent their anger, frustration and hopelessness on somebody - anybody. Years of emptiness, despair and survival had taken its toll on these young lives; and the value of life had long ago lost its impact because of the hurt, pain and sin that were part of their everyday existence. Now to simply take what they wanted was not enough. They would get what they wanted anyway. There seemed to be a score to settle and Tom was caught in their midst - helpless!

"Is it money you want?" was the only thing Tom could think of to say. "There's about twenty dollars in my pocket. Take it - it's yours."

"Oh, we'll take it!" came the reply. "But first maybe you should..."

"Maybe he should what?" came a voice from the shadows. At the sound of that voice, the man with the knife pulled back

25

cautiously and the man who locked Tom's arm and head in position sprang back into the shadows like he'd been contacted by a stun gun.

"Oh Lord, I think I'm going to be sick," Tom thought as he turned and saw where the voice came from.

"I said, maybe he should what?" the voice said again to the three men, as Tom's widely opened eyes caught sight of the most imposing gun he had ever seen. It was pointing in their direction.

"Train," as he was called on the street because of his power in warfare and almost unstoppable battle prowess, stood looking past or through Tom - actually over him - directly at each of the now immobile men. One of the largest men Tom had ever seen - at least seven feet tall with arms and bare chest bursting from a former bluejean jacket, now minus sleeves, buttons and anything else that defied his freedom of movement- Train was somehow his ally in this time of need.

Known and feared on the street as one of the most vicious warriors, nobody - not even two or three - would attempt to try anything against him. His size alone almost guaranteed that someone was going to get badly hurt if they should be foolish enough to risk a confrontation. But more than that, it was well known that Train just didn't care. Past recklessness, past fearlessness, Train defied pain, defied death - even seemed to welcome them - at any opportunity. It was well known that once something was started with him, only death would stop him - his or yours! And street talk said that more than once that's what happened to an ignorant challenger.

Tom could only stare at his massive rescuer.

"We don't mean nothin', Train," one of the men said.

"You can have him," said the steely-eyed man, folding his knife as he continued distancing himself from Tom.

Train stood poised, ready for anything. His eyes danced from one man to another; his gigantic muscles were tightened, gun held steady. Tom stepped to the side, gently massaging his throat as Train moved steadily past him in the direction of the three intruders. The smoothness of his movements defied his massive structure. Tom thought of a poised mountain lion he had seen in a recent movie.

Understandably, the trio's macho toughness dissolved as if masks had been removed from their faces. At a precise moment in time each knew that they had lost. There was nothing to do but retreat.

Almost as if on command, the three street toughs, now looking and acting more like little boys, turned and ran at breakneck speed. Tom watched them as they disappeared into the darkness. By the time Tom remembered where he was, Train had turned away from the fleeing men and was looking straight at him. Because of his focus on the men, Tom hadn't noticed that Train had moved within several feet of him. Awestruck by the immense size of the man standing before him, Tom could hear nothing but his own heart beating so loudly he thought that Train must have been able to hear it, too.

"Which was worse," Tom asked himself, "my fate with the three men whose intent was obviously not the best, or now this- this gorilla minus hair standing in front of me?"

Past feeling, past emotion because of the events that had just occurred, Tom was almost comatose. The man in front of him was so big that Tom felt like he was standing in front of a small building. "Thanks," was all he finally managed to say from a throat that felt like it had a lump in it the size of a tennis ball as his rescuer placed the revolver at about Tom's eye level in a pocket on the inside of his jacket. Tom hoped that this actually was a rescue and not someone stealing prey from another, not willing to share the prize.

Tom noticed that the street had become silent. The two men on the bench had disappeared, the sounds of doors and windows closing, even the distant barking of a dog had ceased.

So much was happening - so much to think about. Unanswerable questions flooded Tom's mind: "What should I do? How can I live through this? Is there anyone to help me? Is there anywhere to go?"

Time seemed to stand still, but Tom's mind raced on. He scanned all of his surroundings, looking for a way out, never even thinking what he would or could do if he found some sort of escape. His legs wouldn't move. As a matter of fact, the only things he knew to be working in his body were his eyes, which were probably bulging and extremely wide; and his heart, which was beating so loudly he was sure the people behind closed doors could hear it.

Train took about five steps away from Tom to position himself under the street lamp, which stood just outside of the shadows. Tom just stood and stared. Train reached into his outside jacket pocket with his left index finger and thumb and pulled a cigarette from the pack he kept there. With the same movement, his other hand produced a match, which he struck one-handed and held the flame, lighting the cigarette. Tom watched as the man who had just rescued him leaned against the black, steel lamppost. His size made the lamp sway, casting moving shadows against the pavement. For what seemed like an eternity, Train just stood against the lamppost, shoulders slumped, looking at the sidewalk. Finally, he looked at Tom.

"I'm Train. I been watchin' you. Been listenin', too," he continued. "You didn't see me 'cuz I been hidin', but I been listenin' while you talked to them busted up guys on the bench. I need to ask you some questions. I'll stand over here so you won't be so afraid. I'm not gonna hurt you," he said quietly, much to Tom's relief.

It was about then that Tom felt his heart re-enter his body. "What do you need to know?" he forced himself to say, his throat still hurting from the pressure of the knife.

Train shifted his weight away from the lamppost, and with one fluid motion threw the burning cigarette on the concrete and moved back toward Tom, who instinctively stepped back a few feet. Train kept coming until he was only a foot away from Tom's face. An intensity shown in Train's eyes – the kind Tom had only seen in his son, Tommy, when he really needed an answer.

"Is it true?" Train asked earnestly. "Is it true about this guy you called Jesus - that He can take away hurt and forgive me no matter what I done? Is it?"

The question startled Tom. Of all the things this man could have asked, this sure wasn't what Tom expected. Tom didn't know how to respond. He saw more pain in the man's eyes than he had ever seen before. The sincerity and pleading need to have it be true almost overwhelmed Tom.

"Yes, it is," Tom said hesitantly, timidly clearing his throat again. "It is one of the only absolute truths."

Tom had no idea how he came up with that response. He also didn't know why his hand started to reach into the inner pocket of his suit coat. There he discovered his little Bible in the place he'd put it right after talking to the men on the bench.

In an instant, Train's pleading expression changed to one of relief. He straightened for a moment and released a great sigh. As quickly as relief had come, his countenance changed once more to an expression best described as terror. He paced in front of Tom, his voice getting louder as he spoke.

"Why would He let them do that to Him? He coulda killed them all, couldn't He?"

Train again stopped directly in front of Tom, his piercing eyes demanding an answer.

"I heard you tell them men on the bench He was God. He coulda killed them, and nobody would be able to put Him in jail or nothin'; but He let them hurt Him and He didn't even say nothin'. Why did He do that?"

29

"Because He loved you and me," Tom choked, remembering the response from a Sunday sermon. Tom grabbed the small brass snap on the leather cover of his Bible and shakily opened the unworn pages. For a moment, his thoughts were paralyzed.

Was John in the New or Old Testament? "Oh, help me, Lord," Tom mumbled. "Matthew, Luke, Acts, Romans.... No, there it is - John, John 3:16."

Tom's hands were shaking so badly he could hardly read the words. He had to bring the little book close to his face. "See, it says 'For God so loved the world that He gave His only begotten Son, that whosoever believeth in Him should not perish, but have everlasting life.'"

Tom kept paging back and forth through his Bible as if looking for verses, never taking his eyes from the pages. And he talked. Almost afraid to let the man in front of him say anything, he talked. He talked about the cross and love and God and whatever came to mind. Where was it coming from? Tom felt like he was on Bible knowledge autopilot. Bible verses he hadn't quoted or even read in many years were pouring from him; he wasn't reading them. He was just mouthing what was in his heart. For what must have been quite some time, Tom was used by the Lord to say what needed to be said. When Tom finally looked up, he could hardly believe what he was seeing.

Tom was looking into the face of a man so much in pain that if he hadn't known better he would have thought Train had been stabbed in the chest. Train began to double over in agony, holding his stomach. Tom put his hand on Train's back as he let out a long, suppressed groan, releasing tears that he had never been able to release before. Tom kept his hand on Train's back while Train walked in a continual small circle on the sidewalk, still bent over, almost as if trying to escape the horrendous pain.

"Nobody ain't never loved me," Train whimpered as memories of rejection and abandonment started to visibly wrack his gigantic frame. "Nobody ain't never loved me like that."

After several minutes, Train stood erect again, sobbing and wiping his tear-streaked face with his calloused, massive hand. He turned toward Tom.

"I gotta do somethin' to thank Him for what He done. Can you tell Him for me, Preacher Man? Can you tell Him thanks for what He done?"

Tom looked up at the most broken man he had ever seen. Without hesitation, Tom put his hand on Train's arm - something unthinkable just a short time ago.

"I think Jesus would like it very much if you'd tell Him yourself, Train. I think He would be very pleased to have you talk to Him."

Shocked at the thought that God might listen to something he might say, Train stepped back a couple of steps in disbelief. Then he looked directly into Tom's eyes. Tom looked directly back into his, assuring him that it would be all right.

"Do I gotta go to a church or somethin'?" Train questioned.

"No," Tom smiled. "We could just sit here on the curb and you could just tell God what's on your heart."

Tom started to move toward the curb to sit down when he noticed that Train had dropped into a kneeling position right where he'd been standing. Tom moved next to him, giving a quick look to see if anyone was watching. Train knelt silently for a long moment, his head bowed and his hands folded in front of him, resting loosely against his body. Quietly he began.

"God..." he hesitated to wipe the tears from his eyes. "God, this is me, Train. I ain't never talked to you before 'cuz I been afraid..."

The next few minutes was one of those rare instances in life when you have the privilege of seeing the God of the universe once again come to visit one of His chosen ones. Quietly, peacefully, almost too wondrous to relate in words, the work that was accomplished on the cross at Calvary two thousand years ago once again became real and alive in one of His creations.

A lifetime of the disease called sin was banished, never to return, as this mountain of a man was visited by the One who loved him most. Anger melted in the light of love; rejection was washed in the love of acceptance; loneliness was erased by the Spirit of Adoption as this lost, wayward lamb was gently led home to warmth and safety. Tom knelt in awe on the cold, hard pavement with Train as he watched a transformation from death to life take place. Cleansing after cleansing became evident as tides of tears flowed from a freed heart so long held captive.

Silence... peace... hope... restoration... healing... right there on the street which only moments before held fear, anger and death threats. Oh, the wonder of God!

Both men remained momentarily silent following the most tender, loving communication Tom had ever heard anyone have with God. Tom stood to his feet and waited for Train to speak.

"What do I do now?" Train said as he got up. "How do I do what He wants me to?"

"You need to read His Word, believe what it says and live your life like Jesus did," seemed to be the right thing to say.

"How do I do that? I ain't got no Bible," Train questioned.

"Take mine," Tom said, almost without thinking, extending the little book toward the massive man. "I have other ones."

Big hands reached to touch, then caress, what he must have previously spit upon. Now, however, nothing seemed more dear as he held the Bible close to his expansive chest. It almost disappeared amidst the sheer size of his clasped hands.

"Thanks, I ain't never gonna lose this," Train said, wiping the last residue of tears from his face and straightening to his full height. He let out another long sigh of relief.

A big smile, revealing magnificent white teeth, turned to a questioning, quizzical look as Train grabbed his stomach.

"Hey!" he exclaimed, feeling different parts of his stomach as if looking for something. "Hey! I don't hurt no more. Every day I hurt here," he said, pointing to the middle of his stomach. "Now I don't hurt no more." Train smiled again. "I don't hurt no more."

Darkness had now completed its cover, hiding the filth of the street for another day. Tom had lost all track of time. But then, time no longer seemed all that important.

Tom noticed his knees beginning to weaken. In fact, he felt as if he were going to faint. The gravity of the encounter with the three men suddenly hit him like a brick wall. If Train hadn't intervened, he'd be dead.

"Those guys almost killed me," he said, remembering the edge of the knife and pointing to the spot where he'd been held. Everything happened so fast with Train, and because his focus had been on answering the questions Train asked, Tom hadn't had time to think about what could've happened. Now that he had time to reflect, he felt queasy. He leaned against the building.

"You O.K.?" Train asked.

"I don't know," Tom stated, staring at his hands, which were shaking uncontrollably. Knees buckling, Tom slumped against the building. As he did, Train knelt beside him, putting a comforting hand on his back very much like his mother had often done when he was a little boy. Of course, her hand didn't cover as much territory as Train's.

"That your car over there?" Train questioned, nodding his head in the direction of the parking lot where a lone BMW glistened under the lights. Without waiting for a response, Train easily lifted Tom to his feet and headed him toward the parking lot.

"Make sure you read that Bible," Tom said as they neared the car.

"You know I'm gonna," Train replied.

Tom groped for his keys and then opened the locked door with his remote. Train handed him his briefcase, which he'd picked up off the sidewalk. In the commotion, Tom had forgotten he even had one. Train smiled, responding to Tom's surprise.

"I didn't take nothin'," Train stated defensively and out of habit. Realizing that the statement was unnecessary, he raised his shoulders sheepishly.

"It's O.K.," Tom responded, trying to make him feel better.

"I…" Tom hesitated with his hand on the door handle. "I guess I don't have much to say right now. How can I ever thank you for what you've done? You saved my life."

Train quietly put his head down.

"I think you saved mine, too," he said, tearing up again.

Not knowing what else to do, Tom got into his car and started it. He sat and stared at the steering wheel for several moments and then slowly shifted into gear. Train backed away from the car a few steps. Tom gave a small wave as he pulled away. It seemed that there was little to say that could adequately complement the experiences that both men had just shared with each other.

Tom glanced in his rear view mirror at the man who meant more to him in the space of a few short minutes than anyone else would mean in a lifetime. Train stood quietly, following the car with his eyes as it pulled into the street. Tom saw him light a cigarette, turn and walk slowly into the darkness.

34

As the world grows darker, My people will shine brighter because of the love they have for Me, each other and their enemies.

This love has already been established in the heavenlies and is about to be poured out in its fullness upon My people. Holy alliances will be made one with another.

Kinsman friendships will be established that cannot be intruded upon by the vile jestings and coarse intrusions that are part of those who do not know Me.

I call you to separate yourselves, but in that separation, I am also calling you, My children, to come together.

Some of you know the bond of adversity, some know the bond of fleshly desire and adoration, some know the safety of a kindred spirit; but no one has known the heavenly bond of the holy alliance that will knit My bride together for My work to be done and for Me to pour My love upon them.

Establish it in your hearts now. Those I call to Myself will know Me, and each other, with the love My Father and I have had from the beginning. Make no provision for the flesh in any relationships I bring your way.

In My way, there's safety, power, freedom and love.

# CHAPTER THREE

*"...If anyone is in Christ, he is a new creation; the old has gone, the new has come!"*　　　*2 Corinthians 5:17 NIV*

Days became weeks, which became months after that fateful night of ultimate terror. Tom and his wife, Sally, constantly prayed for Train even though she'd never met him and Tom couldn't find him. Because of the quickness of all that happened that night, Tom never thought to leave his name or how he could be reached if Train had any questions. Often, Tom would find himself driving downtown to see if he might make a contact. It must have been quite a contrast to the surrounding area as a well-dressed man driving a new BMW would stop anyone who looked like he or she might know a man named Train. It seemed that no one had seen or heard from him since that night. How could someone that big just disappear from the face of the earth?

After about six months of fruitless searching, all previous events mixed into faded memories and somewhat tiresome stories. Sometimes Tom would think of the incident and wonder if it wasn't all a dream, something he had conjured up.

Sally and Tom settled back into the groove of their social, church and family involvements. Tom's design work at Henderson Architectural Firm, one of the most prestigious firms in the nation, was prospering. Several of his designs had been featured in <u>Architecture Today</u>, and he was fast becoming the rising star in the area.

The Lord was prospering on all fronts. Tom and Sally had just completed the plans for their new home, which would be built in spring. They really didn't need a larger home; but since things were going so well, in spite of the war, they felt it was okay to move to Brittany Estates. They both had to undergo scrupulous interviews, financial reports and social registration by the subdivision Control Committee and were accepted, so why not? Sally, a successful fashion designer herself, felt it would be good for their professional image if they moved; and even though they only had Becky and Tommy, four extra bedrooms might someday come in handy.

"There's a Mister Horace Winslow to see you, Mr. Bracken," Tom's secretary, Connie, said over the intercom. On Monday mornings it was always hard to get started and organized, and this day was no exception.

"Connie, I told you that I am in for no one," Tom responded. "I don't know a Horace Winslow. Tell him to leave his card and I'll call him when I can."

"If I want to..." Tom thought as he turned his back on the infernal box that kept interrupting him. "It sure would be nice to be left alone."

"Mr. Bracken, I - I think you had better see this man," Connie said in a voice somewhat unusual even for her. "He... he insists on it."

"This better be good," Tom thought as he responded to her. "O.K., bring him in."

Shortly thereafter, Connie came to the door. "I think maybe you'd better come out here and see this."

"This had better be really good!" Tom muttered, throwing his drawing pencil on the desk. Connie, wide-eyed and looking a little like a lost puppy, followed Tom down the corridor to the main lobby just across from Mr. Henderson's private suite. As they neared the lobby, people were whispering to each other and heading in the same direction. The whole firm seemed to be focusing and congregating around some activity there.

As Tom and Connie made their way through the people, they began to hear low, quiet talking...even what sounded like several people crying. Tom stood in amazement, as there - in

38

the middle of the lobby - were several people, including Mr. Henderson, praying to receive Jesus into their lives. Leading them was this seven foot tall giant of a man named Horace Winslow, known only to Tom as "Train!"

Nothing like this had ever happened at the Henderson Architectural Firm before. In fact, the whole scene before Tom was almost surreal. Proud, stiff-necked business magnates and their "wanna be's" simply wouldn't stop in the middle of their "important" day to even speak to the likes of Train, much less really listen to him. Tom shook his head and made a concerted effort to focus on his surroundings to determine if what he was seeing was really happening.

It seems that Train had walked into the lobby approximately thirty minutes earlier, followed by several security guards who took notice of the giant, bluejeaned "hoodlum" as soon as he hit the lower lobby ten floors below. From there, he seemed to gather people like a magnet. His size, dress and demeanor all demanded attention in this traditional, almost stuffy, atmosphere.

As Train presented himself to Connie, followed by his pick-up entourage, Mr. Henderson noticed the commotion and came to see what was going on. Then the miracle happened. Taking full advantage of the opportunity and under the full anointing and appointment of the Holy Spirit, Train began to tell all those who had gathered about his very best friend, his Lord and Savior Jesus Christ.

So simple was his presentation, so loving was his countenance, so refreshing was this wondrous truth, that the hardened, the cynical, the proud were pierced to the heart. Mr. Henderson himself, who hadn't even thought of God - if there was one - in twenty years, asked if Train would lead all those who had gathered to pray to the God Train loved so much. Those who turned their backs on receiving Jesus that morning knew that something wonderful had happened, even if they didn't understand it. It was obviously the power of the Holy Spirit at work in a way that Tom had never seen before.

Precious, intimate moments of people surrendering and turning their hearts toward home having passed, Train looked up and wiped the tears from his own eyes. Grinning broadly, he looked directly at Tom and said, "Hi there, Preacher Man. I come to see ya."

Tom just stared in disbelief. Finally, after standing there awhile with his mouth open, he realized how ridiculous he must have looked. Extending his hand, he walked toward Train. When they got close enough, both men rejected the formality of a handshake, and instead, shared a big, brotherly hug. The remembrance of probably the most significant event in either of their lives was simply too important to both of them. So they hugged, or more succinctly, Train picked Tom up and Tom in return did what he could to hang on while he was being squeezed.

After Tom was put back on the floor, he began straightening his clothing to a round of applause. No one really knew why they were applauding - it just seemed like the right thing to do. Both men smiled, being somewhat embarrassed, so Tom motioned for Train to follow him back to his office. After closing the door, Tom directed him to have a seat. Train pulled a chair from Tom's conference table and straddled it backwards.

"How did you find me?" Tom asked Train, as he studied this man across the conference table in his office.

"Your name was in this Bible you gave me," he said, holding up his now ragged-edged, love-worn friend. Then he placed it next to him, almost as if it had a life of its own and needed a response as any person would. "And your card here - you must have used it as a book mark. When my Lord said I could, I came to thank you," he said with a smile that lit up the room that only moments earlier seemed cold and business-like.

"I don't need nothin'. I just wanted to tell you what's happened to me since I met my Jesus last year."

Through several unscheduled, seemingly unnecessary interruptions by Connie, Mr. Henderson, several secretaries offering coffee and even some others Tom hadn't seen in months, Train settled in to unravel the mystery that surrounded his life for the last year. Before he could begin, Tom's intercom again invaded the room. "Mr. Bracken," Connie said, only to be interrupted by a harsh, "Bracken, this is Hen…" He quieted as if he were taken hold of by some new control in his life. "I mean, Tom, this is Carlyle Henderson. Tom, it seems our new friend has caused quite a stir around here. Even people from down the hall, other offices from other floors and our own staff would like to hear more about Train. Would you mind if we met you in the main conference center?"

"Of course not," Tom said, glancing at Train with questioning eyes to see if it was O.K. He simply smiled and nodded his head as a sign of approval.

Tom headed for the door, a little off balance because of the slightly unusual turn this day had taken. As he went through the door, he noticed Train had not followed him. Going back, Tom saw him kneeling in front of his chair. Peacefully, quietly, as a submissive child, he had chosen to talk to his Father first. "Father, it seems You have made an appointment for us. We surrender to Your perfect will. Let them see You and Your Son Jesus. We now choose to move and say only what You choose. Thank You for everything. Train."

"I'm ready now," he said, rising to his full height. "Just needed to say thanks for what we are about to see. Father's awesome, isn't He?" Train said as they opened the door to the conference room.

"Yeah, awesome," Tom thought, discovering that maybe he didn't know his Father as well as he thought.

When they entered the conference center, which was a small theater with a raised platform used by speakers at seminars, it was teeming with people. All three hundred fifty seats were filled. People were sitting on the floor in front of the seats and the aisles were beginning to fill up as more businessmen and women - staff and some passers-by - flowed in. Tom had to laugh to himself as he thought of the animals as they were drawn by the Lord Himself into the ark; foreign to their natural patterns, they humbly obeyed. Now, another group of obedient wanderers quietly submitted, some of them not even knowing why.

"I am once more in awe of our Father in heaven," Train began as he refused the podium or chair on stage, but sat as a child would on the edge of the platform. "Last night, when I started to walk to meet Preacher Man over there," he said, pointing to Tom who was somewhat embarrassed that few even knew he had given his life to serve Jesus, "my Lord told me to expect Him to be with me and to not be surprised by what He was about to do. All night as I was walking here, He kept tellin' me about lost sheep that don't know they're lost. I didn't understand until now what He meant."

Tom was reminded of what it must have been like when Saul of Tarsus, now Paul, would tell of his life to those gathered in the local communities. How the Spirit of the Living God must have fallen to nullify the objections, the doubts, the false wisdom of the learned. For at the throne of God, in His presence, there is no special elite, no rank because of money or talent or status esteemed by men. There we all become equal - sinners silent before a holy God.

Tom's thoughts turned back to the conference room where people representing every conceivable walk of life, every circumstance caused by sin, were bathed in the love of the Father. As in the days of Paul, they were becoming enraptured by the story of the life of a wayward lamb that found its way home through the loving Shepherd of our souls, Jesus Christ.

Train was born in a back alley room, which was used as a shoot-up room by heroine addicts. His mother was a user and sold herself to maintain her need. Ears strained to listen and broad shoulders slumped as he told of nights in the same bed with her as "uncles" would come to use her. At times, he would hide his head in his pillow to make it go away; and even as a small child he would try to defend her from the beatings by those men, only to be beaten himself.

Once it was too late and he was not strong enough. All night, he tried to wake his momma. He washed the blood from her face and tried to make her hurt go away. Early that morning, he was pulled from her by another "uncle" and thrown out in the hall. "Never come back here, kid," he remembered hearing. "Your ma ain't never coming back, so get lost."

Silence, except for an occasional nose blowing or quiet sob, permeated the room as Train told of his life on the street from the age of five. Survival was the only way of life he knew and being tougher than the street itself was the only way to make it. Hours flew by as a story of rage, hostility, gang warfare, theft and crime heinous enough to defy any imagination unfolded before the wide-eyed audience of "straights" as they were brought through the events that took them to the night Tom met him.

"I was on my way to settle a score with the Kings," Train said as he stood for the first time, seeming to again breathe in the new life he found in Jesus. Almost refreshed now and recovered from relating the life of darkness, he continued.

"They had taken out my friend, 'Boney,' and I was on my way to take them out. I didn't know it was a set-up. They were waitin' for me and were gonna blow me away, too. On my way there, I saw this guy," he said, again pointing in Tom's

43

direction. "He looked outta place on the street, but somethin' made me stand at the corner of a building in the shadows and listen to him. He was talkin' to these two guys on a bench about this guy who had let a bunch of people take him out by hanging him on a cross. But He asked His Father to forgive them. Somethin' inside of me told me to follow him to find out more. That's when Steely, Mic and Tony tried to kill him."

Tom was quieted in his heart for the first time in many months as Train related to the crowd the new life that he felt come into him as he was washed by the blood of the Lamb that night. Just like Saul in the Bible, Train was taken aside by his new Lord and taught from His own mouth. For eight months, Train received as the Lord of the Universe gave. Forgiveness, healing, love and freedom replaced the grimy sin of the street in this special child. The verse "He who has been forgiven much loves much" became a reality to Tom as he heard and saw and remembered once more the covenant promise fulfilled in the "tabernacle of the Living God" that stood before the awestruck crowd.

"He wants to help you, too; you ain't no different to Him. He wants to show you His love, too. All you gotta do is take it."

With that he began to pray. Simply, honestly and naturally he invited anyone who desired to pray with him. And many did. The miracle of new life became a reality to Judy, who tried to find love with every man she met; and Dick, the office "wolf" and ridiculer of everyone. Even Mr. Henderson, or "Carlyle" as he was now known to Tom, was found on his knees again in the back corner of the platform behind the curtain, alone with his newfound Lord.

To say the least, it was an unusual day at the Henderson Architectural Firm! How could Tom have known that the biggest surprises were still to come?

*I call you to holiness, but you are too busy to spend time with Me. I call you to a crucified life, but you cannot die to yourself. I call you to present My Son to those who are dead that they might receive His life, but you curse them in My presence.*

*Can you not see how cold you really are? Can you not see how far you've strayed from My purposes for your life? Who are you saving by your actions? What are the purposes of your comings and goings? Whose agenda are you following, and what is its end?*

*Wake up. The harvest is white and the workers are few. Pray to the Lord of the harvest. What are His purposes? What is His agenda? Pray for wisdom that you might see with His eyes and move with His heart. The time is short and much is to be done.*

# CHAPTER FOUR

*"But we have this treasure in earthen vessels, that the excellency of the power may be of God, and not of us."*
*2 Corinthians 4:7 KJV*

The new BMW that had seemed so important to Tom that morning was somewhat out of place in light of the purity of what had happened throughout the day. With the front seats more than filled with the two men, Tom and Train made their way to Sally and the kids, who were waiting at Tom's home. Tom had called first, to prepare his family for the grinning mountain by his side. Sally immediately insisted on having Train stay for at least a couple of days and Tom agreed, thinking it would be good for Train, also. Fresh air, good food and a comfortable bed would be a welcome change to someone who lives like he does, they reasoned.

Even after the countless stories Tom had told about him, Sally was not prepared to meet Train. Obviously taken aback, she still greeted him enthusiastically, but gave Tom shocked glances when she knew Train wouldn't notice. As he unfolded himself from the front seat of the car and ducked his head on his way through the front door to become the main object in every room he occupied, Train had finally arrived. Now Sally, Tommy and Becky could see for themselves what Tom had been trying to explain all these months.

As a family, the Brackens vacationed with Train in their home on Tuesday, Wednesday and Thursday. Events such as those that happened recently at Henderson's seemed to be everyday occurrences in the life of this surrendered vessel of God. Simple walks became spiritual journeys as the Lord led the hurting, the "empty in the lap of luxury" and the "hardened by life" to His trusted child, who was always available and

47

obedient to share new life.  Tom laughed out loud often as the children - so many children! - found Train willing to be their "mobile climbing tree."  They, en masse, would hang from every accessible handhold and literally crawl to the top of him until he would feign weakness and gently fall to the ground, to the delight of the giggling horde.  Once Train was on the ground, they would swarm after him until they were exhausted with joy from the tickling, struggling and just plain foolishness.

Timmy Carlson, a boy who had never said a word in his seven years, exclaimed to his parents Wednesday evening after a day of romping and storytelling by Train, "Jesus loves me," pointing to his chest.  It seems that the Lord broke through years of being considered less important than work, travel or things, and filled his heart and opened his mouth.  All day Thursday, to anyone who would listen, Timmy was a waterfall of stories and expressions that he had saved all of his short life.

Margaret Miller took the brace off of her small, twisted leg to crawl around on the ground.  In the spirit of the afternoon and in the heat of the chase, she ran, jumped and scurried.  Only after the roar of life quieted to a normal din (for children) did Fred Smithers yell, "Hey, Margaret, your leg ain't funny no more."

In the midst of a stride, Margaret stopped, looked down and said, "Wow!  Jesus musta touched it."  He had, and everyone cried.

Each encounter seemed to give Train new life or somehow impart to him the joy he had missed, himself, as a child.  He played as he loved and as he prayed - in absolute fullness, total abandon, and childlike endeavor.  There was no reason other than God's reason, no encounter other than God's appointment, no situation other than God's desire to show Himself to those involved, as far as Train was concerned.  D.L. Moody once said that he wondered what would happen in the life of someone totally sold out and surrendered to God. The Brackens were beginning to get a glimpse of what could happen.

In three days, neighbors - some whom Tom and Sally had never seen - became friends. Cold relationships were warmed and all were pointed to the Sustainer of Life and Healer of their Souls. Old Mrs. Grimshaw smiled for the first time after meeting Train and his Lord. Many neighbors who had encountered her wrath for not mowing their lawns right or cutting shrubs too short or picking flowers too early and not in full bloom, were startled the first time she smiled. Micky Tournet, much to the embarrassment of all, pulled his mommy's dress as she was talking to Mrs. Grimshaw and loudly screamed, "I didn't even know she had any teeth!"

Tom, Sally, Tommy and Becky were enraptured by their guest. Although Train remained quiet unless he was asked a direct question, there was never a hint of tension or uneasiness. Over the three days that Train was with them, an unquestionable friendship - no, more than that - an alliance was made that defied human reason. The simple love, the holy peace that permeated this man of God left no room for formality or decorum. It seemed that Train was family in a very new sense of the word to the Brackens. Even Tommy and Becky talked of "making a part of their new house for Train to live in forever." But Tom and Sally somehow knew that that could not happen.

The ride to the Thursday night church service was uneventful, at least in light of the newness of life that had been found over the last few days. One stop at a stoplight to bring a young boy with purple hair to the Lord, an event that would have been enough for at least a few weeks of marveling at any other time, was the only circumstance of note.

Upon arrival at His Holiness Christian Fellowship, an architectural marvel given much press for its beauty and awe-inspiring design, things took an unexpected turn. For the first time since their initial encounter, Tom noticed that Train was somewhat uneasy. An unusual gloom seemed to come over him. Downcast, even morose, he sat and watched as the expensive, shiny luxury automobiles parked and presented their proud, colorful cargo to those who had arrived before them.

"I'm gonna sit here for a while," Train stated flatly. "You just go in by yourselves. I'll come in after I talk with my Father for a while."

"Honey," Tom said to Sally as they walked toward the front door, "I never even noticed that he's wearing the same clothes he had on when he came. Do you think he's embarrassed about how he looks? I could kick myself for not being more sensitive. Lord, please forgive me."

*"In the Name of the Lord," you say. You go about your business doing your works and call them Mine. How can what you do be truly Mine if you don't spend enough time with Me to hear Me, to search My heart, to find My ways, to know Me?*

*I am not in your feasts. I am not in your programs. I am not in your fellowships. A time is coming when those who think they hear My voice will see and understand who they have really been listening to. It is not Me. All the works of the flesh will wash away as so much grime. I will not complete what I did not initiate.*

*Stop praying for things. Stop working for men and their desires. Begin praying to search Me out. I can be found. I desire to be found. Those who choose to know Me are wise. Those who come to Me will walk the straight, safe path. My ways are sure. My time is well spent for those who have heard Me.*

# CHAPTER FIVE

*"...Forasmuch as this people draw near Me with their mouth and honor Me with their lips but remove their hearts and minds far from Me, and their fear and reverence for Me are a commandment of men that is learned by repetition [without any thought as to the meaning], Therefore, behold! I will again do marvelous things with this people, marvelous and astonishing things; and the wisdom of their wise men will perish, and the understanding of their discerning men will vanish or be hidden."*     *Isaiah 29:13-14 Amp*

Heralding itself as "one of the fastest growing churches in the land," His Holiness Christian Fellowship took much pride in its impact upon the community it served. From the long, winding entrance sidewalks, past majestic fountains and manicured lawns, to the three-balconied superstructure with its orchestra pit and tiered choir platform that was filled as usual to capacity with a three hundred fifty member choir; it spoke of the commitment of its congregation to receive the blessings God had for them. Each Sunday, ten buses would go to local communities and return with the poor, the infirm, the children who could not make it to His Holiness for some reason or another, and then return them home after the service.

Because of the commitment of Pastor Wickham to be "salt and light" to the world, the activities of the church body were unparalleled. Due to its vast financial resources and the commitment of its people, His Holiness had a powerful influence within its vast outreach arms. Three abortion clinics could no longer stand under the pressure applied by the church and its connections. In fact, the slogan, "A Clinic a Week for a Year," boldly stated the commitment of the body of believers to "clean up" their community once and for all. In short, much social involvement and its immediate and long term impact served notice to anyone who attempted to defile the community in which they functioned, that the church was truly a force with which to be reckoned.

Thursday evening service at His Holiness Christian Fellowship was a time of testimony, praise and Bible study. Mrs. Fontaine testified of her inheritance coming through after a long and drawn out court battle. Tom Dilling thanked God for his new job, and Mike and Cindy Lackinger praised God for their new mortgage. They felt it must have been God's hand on them for they really didn't qualify for a mortgage that size, but somehow they got it anyway. Tom and Millie led the gathering in praise that seemed unusually sweet, at least to Tom and Sally; and prayer was offered for the sick and the lonely.

All in all, it was a good evening. Pastor Wickham spoke of laying down our lives to become more like Jesus and people came forward to commit to doing that. In fact, it seemed that they were the same people who usually came forward. Pastor noticed that Train, who had slipped in sometime during the service, was sitting in the last row under the first tier of balcony seats.

"I'm sure by now you all have heard about this man," Pastor stated, extending his arm in a gesture of welcome toward Train. "He has caused quite a stir around here and is gaining a reputation for himself," he continued. "Train, would you come forward and share with us what the Lord is laying on your heart?" Pastor called with a warm smile.

All eyes turned toward the person whose name had been on the lips of many, with stories that sometimes even surpassed the immense impact that they, in themselves, had. Slowly, Train stood to his feet. His countenance seemed heavy and gone was his characteristic smile and the brightness it invoked. As he lifted his head, Tom saw that tears had filled his eyes.

For a moment, Train surveyed the church body, which was now also sensing that something was not in order. He gazed upon all that were there with Christ-like compassion. Then, in quiet reverence, he turned and slowly walked out the door.

"I had better go and see what's up," Tom said to Sally. "Try to find a ride home, O.K.? I might be late."

Tom left the startled crowd behind, almost running as he passed faces expressing wonderment and questioning what had just transpired. He leaped down the front steps and slid past a startled group of teens who tried to quickly conceal the one cigarette they were sharing in secret.

Tom asked a pimply-faced boy of fourteen years of age, who was attempting to give the cigarette to anyone who would take it, "Have you seen a really big guy come past here?"

"Yeah. He scared the pants off of us," Billy Cameron said, waving his hand around in a vain attempt to remove the cloud of smoke that encircled all of them.

"We thought he was an angel or something he was so big. I think he's over there behind that garage."

Running in the direction Billy had pointed, Tom began to pray. "Lord, help me to help him. I'm sorry if I've hurt him. How could I know all of this would be too much for him?" Then, at the corner of the family resources building, Tom saw him. Sobbing like a little baby, his immense frame jolted with each new burst of tears, he was bent over a yard tractor in weakness from the pain.

"I'm sorry, man," Tom said. "Is there anything I can do?"

"I need to go home," was Train's response through continued tear bursts that defied his rugged features. "I want you to come with me," he stated in a tone that left no room for discussion.

The sun had set over the well-lit street lamps, sculptured lawns, and expensive homes, filled with all the finery money could buy. Now, the darkness had again encapsulated the dingy corners, grimy alleys and stark homes that had given up on trying to overcome their age and hopeless surroundings. As Tom drove deeper into the home of the cancer-infested society with its gangs on every corner waiting for who knows what, the hideous acts done in dark places, the hopeless attempting to find hope; he silently prayed for the Lord to protect him, hold him and help him to understand what was happening.

The shiny, new and now in this setting, ridiculous-looking BMW pulled to a stop in front of a building that looked as if it had been abandoned for years. Tom realized that he was very near to the place where he'd first met Train. As soon as the car stopped, Train disembarked and stretched to relieve his cramped muscles. He stood silently near the right front fender of Tom's car as a crowd started to gather. Tom was amazed at the number of people who came from nowhere to look at him, his car, and just to be there for whatever would happen next.

As the crowd got bigger and closer, Tom felt the best place to be was as near to Train as possible. As he attempted to move in that direction, something happened that he had never experienced before. Even though he tried to excuse himself to get to Train, no one would move. In fact, no one would look directly at him. He remembered the open defiance he had met with the two young boys playing ball the night he met Train, but that was nowhere near as frightening as this. The common courtesies that were a part of Tom's normal life did not exist for him here and it made him frightened beyond belief.

What chance did he have if anything dangerous happened? What would he say if anyone even spoke to him? He was truly the odd ball with his expensive car and clothes, and instantly he wished he were not so different. He knew he didn't belong here and was sure that everyone was purposely letting that be evident to him. It was almost as if the strongest mass became the "owner" of any given event. Showing that you are able to maintain control, gives you control. Sometimes that might be a gang, some loud gesture or simple street toughness, depending on the situation.

As Tom watched, pockets of forces began to form, making elementary attempts at being noticed. A gang of youths began pushing each other, some girls began to giggle loudly and jitterbug to imaginary music; several larger men moved near the car and began appraising it as if they were potential buyers.

As Tom was preoccupied with the people and his immediate surroundings, he hadn't noticed the subtle change that had taken place. From the moment Train had moved to the front fender of the car, he began to pray silently. His Father, knowing his need at that specific moment and using the means available, equipped Train with street authority. Everyone knew that he had sold out to Jesus, that he also fought no more and that he wasn't the same as he had been a year ago. But still, a spirit more powerful than his former spirit embodied him.

No matter what anyone else may have had in mind to do, God's will would be done. Tom saw it in his face. His countenance had changed from morose to determined right before Tom's eyes. Everyone else noticed it also as soon as he spoke.

"Let it be known on the street," he said in a voice Tom remembered hearing only once before at their first meeting, "that this is my friend's car. Do you understand?" he said with added directness.

They did. The crowd immediately quieted and began to disperse. Train took the most unlikely candidates, the "appraisers," and called them aside. "I need you guys to make sure nothing happens to that car. You are going to do that." He spoke in surprising gentleness.

"Yes, sir," they agreed in unison, almost childlike. Train thanked them and expressed in street talk how confident he was that the car would be safe.

57

As Tom and Train walked toward the building where Train lived, he could hear the men making plans and discussing who might do the best job protecting the car and which shifts they should take through the night. Tom didn't understand why he knew his car would be all right, but he did. Tom's reasons were justified, for silently, in addition to the men, several invisible warriors positioned themselves near the car and around the entrances of the building before them.

*Your carnal mind cannot begin to understand what I have planned for you. I call you My children. That you can understand. When My glory is manifested, My Word says you will be as I am. (I John 3:2.)*

*If you could only believe. If you would only come close enough that I might express Myself to you. Your eyes are big towards what is happening around you. In your disloyalty, the world is powerful. In your obedience, you can see a little more of My perspective. There is nothing too hard for Me. There is nothing to fear if you choose intimacy with Me over activity in the flesh. My plans for you - who you are now and what you shall become - do not depend on the world and its ways. They are not changed by loud voices.*

*Understand I do not change. I do not waver. I do not fail. My Word is true and at work even now in the din of life. To see My purposes, you must turn to Me. I don't mean for you to pray about things; I ask you to come to be changed.*

*I am not interested in what you do as much as I am interested in who you are becoming. How can old things pass away if you remain in them? You are no longer part of this world. Separate yourself from it, for it is soon passing away. Only My Word, My ways, will remain. Come to Me now. I love you.*

# CHAPTER SIX

*"Consider it pure joy, my brothers, whenever you face trials of many kinds, because you know that the testing of your faith develops perseverance."*        *James 1:2-3 NIV*

"We'll talk tomorrow," Train said. "Tonight I need to pray by myself."

With that, he moved to a main entrance landing through the unlocked, broken-hinged door that long ago needed paint to stop it from cracking and decaying. Tom had moved so close to Train that he almost stumbled when his big friend moved. Feeling very much like a frightened child clinging to its parent, Tom walked in unison with Train.

"I live on the sixth floor," Train said halfway up the first flight of his two-steps-at-a-time climb to that location.

Tom's mind was numbed and racing at the same time. "What am I doing here again? How did I even get here? I don't know if I should be frightened or excited."

The pungent smells, dark stairways lit only by a single bulb where there was one; the humid, neglected atmosphere all foreign to Tom's world of clean, new and bright, invaded his consciousness in unwelcome bursts as he followed his companion - now his only visible security - down a dark corridor past voices unmuffled by the thin walls. On every level, seemingly from every door, voices - most of them angry and argumentative - could be heard. The closer they came to the sixth floor, however, the noise was less noticeable to Tom. In fact, Tom became aware of the absence of the noise heard on the landings on the preceding floors. As they walked past apartment doors toward what Tom perceived was Train's apartment, a noticeable peace began to envelop them.

"We're here," Tom heard as the key entered the lock on door #608. From the doorway, the entire single room Train called home was visible. Stark, old, repaired and poor, flashed through Tom's mind as the two men entered. Scrubbed, polished, clean, neat and… and peaceful. A refreshing, almost restoring sense surrounded Tom, compared to the invasion of sights and sounds of the past few moments. Tom continued in further as Train opened some windows to let in the cooling night air.

"I need to know why you've brought me here," Tom said as he moved to the single, threadbare, overstuffed chair offered to him.

Train pulled a "kitchen" chair directly in front of Tom. Thoughtfully, he sat and looked at his friend, his massive frame leaning toward Tom, elbows on his knees, hands folded in attentive friendship. "Tom," he started slowly, "I'm sorry for doin' this without explainin', but things were happenin' so fast inside a' me at your church that I just needed to get some place familiar to pray and think. I think it was right to ask you here and I ask you to kinda trust me on that."

"Kinda trust him," Tom thought, trying to imagine the foolishness of leaving this room, walking down the hall by himself, down the stairs and then outside in this neighborhood, not to mention trying to get past those gorillas who voluntarily impounded his car. Even in the car, if he made it that far, what chance would he have to make it out of the neighborhood without Train's protection?

"I'll say I'll kinda trust him!" Tom was in Train's world now. A world that physically may have been only twenty or thirty miles from Tom's, but it might as well have been on the moon. All that Tom had ever been taught, valued and sought after meant nothing here. He was totally dependent on Train to simply survive. Outwardly, at least, Train seemed to do a whole lot better his first few moments in Tom's world than

Tom was doing in his, he mused as he reflected on Train's visit to his office. Could that have been only four days ago?

"Lord," Tom thought, "when You start to change someone's life You don't mess around, do You?"

Train's voice brought Tom's mind back in focus. "When I came to see you," he continued, "I just thought I was gonna say 'thank you.' I thought maybe we'd have a meal together and then I'd come home. I didn't know that my Father wanted me to learn so much. See, I ain't never been out of the neighborhood before. I didn't know what it was like. I ain't never met people like you before, so I gotta go pray. I gotta get some stuff straight in my head and in my heart. I don't think it would be too good to talk too much now before I go pray. I do know you gotta see my world and I think Jesus wants to learn you some things. So you and me, let's pray, O.K.? Then you can rest and I can go be with my Father."

With that, he started, "Father, it's me, Train. Help us to learn what you want. Protect us and protect Tom's family from worry. We love You and thank You. Amen." Tom, not used to such short, direct prayers, was startled that prayer time was already over. The thought of some "spiritual" people in his church who said longer meal prayers than this flashed through his mind.

Train put his big hand on Tom's shoulder as he got up. Tom knew that he need not argue or continue to ask questions. Silently, he watched as Train walked toward the door. After opening the door, Train turned toward Tom. "You'll be O.K. if you stay in here," he began. "I'll be on the roof. It's quiet up there and I've built a spare room to get away." He turned to close the door, but at the last minute he opened it again. "I'll have someone get a holda Sally, O.K.? Just to tell her what's goin' on." With that, he closed the door. Tom sat for a moment just looking at the door as he heard the key being inserted in the lock.  He could hear Train walk all the way down the hall to the stairs.

"What is this all about?"  Tom said quietly to his Lord. "For what possible reason could you have brought me here again?" he continued, as he moved over to the window and looked down at the street.  For several minutes, maybe even longer, Tom watched the beehive of activity below him. "People," he thought.  "So many people that I never really knew existed.  People surviving on nothing, many hopeless beyond imagination. But each one loved by You, Lord.  What does it all mean?"

Tom moved to the bathroom to clean up as best he could before going to sleep.  It was small and stark with a toilet, wall-hung sink and a medicine cabinet.  A single, bare bulb light with a pull chain was the only source of illumination.  As Tom dried his hands and placed the towel on the hook on the wall, he noticed the old, old bathtub behind the shower curtain. It was one of those that had legs and feet like tiger's feet, holding a ball of some sort.  Even though it was old, somehow it seemed in very good shape.

"I know some people who would pay good money for that thing," he said quietly to no one.  He laughed to himself at the irony of that statement.  "Hidden value in the midst of poverty," he continued.  "Isn't that a lot like those people on the street."

Tom took a blanket from Train's bed and laid it on the couch where he had decided to sleep.  He laid his shirt and pants on one of the "kitchen" chairs and placed his shoes neatly on the floor under it.  After sitting on the couch for a moment thinking about nothing, everything, Tom laid back and pulled the worn blanket over him.

The peace that could only have been the presence of the Holy Spirit allowed Tom to fall into a restful sleep.  The din of street activity, the quarrels, the screaming tires, sirens and an occasional loud noise that Tom would not admit might be gunfire - sounds so unfamiliar to him - seemed not to really involve him at this time. What should have been fearful, and definitely would have been at some other time, was denied an audience with Tom as his Lord held him through the night.

From My perspective, some of you are acting no differently than the world that is perishing. You are using its methods to change its unchangeable heart. Why would you think that true, lasting change can be accomplished by the ways of man? Laws never change hearts, for the heart is wicked. When you move in the flesh, fleshly changes result.

I have never called you to pursue anything but Me. When you do that, We move in the spiritual realm to change hearts, to save those who are perishing. My Word shows how fallen man is helpless to even see the need to repent and change his ways. My Word shows how My covenant is invoked when My Spirit moves on the heart to come to repentance. When that happens, eternal changes result. That is My way.

You cannot see, however, because you want changes your way and you are ineffective because I cannot be with you to empower you because it is not My way. It never will be.

I have one purpose for you now that you are Mine. It is the purpose My Holy Spirit, Who is now in you, has always had. He has always proclaimed the beauty of Jesus to a world out of answers, a world dying in its sin. He has always moved so that those who are perishing might see, and come and be saved.

Why are you not moving in that same direction? All else that seems important is folly. I am not in it. Why would you be?

# CHAPTER SEVEN

*"A new heart will I give you and a new spirit will I put within you, and I will take away the stony heart out of your flesh and give you a heart of flesh. And I will put my Spirit within you and cause you to walk in My statutes, and you shall heed My ordinances and do them."*

*Ezekiel 36:26-27 Amp*

"Wake up, Preacher Man. Yeah, man, time to face the day," Tom heard as he felt a strong arm shaking him awake. Dreamless reverie at an end, Tom was startled into the realization that it was morning, but which morning? Where was he? As he rolled over in early morning stupor, his mind could not comprehend what his eyes were telling him they were seeing.

"Bet you never thought you'd see us again," said the steely-eyed man that had shaken Tom awake and was standing directly over him in giant-like form as Tom lay there, startled beyond reason, beyond thinking.

"Yeah, man," came a voice over his head, "but this time things are on much different terms, ain't they?"

Bolting upright in reflex action and jumping to his feet, Tom found himself face to face with two of the men who had tried to kill him that first night on the street - the night Train had made them flee. Where was Train now?

Tom backed toward the window for no real reason, looking for some form of protection, a knife, a vase, anything he might be able to use to defend himself. He never gave any thought to the folly of his actually attempting to fight off these street toughs who were no doubt experienced fighters. Suddenly realizing he was still in his underwear, he stopped, knowing that he couldn't leave even if he made it past his present assailants. The keys to his car were in the pocket of his pants, which were draped over the chair that the steely-eyed man had his hand on. Both men were grinning as if they knew the folly of Tom's thoughts.

"Cool it, man. You don't need to be scared of us no more. We're like you now. We've given our lives to Jesus and work for Him."

"Yeah," said the other, "instead of rippin' people off on the street, we give 'em Jesus now. It freaks 'em out, man - especially the tough ones. They knew us before 'cause we used to hit on 'em regular; but now when we walk up to 'em and they start gettin' scared like you, we tell 'em Jesus loves 'em and so do we. They think we're nuts until they know we're serious. We don't let 'em go 'til they hear the whole story."

"Yeah," said the steely-eyed man in front of Tom, breaking into a broad, mischievous smile. "We figure as long as we got their attention, they might as well get the whole ball o' wax. Right? Anyway, what better way can we pay them back for hurtin' 'em all these years? Think about it. They gave us stuff and now we can give 'em eternity with Jesus in return. Pretty good deal for them, wouldn't ya say?"

"Yeah, right. I mean, yes, I think so," Tom found himself saying, groping for anything to give him time to even begin to comprehend what was transpiring. Both men broke into hearty laughter.

"Look, man," said the one behind Tom as he placed his hand gently on Tom's shoulder, "we're changed like Train is; we really do love Jesus, and for the first time in our lives we can love other people."

The broad smile gave way to a dead-serious expression as he dropped his head, remembering his shame as he continued. "I hurt a lot of people; but see, I didn't know no better. The street was all I knew. If I didn't beat it, it would beat me; so I got tough. There was no room for bein' friendly, ya know.

"But when I found out I could get a new start, I mean, that I could get forgiven - a clean slate - I wanted that more than anything. Jesus made my heart soft. I don't want to hurt nobody no more. If they wanna hurt me, that's O.K. They wanted to hurt Jesus, too! But I ain't gonna hurt nobody no more."

As tears wet the shirt of this broken, humble man before him, Tom realized the miracle that God had just manifested before his very eyes. Social, financial and educational barriers had been vaporized by God's love born in the heart of these new brothers. Lifetimes of differences and generations of separation disappeared on the level ground at the foot of the cross. The miracle of the cleansing blood that poured full strength through the corridors of time to restore each of us, transformed the three people in that room from two street hoods and an architect into three brothers in Christ, linked forever by Him to the glory of the Father.

For the next few minutes, in the starkness of a room Tom had first seen the previous night - with two people whose presence moments before evoked only memories of terror - the story of how these new friends met Jesus unfolded, like a drama interwoven with wondrous new life, before an enraptured audience of one. Tom sat in awe and listened to the story as the miraculous came once more to flesh and blood.

It seems Steely, Mic and Tony – Tom's former assailants - had been looking for Train for months after that evening, the same as Tom was. While Train was alone with his newfound Savior, their lives continued to seethe with anger, hatred and revenge toward anyone who crossed their path. Street pride demanded they make Train pay for the humiliation he had dealt them. Street talk had them labeled as cowards for running, which made them all the more dangerous because now they had to show the street they had not turned "chicken." Possessed with finding Train, and festering with the need to get back their twisted concept of honor, the three went on a spree of robbery, rape and even murder.

"All we could think of was gettin' him back, ya know," Steely said, his eyes wide. "It was like there was nothin' more important to do. Now I think we went crazy for awhile." Steely looked at Mic who nodded his head in confirmation. The animation and childlike enthusiasm made Tom think of two little boys telling someone a wild story they had conjured up in their minds. It was hard for Tom to remember that these two men were the same men that had frightened him so horribly that first night.

After months of searching, they finally got the breakthrough as to Train's whereabouts. Tommy Nichols, a slightly built, somewhat mentally slow friend of Train's, had the misfortune of crossing their path in Kelley's Bar one evening. Having an honor code of his own, he said nothing despite the horrible beating he incurred. Only after emptying his pockets and finding the address to Train's temporary home above Casey's on East Street was Tommy left alone.

"We went to hit him," Steely said. "We were loaded for bear, man; we were really gonna take him out. But he got wind we were coming and left before we got there. Boy, were we mad."

"Yeah," Mic chimed in. "We were out of answers and too mad to even think straight. We decided we were gonna go to my place and get stoned. We had this really good stuff and were really cruisin' when all of a sudden the door comes flyin' at us and there was Train. Can you imagine being so stoned you can't stand, and all of a sudden this mountain you had been lookin' for for five months is standing in your doorway on top of the door he just kicked in. He was just there -bigger than life - right in our face."

Mic hesitated for a moment, arms in front of him in silent wonder, remembering the scene. His silent freeze seemed to indicate that he was reliving the incident all over in his mind. "It blew our minds, man! All we could do was look up at him with our mouths open and eyes bulging. We knew we had 'bought the farm,' especially when he started to tie us to our kitchen chairs."

Tom couldn't help but laugh out loud as the picture was shown to him with demonstrative enthusiasm of these three hoods, tied to their chairs for three days and nights while Train read from the Bible, preached at them and made them read themselves. Slowly, the love of God broke through their sin-sick souls as they saw their need and embraced the only hope ever presented to them. All three became new.

"It was good it happened, too," Mic said, "cuz Tony got taken out by the River Edge Gang two days later."

"I think they're still waitin' for us to come get 'em for Tony, but we ain't gonna. It's over for us. We're lettin' 'em alone."

"Unless we get 'em for Jesus," Mic added with a determination in his voice that punctuated all that Steely had said.

The two men gave each other the high five and backhand slap and then did some things that Tom didn't understand with their hands and fingers as they passed one another in front of him.

"We'll get 'em," Steely confirmed as he walked to the window to look at the street.

The men were silent for a moment, as they realized just how much their hearts had been transformed. Mic joined Steely at the window, bracing himself with his powerful arms against the sill, staring at the street. Tom noticed the tattoo on his bicep - a knife dripping blood.

"Old things made new," he thought.

71

"Ya better get your pants on," Mic said, slowly turning from the window. "We got lots of stuff to do today."

"We're your bodyguards," Steely chimed in brightly. "Train had to go to the hospital to see a buddy that got cut up real bad last night, so we're gonna take care of you and give you the nickel tour of the countryside."

Tom knew, even with the jesting, that these two had been commissioned by Train to be with him. He still didn't know what it all meant, but he was sure he would find out soon.

My holding power is much more powerful than the sinning power of your flesh. When will you grasp the reality of what has been done on the cross for you? Its work runs deeper than any force. Its power is so much greater than anything that may attempt to come against it.

When Jesus died, all that hindered My presence from becoming active and available in your life was removed forever. When He arose, death itself was defeated. Think on that. What that means for you is the freedom to receive My life, My eternal life, and the wealth that comes to you by My presence being with you in your life forever.

When hardship comes, don't attempt to deal with it by your knowledge or ability. Apply My life to it. Wait for My presence to move. Rest in Me. See My work being done in all situations. Be free by My Spirit and you will have an abundance no matter what the outward circumstances might appear to be.

# CHAPTER EIGHT

*"The Angel of the Lord encamps around those who fear Him [who revere and worship Him with awe] and each of them He delivers."*                    **Psalm 34:7 Amp**

Tom took his clothes into the bathroom and dressed while Mic and Steely moved to the kitchen area. He could hear drawers and cupboard doors opening and closing as they helped themselves to whatever was there to eat.

Their familiarity and ease of movement in someone else's home reminded him of relationships he'd had with some of his college buddies. The remembrance of real friendships, not simple business or social friendships, made him stop to reflect as he was buttoning his shirt. The stark coldness of his surroundings, the unsureness of what was ahead for him this day, his two new companions - what was it all about? He felt like running again.

"Lord, You gotta help me out of this one," he spoke to himself as he pulled his left sock on. Slipping into his shoes, he took one deep breath, reached for the well-worn door handle and went to face whatever was in store.

"Hoo whee, those are some fine looking clothes you have on there," Steely commented, looking over his shoulder on his way to the refrigerator for the third time. "You sure do look purdy."

Tom stopped to appraise his clothes in comparison to the jeans and undershirts both men were wearing. "I guess I do look kind of dressed up," he said sheepishly. "If I'd known I'd be hanging around with you guys, I'd have brought some jeans or something, but I didn't have time to change last night."

"That's O.K.," Mic said, somewhat unclearly, his mouth full of peanut butter. "That's O.K.," he said again after

75

washing it down with some milk. "Me and Steely here are supposed to take care of you Train said, so we'll just get some dirt on you or hide you if we see anybody we know," he continued, giving Steely a knowing grin. "Won't we, Steely?"

"Uh huh," Steely responded from a crouched position, staring into the now empty refrigerator. "We'll get him dirty or something just to get the shine off him." Tom tried to catch Steely's eyes to no avail, just to make sure he was kidding. Boy, did he ever hope that this guy was kidding.

Having finished their "meal," and satisfied that there was nothing left that was worthwhile to eat there or take along, Mic and Steely started walking toward the door. As they did, they almost in unison pulled baseball caps from their back pockets and placed them squarely on their heads, brims curled. "How come your hats aren't tilted anymore?" Tom questioned, remembering how their caps were at an angle at their first meeting.

"What? Oh, we can't do that no more," Mic said. "We quit the gang, so we'd get shot if we still looked like them." Tom didn't question if he meant they really would get shot with bullets. He thought it better that he didn't know for sure.

The irony of having Mic and Steely as Tom's tour guides, for what became his first morning on their turf, made his heart glad for his Father in heaven. If he had to be here, it made sense that they would be with him. It was because of them that this all started and now here they were, new in heart, assisting an outsider. He had tasted who they were in their old life. Now the taste of who they were becoming brought joy to his heart.

The sounds, sights and smells that greeted Tom as he began his venture into this new land were so foreign to him that he had to stop and think to make sure that he was in the same country. Could anything so close in geographical proximity be so far away in every other aspect?

76

At home, Tom's normal Friday morning would have started with the dancing sun cascading into the breakfast room, and myriads of flowers blooming as a colorful border for the well kept, freshly landscaped yard. Sally and the kids would be at breakfast with Tom, talking of the meetings, sports or school events that they needed to attend.

About this time, Dick and Marv would be at the end of the concrete drive waiting to pick Tom up for the commute to the Henderson Architectural Firm. Conversation would be about some seemingly important event that had already or was about to take place. As Tom thought about it, he couldn't remember even one really important topic – other than some events concerning the escalation of the war - having been discussed in their four years of commuting together. "Somewhat of a contrast to this morning," Tom said with a grin, half thinking, half talking.

"You say something, Preacher Man?" Steely asked as they passed the third landing on the way to the street.

"Huh? Oh, no. Just talking to myself," Tom responded.

The bright morning sun eliminated the fear that was ever-present in darkness as the three stepped into the street from the unpainted doorway. The "street" was a perfect example of life contrasts. At home in Tom's world, the street was something you simply drove on or crossed. It had no life of its own; it didn't really have significance other than it was used to go somewhere.

Here, the "street" takes on a very different connotation. When you talk of it, you go far beyond concrete or asphalt into culture, lifestyle and survival. Making it on the street means life or death, win or lose, an absolute. Not making it on the street means you're never heard from again at best, for the alternative is less than human in most cases. The street is your entire world for better or worse. It's home, or you hide from it or beat it, depending on your savvy and strength; it has no tolerance for the weak, the fearful or the uninitiated.

As the trio hit the street, Tom felt his vulnerability surface and became well aware that without his two new companions, or someone like them, he would be like red meat thrown to a hungry lion. However, Mic and Steely were well aware of the same thing and vowed to Train to take good care of their charge.

"We took good care of your car for you, Mister. Matter of fact, we're going to stay right here as long as you want," the small, well-built man said with a salute that mocked sincerity as he slid off the hood where he had been seated most of the night. Tom thought it best to be grateful for that rather than examine the hood for scratches from his boots.

"Thanks," Tom said with a wave as he walked past the driver's side window. He even noticed that the phone and radio were intact, which for some reason didn't surprise him.

"Where're we going?" Tom inquired of the only two familiar beings he knew in this very unfamiliar world.

"Headin' to Papa Joe's," Steely returned. "We gotta give him something before we meet Train. He said it was O.K. you come along."

"What's at Papa Joe's?" Tom asked, testing the waters of conversation to see if he was still free to ask questions.

"The only thing at Papa Joe's is usually Mama Joe," Mic said with a grin, and winked at Steely as they headed in a direction unknown to Tom. Then, realizing that Tom was too uninitiated and naive to appreciate the normal banter given to a "tag along," Mic said, "We gotta give 'im something we owe him."

"Yeah, he's about the last on our list to make it right," Steely stated as he smiled broadly.

The trio walked for several blocks. The continuous conversation between Mic and Steely, their childlike bantering

78

and playful attitude, let Tom momentarily forget that he didn't really belong. In fact, Tom had to consciously force himself to remember the recent events that brought them all together. The Spirit had so unified their most recent moments, that it seemed like he'd known them all of his life.

Suddenly, both men stopped dead in their tracks. Tom, who at that precise moment had his eyes on the unusual pattern the cracks in the sidewalk made and the fragile little flower that had bloomed through one of them, hadn't noticed the actions of his companions. As they stopped, he kept walking and ran right into Steely.

"Wow!" Tom exclaimed, holding his nose, which had jammed into the back of Steely's head. "You guys better signal before..." his sentence was cut short as he saw what caused his friends to halt.

Paralyzing fear, similar to what he felt during his first encounter with Mic and Steely, chillingly penetrated every cell of Tom's immobilized body. Tom watched helplessly as twelve to fifteen people - he couldn't even count straight - approached.

Mic and Steely held their arms in front of Tom in a silent command to stand still and be quiet as they moved instinctively to protect him. Unaccustomed to the street and the need to react before - and sometimes even without - thinking, Tom found himself sandwiched between his friends and now bodyguards as they went back to back to face the group that had surrounded them and were closing in slowly. The statement Mic had made earlier about purchasing the farm, or something like that, came to mind as Tom said his own silent prayer.

"Well, lookee what we have here!" said the tall, Spanish-looking man who had darkened eyes set deep in his olive-skinned face. Emilio, the obvious leader, was the only one who spoke. The others, armed with an assortment of weapons, moved in choreographed unison around the caged trio.

"Could this be Macho and the Iron Marshmallow?" he continued. "Where's the big man...what's his name... 'Caboose'?" he spat out with evident loathing and sarcasm. "The street says he's outta reach right now and you boys are all alone with this new puppy in town.

"We like your shiny, bright car, Little Puppy," he said with growing intimidation in his voice as his eyes burned a hole straight through Tom. "Maybe we'll take it for a little ride after we finish this business. That O.K. with you, Little Puppy?"

His senses having gone numb, and being unable to reach for anything from within for help, Tom could only stare. His mind raced: What was in store for them - him in particular? Were Mic and Steely any match for these men? Where was he going to run? Tom soon discarded any hope short of a miracle that the three, or rather the two of them plus whatever help Tom might be, could go toe to toe with all of them. Because of what had been said earlier about Mic and Steely being finished with the street, the situation looked less than favorable.

"Street says you got something for Papa Joe," Emilio snarled. "Maybe we should take it to him. What you say, huh? You wanna let us take what you got for him?" he continued, moving forward from the ranks of his men.

Tom's mind raced as he saw the man move closer. "God, why did you put me in this situation? If I die, who will take care of Sally and Tommy and Becky? Maybe I should've just stayed in my car, dropped Train off, and then driven back to my safe, secure home where I belong. This is Train's world. I don't know how to function here. I don't even know the rules."

Panic was about to overtake him when he heard a strange clanging behind Emilio. It caught everyone's attention.

80

"Maybe this is my chance to run," Tom thought to himself while everyone turned in the direction of the noise. "But where do I go? Oh, God! Help me!" Tom whispered a fervent, desperate prayer.

Almost as a small breeze that would bring refreshing on a hot, still day, a calm settled in his heart. At that moment, due to a power that was not his, he chose to completely trust his Lord with his very life. Peace replaced panic as the presence of God rested on him.

"Be still and know that I am God," settled in Tom's heart as his attention was again drawn to the rhythmic clamor.

The morning sun danced off the silver hair of the aged, bent, diminutive man who leaned heavily on the cane that he had just used to pound on two garbage cans. He was wearing a tattered, outdated, drab suit and his feet shuffled as he slowly moved across the street toward the gang and trio. As he got close enough, Tom noticed something extremely unusual. The man's movements, his clothes, his leather-like skin all indicated that he was very old. But his eyes – bright, blue pools of calming waters - indicated a clarity, a youth and wisdom that Tom had never seen before. It was as if eternal youth had been captured in an ancient body.

As all watched silently and immobile, Tom was reminded of an orchestra looking to its conductor as he ascends his podium. Without a word, this "maestro" had been given complete control, and all were awaiting his first command. A very large man, who wore a bright red bandana that partly concealed a long braid of raven colored hair, obediently stepped aside to allow the man access into the circle that had imprisoned Mic, Steely and Tom. Before proceeding, the man took a brief moment to put his hand on the big man's chest and look up into his face. He, too, saw those eyes and could only look down at the sidewalk in humbled obedience.

Turning again to Emilio, and in essence, tapping his conductor's baton, he began.

"Emilio," the man said with a confident, friendly smile, "venga aqui."

The tall, muscular Spaniard stood silently, as if held in position against his will, waiting for the man to come closer. Still smiling warmly, the old man motioned with his gnarled index finger for Emilio to bend closer so that he could whisper something to him. Perhaps in a state of shock, and realizing he was no longer in control, Emilio could only obey. The trio, the gang, and time stood still as the power of what was being said held captive this one who had spent his adult life making sure no one controlled him.

Tom noticed that Emilio - who had at first done the old man's bidding reluctantly, as if forced to by some unseen greater power - slowly submitted to what was being spoken to him. Several times, he would straighten up as if trying to escape the words given to him only to be again bent almost in half in order to hear what was said next by the much smaller man. At times, looks of shock and even horror were evident on Emilio's face as the old man spoke. At the same time, the old man held on to his captive's shoulder. Tom wondered if he was forcibly holding him or simply comforting him. At last, the little man gave two reassuring pats on that shoulder, signifying that all had been said and that he was finished.

Emilio stood silently, simply looking at the old man. The expression on his face was one of guarded wonder. The old man responded to his look with a calming smile. After what seemed like many moments, Emilio who was visibly shaken, his face having taken on an ashen hue, turned toward his hideout and walked away. His gang obediently followed like ducklings following their mother; there seemed to be nothing else they could do.

For as long as it took for the quieted wolves to turn the corner of the next block and retreat out of sight, all remaining players simply stood quietly and watched.

"It's safe to go now," the old man said with a smile, shocking the trio into awareness. "No one else will harm you today," he added as he turned and shuffled back across the street.

The three watched him in silence for as long as they could see him. When he was gone, they continued on their way. It seemed the only logical thing for them to do.

"What happened back there?" Tom blurted through the silence after walking about two blocks. "And isn't it about time you guys told me what's going on around here? Who's this Papa Joe? Why are we going to him? Who were those guys and what do we have that they wanted...and who was that little guy?" By now, Tom's voice was a whole lot higher than when he first started talking. He found himself on the verge of being sick to his stomach as his mind began recalling the recent incident. "Come on, you guys. You gotta start letting me know what's going on around here," Tom said somewhat out of control and feeling like he did when he whined to his older brother when they were both kids.

"Preacher Man, I think we all just became part of one of our Father's miracles," Mic said slowly, almost reverently. "Let's sit on those steps and thank Him," he continued, pointing to the front steps of the small shop just ahead. "Then we'll talk; we'll start from the beginning."

As My people go about their own version of what My Word says, I the Lord God am used as a license for them to remain in their sin, or I am left out completely.

Where in My Word does it say that My people are to be political or moral watchdogs? Where in My Word does it say that My people are to condemn the sinner? Where in My Word does it say that My people are to search out those things that give them comfort?

I have called My people to holiness. I have called My people to be set apart from all that resembles the world. I sent My Son that the dead may be given life. All do not receive that life. They choose to remain dead.

Your flurry of activities, your agenda of issue involvement, your moral judgment and all of its associated activities have not and cannot bring life to those who choose to remain dead. I am not in your outcry against your world. I am only in your outcry for mercy for your hardened heart.

Repent and turn now. See your spiritual adultery. See your hardened hearts. See your dead, cold churches and weep for them. I have called you to tell the blind of a way that they might see My Son, Jesus Christ. Why do you insist on doing your own will rather than submitting to Me to have your heart changed that they might see Jesus in you?

# CHAPTER NINE

*"...be strong in the Lord and in his mighty power. Put on the full armor of God so that you can take your stand against the devil's schemes. For our struggle is not against flesh and blood, but against the rulers, against the authorities, against the powers of this dark world and against the spiritual forces of evil in the heavenly realms."*

*Ephesians 6:10-12 NIV*

*"The weapons of our warfare are not carnal..."*
*2 Corinthians 10:4a KJV*

Mark Deider sat quietly, pensively, swirling a glass of ice water. Not noticing anyone else in Marie's Cafe, Mark was in silent prayer as he waited for Stephen MacDougal to arrive for their early morning meeting. For many weeks, Mark was not at peace. An unsettling, somewhere deep within him, had begun to grow some time ago. At first, he could shake it off; but more recently it was all that he could think about. Now he had to do something about it - to tell someone - someone who could help him straighten out his thoughts, make some order of his feelings, and give him peace again. Maybe this meeting with Stephen could give him some answers. Stephen always had answers, and it seemed to Mark that he could help.

As he waited, Mark began thinking of how much of an impact Stephen exerted on his life recently. In fact, Stephen was instrumental, it seemed, in giving Mark direction - even purpose if you will - something he had been looking for for many years. Mark was so caught up in his thoughts that he didn't notice Stephen until he was standing at the table about to sit down.

"You sure were lost in thought there, brother," Stephen said as he slid into the booth opposite Mark. "If I didn't know you better, I would have thought you had some real problems like losing your salvation or something like that," he continued in jest to lighten the formality of the moment.

"Hi, Stephen," Mark said with a smile. "I didn't even see you come in. Guess I must have been pretty involved in my thoughts. Sorry, brother."

"It's O.K.," Stephen responded. "Let's pray before we get started to invite God here, all right?" Both men dropped their eyes and dedicated their conversation to the Lord, asking for wisdom and requesting that the Holy Spirit guide their dialogue.

After their prayer ended and coffee had been ordered, Stephen spoke. "Well, what's on your mind, my friend? It must be pretty heavy because worry and tension are all over you."

Stephen had a way of getting right to the point. His ability to communicate and his natural leadership qualities, combined with his great zeal and definite purpose, allowed him to prosper greatly in his calling. As president of God's People for the Restoration of Morality, Stephen was very prominent in the community. His involvement in and commitment to the issues dealing with morality, or immorality as he voiced it, made him a much sought after figure. Mark felt somewhat honored that Stephen could find the time for this meeting.

"I guess," Mark started slowly. "I guess I'm somewhat confused," he said.

"About what?" Stephen queried, stirring his coffee and adding more cream.

"I guess about a lot of things. Things I haven't thought about for a long time. Like...like," he paused, feeling as if he were about to explode with a word flurry towards Stephen as release for all the thoughts that had been going on in his mind lately. "...like, are we really doing what God wants us to be doing?"

There! He said it in a nutshell. All his worries, concerns and sleeplessness could be summed up in that simple question. Mark was somewhat startled himself at how much the question precisely consolidated all of his emotions. Spurred by this, he continued as he recalled the recent barrage of activities, protests, court battles, pickets, rallies and meetings - oh, the meetings – abortion strategies, elections, committees, etc. etc.

"I mean, are we really doing what our Lord wants us to do?" Although it almost made him feel sacrilegious, it seemed impossible to express the weariness he was feeling without speaking negatively.

"Look, Mark," Stephen interrupted, "we are living in perilous times. The world has gone mad with its sin. All around us there are people demanding the right to do things that will destroy this country. If we don't stand up for what is right, there won't be any freedoms as we know them now. If we let them have their way, you and I won't even be able to pray like we just did in public. The Bible says, 'When the enemy comes in like a flood, the Spirit of the Lord will raise up a standard against him.' We are that standard - you and I, Mark. We must stand for what is right."

Mark sat and listened as Stephen continued regarding all that had been accomplished and, as usual, it all made perfect sense. Much was being done for the good of the community. Salt and light were being shown, it seemed, and Mark felt almost ashamed for even taking Stephen's time with his concerns.

"...And we must stand together so the world can see the strength that they are dealing with," Stephen concluded and paused to sip his coffee.

This gave Mark time to ask, "But what about Tuesday night?"

"What about it?" Stephen responded.

Tuesday night - the culmination of months of meetings, rallies, legal threats and much more against Katie's Naughty Toys Adult Book Shop, which threatened to invade Brookville, a suburb just left of Smith's Corners on Highway 21. Tuesday night was the final showdown. The community, well-organized and prepared for battle to stop any threat to their lives, was there in full force. The local papers had fueled public interest by stating reports that Katie had hired the best Chicago lawyers to insure that her right to build what she wanted, where she wanted, was not infringed upon. Everyone was prepared; no one was going to budge. It was determined that no matter what decision was made by the local board, the matter was far from over. Each side vowed to carry their cause to the highest court before they would concede.

But when Tuesday night came, something strange and unexpected happened. God's People for the Restoration of Morality had done their homework. The community was there en masse. The value and clarity of purpose were evident in the eyes of everyone and resolve for the mission was very apparent. What surprised everyone, however, was that Katie came to the meeting by herself. No legal counsel, no friends - just Katie.

As testimony after testimony of the dangers of what she was trying to introduce into the community rolled on, she sat quietly with her head down. Finally, when it was her turn to speak, Katie startled everyone by withdrawing her petition.

She quietly related that all of the noise and turmoil of the recent months had made her very discouraged and angry. She stated how much hate she had for the people who were demanding their way when she didn't even mean to hurt anyone. She didn't understand how one harmless little shop, which made people feel better, was worth all of the "rigmarole," as she put it. For many years she had scrimped, saved and worked very hard to open her own shop and was very excited that her dream was about to come true. But when all of the commotion started, it left her hurting and almost dead inside. So she quit.

"It was a great success, wasn't it, Mark?" Stephen said. "I think it will be a long time before anyone tries that around here again."

"But did you see her face while we were all jumping around celebrating the victory?" Mark continued. "I mean, I thought she was going to be this hard broad, bigger than life, you know. But she wasn't. She was this lonely, rejected, broken little woman that just slid off into the darkness."

"But we won! We made sure everyone knows that her kind is not welcome in this town."

"What is 'her' kind, Stephen?" Mark asked from his heart. "What kind of person does God see her as, and what is our job here on this earth for 'her' kind? What are we called to do with 'her' kind whether they kill babies, or run for office, or rob or steal? What is our job?"

"Look, all I know is that we showed her that Jesus doesn't want that kind of store in this community and she got the point," Stephen reacted somewhat aggressively. "If we don't stand up for what is right, there's no telling what kind of society we'd have around here. Why..."

Mark had seen Stephen like this before and knew that it would no longer do any good to try to reason with him. In his heart, he wondered what Jesus would have done with the Katies of His time. Maybe he would find out. He did know, however, when he could get a word in, that he was going to tell Stephen that he would be less involved in things in the future. He was going to take some time to get quiet and think - and pray - and maybe find Katie.

If only you would learn to walk in the Spirit and not in the flesh. My will would be known to you daily, but you miss out on many blessings I have for you. I have not called you to a walk of life, but death to your flesh and through that death comes life - My life for you. Have I not called you to take up your cross daily and to follow Me; to do away with self and self will? Have I not called you for My purpose and My purpose only?

I see My church and I know the things that go on in My church. Nothing is hidden from Me, but everything exposed by the light becomes visible for it is light that makes everything visible. (Ephesians 5:13-14; Numbers 32:23)

First love! First love! I am calling you. Look to your first love with Me. Many of you make other things your first love. I am a jealous God and I will remove everything that comes between you and Me. I love you too much to have that happen to you. It is not to dishearten you or discourage you in any way, but so that you will really know the love I have for you.

# CHAPTER TEN

*"They devoted themselves to the apostles' teaching and to the fellowship, to the breaking of bread and to prayer. Everyone was filled with awe, and many wonders and miraculous signs were done by the apostles. All the believers were together and had everything in common. Selling their possessions and goods, they gave to anyone as he had need. Every day they continued to meet together in the temple courts. They broke bread in their homes and ate together with glad and sincere hearts, praising God and enjoying the favor of all the people. And the Lord added to their number daily those who were being saved."*  Acts 2:42-47 NIV

Tom moved with Mic and Steely to the steps in front of the shop so they could talk. And talk they did. For the remainder of that morning, Steely and Mic related to Tom the new story of street life in which he unknowingly had played a key role. On that first night, when Tom gave Train his Bible and said that he should read it and do what it said, Train did just that. For six months, all he did was lock himself up with his new Lord and the Word. Having only the Holy Spirit to teach him and not having anyone to tell him otherwise, he took every word as not only truth, but truth for him every day. He walked only where he was told by his Father, said only what his Father told him to say, and told others to do the same, just like Jesus did.

The Bible was not just a book to read, but perfect directions on how to live. Jesus was not just a man who lived two thousand years ago, but the risen, living Lord who loved to be involved in the lives of those who loved Him. As trusting children, the "street" church followed only God. They loved because He said they should, forgave because it was the only acceptable response, and received the forgiveness that was given them as starving children savor every morsel of newfound food.

Dead to self, uninterested in the world and totally sold out, each new convert received the untainted gospel as if it were given to him or her from the mouths of those who had walked with the Lord Himself. Bypassing all tradition, spurning any hint of impurity, the unpolluted truth of God's Word was planted deep in fertile soil. Unhindered by the wisdom of man, the Holy Spirit was able to ignite the truth in hearts pregnant with need and fan it into a flame that spread like wildfire.

Instances of people meeting in homes, warehouses and empty buildings to share God's Word and give their lives to Jesus were commonplace. Meetings of ten, fifty, one hundred would sit in the presence of the Lord and wait for the Holy Spirit to empower them. When it happened, they would go forth and proclaim what they knew in power. Children would stand on street corners telling anyone who would listen about Jesus. Signs, wonders and healings came as a natural outflow of a loving God moving through surrendered, holy vessels.

"It sounds like the first century church functioning right here," Tom exclaimed, needing to say something - anything - to express his astonishment.

Steely and Mic looked at each other for a moment. "We don't know what you mean," they said innocently.

"I mean, it sounds like your church functions like they did just after Jesus walked on this earth," Tom continued.

"Isn't that the way all churches work?" they asked, wide-eyed, reminding him of small children. "How does it work any other way?"

"It doesn't," Tom thought but felt it better that he not say anything. "What are we doing here?" he inquired.

"We're getting to that," was their unison response.

Mic began relating that as soon as people realized they had been living sinful lives, even though they were forgiven, they were willing to pay for what they had done. Pushers, thieves, murderers, cheats, pimps, prostitutes en masse began seeking after the Lord as to how they could make amends for their former actions. It was unanimously decided that the right thing to do was to turn themselves in to the police, so one day they all went down to headquarters to confess their crimes and take whatever came their way.

What they didn't expect was that their new brothers and sisters in Christ, most of them their former victims, followed them to the station. As a sin was confessed, someone else would volunteer to pay for the crime. Thieves would stand up and proclaim the amount they had stolen and two, three or four people would vow to pay the debt if given enough time. It became so confusing that no one knew what to do. If there are no accusers, how can there be any crimes?

"The instance that topped it all off though, was when Mickey Wilson, with great sobs of repentance, confessed to the vicious beating and murder of Mary Kirtland. During the preliminary hearing, he walked over to Mary's dad and asked his forgiveness in front of everybody. And Mr. Kirtland," Mic continued, "stood up, hugged Mickey and told the judge that he would serve Mickey's sentence for him if the judge would let him. He said Mickey was younger and could do more for the Lord on the outside. That judge was so shook that he said he didn't want any of us back unless there were complaints. So God set us free and then the judge did, too! So here we are, free as birds and forgiven."

"Ain't God good!" Steely exclaimed with the joy of a released bird in flight.

"Wait a minute," Tom responded after a moment of thought. "You mean to tell me that everyone in the church here functions just like Jesus did...they lay their lives down for each other, they always love, always forgive?"

Mic smiled. "Not always, but when they don't we get together to pray for them. They either start to live as God says we should or they don't hang around too long. Why?" he inquired as if that were the only way to function.

"Oh, I don't know," Tom said, feeling very foolish for asking. Why wouldn't it be that simple? Loving, uncompromising, immovable standards act as the plumb line and all actions are directed by the Word of God.

"But what are we doing here on our way to Papa Joe's? And who was that old man?" Tom asked, looking back a couple of blocks to where they had met Emilio and his gang.

"You're sure gettin' pushy, Preacher Man," Mic said, emitting a fake growl and winking at Steely. "There was a time that kinda talk woulda cost you something. Maybe we should leave you here for a while to see how tough you really are!"

"Sorry," Tom said, getting the point. This was not Henderson's he thought, and he was not the boss over anyone here nor was he in his own world. There is a truth to all being equal in God's eyes because of Jesus. Never before had this become so clear to Tom as now.

These men - men he would have scorned, passed by and more than likely considered much less important than himself - had become his guide, his wisdom for survival, his help in time of need. Tom was as helpless on the street as a small child. The education, success and savvy that allowed him to excel in his portion in life were useless here. Had he become so hardened that nothing or no one really mattered to him outside of his own little sphere?

"Lord, forgive me. Have I been so blind to what You really desire to do with Your people? Help me to learn."

"You off dreamin' again, Preacher Man?" Mic inquired. "You seem to doze off once in a while when we're talkin' to ya. Have you heard anything we said since you asked what we're doing here?"

"You must forgive me. The Lord is really dealing with me right now. My mind is going about sixty miles an hour. This is all so new to me."

"Speed kills, man! We'll take it easy on ya so you don't crash and burn, O.K.?" Steely said with a big smile that showed he was enjoying being in total charge of this street rookie.

"Anyway," Mic continued, "the Jabowski's - Ray and Sarah - had been saving for a long time for this house in the suburbs. You know, to get out of the city. They even had some land they would go to on weekends. They'd take the bus as far as it would go, then walk the rest of the way. They'd stay overnight and start back Sunday and get home before dark."

Steely jumped in enthusiastically, "And we had this meeting see - those of us that had ripped people off. And God said we should start paying people back. We didn't have no money, but we still all felt God was saying to trust Him. He had it taken care of. That was pretty wild, man, because we couldn't earn money like we used to, ya know."

"So we told the rest of the church at one of our meetings," Mic continued with raised eyebrows, showing signs of irritation at Steely because of his butting in. "I mean, we just told them so they could help us pray. But before the end of the meeting, Ray and Sarah said we were supposed to make a list of all that was needed because God told them to sell their land."

"Not only that," Steely chirped, knowing he was on dangerous ground, "they also said they had about $15,000 saved toward the house they were going to put on the land and they wanted to give that, too. When that happened, we all went crazy. We were cryin' and praisin' and thankin' God. It was wild, man!"

Mic, having had just about enough of his thunder stolen, looked at Steely and said, "Look, man, you can tell the next story, O.K.? This one's mine! Now go pray or somethin', O.K.? Anyway..." Mic paused, looking at Steely with a challenge, "when the land sold and we added up all the money, it came to exactly the same amount as the money we could remember we needed to pay back to all the people we ripped off. Ain't that just like God!"

"Yeah, I mean, yes, that is just like God," Tom agreed, trying to remember when that kind of love had ever been shared within the Christian circles he frequented or when some direction God had given had been confirmed so clearly.

"And that's what we're doing here," Steely offered with new bravado, feeling he had a right to speak because the story was over and now they were answering a new question. "We're on our way to pay back Papa and Mama Joe. They own a little grocery store on Fourth and Bigsby Street, and people have been rippin' 'em off for years. When it all got added up, we figure we owe them about $2,500. So we're takin' it to them. It's the last of our money and the last of what we owe, so we're done."

"You mean you're carrying $2,500 in cash on you - on the street?" Tom exclaimed, realizing his voice was getting high again. He quieted himself to almost a whisper. "Do you realize what would happen if word got out that you were going to Papa Joe's with $2,500 cash in your pockets? Have you any idea how many people would 'take you out,' as you say, for that kind of money if they knew you were coming?"

"They did know. We heard that Emilio found out this morning and that's what just happened," Steely said, pointing back to the place where they had been stopped.

"They knew? How did you...wait a minute," Tom said. "If they knew, and you knew that they knew, what in the world would possess you to walk out here with $2,500 in your pocket?"

"Well," Mic replied, "we prayed and God said we could go today - that everything would be O.K. We all had a peace in our hearts that today was the day. So we went and here we are." As the statement rolled from his grinning lips, he made a wide sweep with his arm, a gesture somewhat like Tom remembered one of those models on some game show would employ as the curtain gave way to reveal a refrigerator or some other appliance.

"You guys are nuts; that's all I can say. You gotta be crazy walking down the street with $2,500 in your pockets when you knew people would be looking for you because they knew you had it on you. We could have gotten killed!"

Mic and Steely looked at each other. A combination of expressions - those of surprise and hurt - showed that Tom at least had not angered them by his latest ignorant statement.

"Maybe we didn't make ourselves clear," Mic finally said. "Our Lord said we could come today. He has protected us every other time. Why wouldn't He do it now?"

The expressions on their faces were ones of true wonderment. All of a sudden, it hit Tom. They really walked in faith with their God. Not like he did, with his own limitations, preconceived notions, and built-in fears; but in absolute, childlike, totally trusting, unquestioning faith. They lived it.

"Less than one year old in their faith," Tom thought, "but having faith and maturity unlike anyone I've ever met." He'd only read about it in the book of Acts, but now he was seeing it in flesh and blood.

Waves of embarrassment, shame and repentance flowed through him as he sat there looking up at two of God's

97

children- His true children - unblemished until he came along. They needed to trust what God said to even survive here. Each move they made, every step they took, was done only after they had consulted their Father in heaven. Just like Jesus did. When they were assured of what should be done, they simply did it, without question, no matter what the outcome.

All of a sudden, Tom felt like a cancer cell that had just introduced itself into a healthy body. His doubts, fears and religion seemed very distasteful to him. Tom almost felt ill again. He certainly felt very ashamed and very, very unChrist-like.

"That kinda stuff's been happenin' around here since we got saved," Steely exclaimed, referring to the old man with the brilliant eyes as they again started in the direction of Papa Joe's. "Sometimes, it's whole gangs of really big guys, or a lone old woman, or even young kids. It's never done the same way, but the outcome is always the same."

"Yeah, boom! Everything changes just like before," Mic broke in, referring to the most recent incident.

Steely continued in childlike awe, so deep in thought that Mic's interruption didn't even register. "Like that old guy - the one that whispered somethin' powerful in Emilio's ear back there. He had to be one of 'em. One of those angels. He must've been sent by Jesus to help us. You gotta admit, we were about outta quarters before he showed up, weren't we?"

While he kicked an empty soup can into the distance, Steely glanced bright-eyed toward heaven in honest praise and exclaimed, "Ain't Jesus wonderful! I mean, He not only died for us, but now He lives to take care of us. Ya know, this would make a great fairy tale if it weren't true." Then he shared a private moment with his Lord as he whispered, "I sure am glad it's true though. Boy, am I glad!"

Mic stopped for a moment as the Lord planted a wonderful thought in his mind and then applied it as truth to his heart.

Tom and Steely kept walking, absorbed in thoughts of their own.

"Wow!" Mic cried, running to catch up. "Father God must really enjoy being involved in our lives," he began enthusiastically. Both men stopped and looked at him, waiting for him to elaborate.

"I mean," he continued, awestruck and not as much talking to Steely and Tom as he was simply expressing what he had been shown, "think of the hundreds, no millions of times each day that He helps all of us. He protects us, holds us close, changes us, teaches us how to live so our lives are worth something; and most of the time we don't even know all that He is doing or..." he hesitated, "or sometimes we don't even care."

His countenance became saddened for a moment, and then he brightened as the Lord assured him of His love. "But even then He is pleased to be part of our lives even if we don't always let Him know how glad we are that He is." Then, shaking his head slowly from side to side while staring at the sidewalk, he said quietly, "Boy, are we blessed!" Increasing his decibel level, he exclaimed, "Man, we sure are blessed, aren't we?"

He made eye contact with Tom and Steely and both nodded in agreement. As the trio resumed their journey to Papa Joe's, each in his own way quietly gave thanks to their Father in heaven for His most evident hand on their lives and for their newly refreshed knowledge of the heritage that Jesus, their Savior, had won for them.

For Tom, the day seemed brighter. His fear seemed much less evident and his curiosity to learn more about Jesus, Mic, Steely, Papa Joe and anything else his Father had in store for him was heightened. "This is gonna be fun," he said out loud before he could catch himself.

His two companions, their eyes bright with surprise, looked at each other, then at Tom, then back at each other before they burst out laughing.

"Oh, Preacher Man," Steely said, putting his arm around Tom and giving him a one-armed hug as the three walked in the joy of the moment. "You might make it after all. Maybe."

"Yeah, maybe. But don't forget who's buying the tickets for this trip," Mic added with a smile, giving Tom a gentle poke in the ribs with his elbow.

*Healthy life comes from pure seed. The purest seed has fallen willingly to the ground and died. It is My Son, Jesus. I have raised Him up and glorified Him for all eternity.*

*Should you not follow the example of My Son? Why do you hang on to rotting seed when I AM the source of a life that is untouchable by the death and decay of this world?*

*Hold on to those things that bring true Life, not those things that are perishing. I have shown you the way; now walk in it. Do not look to the left or to the right, but only to Me for I AM with you.*

*But you must trust Me and Me alone. Your only safety is in the life of My Son, Jesus. That means a complete death to your ways of doing things. It will cost you everything, but it is My way for your best life.*

# CHAPTER ELEVEN

*"...Love your enemies, bless them that curse you, do good to them that hate you, and pray for them which spitefully use you and persecute you."*

*Matthew 5:44 KJV*

"Oh boy, there she goes again," Head Nurse Nancy Terser said to anyone in earshot, hoping someone would volunteer to answer the blinking call light from Room 1122B. "She's probably on a tirade again. Do I have any brave souls willing to face the 'wrath of Khan?'" she said to her staff, almost resigned to the fact that she was really, in fairness, the only one who should answer the call. Her entire staff had born the brunt of the indignation coming from Bed B most of the day and it was up to her this time.

"I'll be right there," she responded into the microphone. Normally, she would ask what was needed, but she and her staff knew better in this case. Personal attention and plenty of it was the only acceptable treatment for Crystal Hollingsworth. After all, she was important and she let everyone know "her daddy could buy this place if he wanted and fire all of them." The trouble was he probably could, and maybe even would, if his precious "Buttons" desired it.

One of the wealthiest, most prominent men in the country - maybe even the world - Brighton Hollingsworth III raised his daughter needing nothing with the possible exception of some long overdue discipline, which most people were very willing to administer after any kind of encounter with her. Known for her fast, outrageous and daring lifestyle by her friends, and her hot-tempered, sharp-tongued vengeance by her enemies; Crystal spent her life in endless circles of parties, social events, clubs, cruises and anything else that would allow her to consume her father's wealth upon herself. With an enthusiasm that would make the most diehard soccer fan proud, Crystal Hollingsworth lived her life at burnout speed.

And burn out she did. The alcohol, dope, sex and especially the emptiness she felt deep inside that made her pursue some unseen, unattainable goal, finally caught up with her. At twenty-six years of age, with endless possibilities available to her to make something of her life, she tried to end it for the third time. And so, here she was at Layton Memorial Hospital - out of town and out of reach of the press so as not to slander the precious family name. Crystal Hollingsworth lay in her hospital bed in the most recent of an endless string of mindless, hopeless attempts to scream aloud that she was in serious trouble within.

"It sure took you long enough, you useless incompetent," she said, glaring at Nurse Terser. "I want you to come immediately when I call you, do you hear me? If my father ever found out how you're treating me here, he would have all of your jobs. Then what would you do with your useless lives?"

"What is it you need?"

"This bed has rocks in it, and it's hotter than hell around here."

"I'll see what I can do about it," Nancy said patiently.

"Don't give me any of your patronizing bull_____, you son of a _____. I want you to do something now or I'll make your life so miserable you'll wish you were..." She stopped mid-sentence, looking toward the open door.

"What are you looking at, you overgrown dung heap?" she yelled at the man standing there with his mouth open, unaware of his foolish gaping. "I said what the _____ do you want? If you're going to be a jerk, go be a jerk some place else, not here, O.K.?"

Momentarily taken aback by the foul language and angry demeanor coming from someone so physically beautiful, Train who had just left his buddy, Tiny, stumbled halfway into the room; almost unwillingly, as if pushed by some unseen force. "You sure must be hurtin' bad to be actin' like such a fool," Train said before he even had time to consider his response.

"Just who in the ____ do you think you are?" Crystal said, enraged at this - this nothing - daring to talk to her like that.

"I don't think I'm anybody special, but I do know who you are," he said, beginning to call silently to his Father for wisdom.

"Are you going to give me some of that patronizing _____ about making something of myself...and 'if I had your beauty and money I'd become something?' Look! I've heard all that before and from people a whole lot better than you, you pile of dumb rocks. So beat it, jerk! No more junk heading my way, O.K? And get out of my room before I call security. From the looks of you, you don't want anybody, especially cops, knowing where you are. Now get lost!" With that, Crystal turned her back on both people to add a final note of total disdain and rejection to her comments.

"Who is John Lassiter?" Train said, moving in the Spirit.

"What!" Crystal turned in astonishment, eyes piercing her assailant. "What did you say?" she demanded.

"Johnny Lassiter. Jesus says to you, it wasn't your doing and He has forgiven you."

"You ____, how dare you! I don't know who you are or how you found out about that, but I'm going to have your ____ for daring to even talk to me about that," Crystal said, her face now flushed with anger, screaming totally out of control and obviously off balance. "Nurse, get security. I want this man arrested."

"You won't need to do that," Train said quietly, raising his hand toward the startled nurse. "I'm leaving now."

Focusing once again on Crystal, who was now livid with rage, he said, "You need to know that Jesus paid the price for all of your sins. Even those you won't admit to right now. He hasn't turned his back on you and He would like you to know it wasn't your fault and that He forgives you. He loves you."

With that, Train turned and walked down the hall, followed by loud expletives and cursings from Crystal, who was now being restrained by several nurses. He simply turned and pointed in the direction of the noise as the wide-eyed security guards stormed past him. He decided not to say anything to them that would interrupt his quiet prayer for the woman he somehow knew he had not seen for the first and last time. For some reason, a wisp of a smile was evident on his face.

The harvest is white right now, but My church is so busy doing good things that they can't see My things to do. I ask you, when did My gospel call you to any activity that did not have the eternity of the souls of men and women as its purpose? When did I ever ask you to protect your rights? Where in My Word does it say that you must occupy your time doing works that have no impact on the salvation of your enemies?

I am not in the midst of your projects of men. The ultimate purpose of these doctrines of men is the preservation of your freedoms, your way. I have set you free My way, so that you might share My light in the darkest places for the good of those in bondage. How pitiful and powerless your works are.

You have chosen this day whom you will serve. All projects that have fleshly motives will fail. I call them wood, hay and stubble about to be burned away. Some of you will stand empty handed before Me on that day. You think that your arms are full to present offerings to Me. They are barren and of no eternal worth.

Turn to Me. Remember My desires. I care about the souls of those who are perishing. You care about preserving your life and call it My desire for you. It is not Me to whom you are listening. Turn now to My purposes.

# CHAPTER TWELVE

*"I know your deeds, that you are neither cold nor hot. I wish you were either one or the other! So, because you are lukewarm--neither hot nor cold--I am about to spit you out of My mouth. You say, 'I am rich; I have acquired wealth and do not need a thing.' But you do not realize that you are wretched, pitiful, poor, blind and naked."*

*Revelation 3:15-17 NIV*

"That's right. He's going to be there a couple of days... No, everything's going well. Look, Sally, I didn't talk to Tom himself, but to a Maria Raphael, a lady who takes care of Sunday school kids or something like that. She sounded very nice and I'm sure Tom is fine... Yes, if I hear from Tom or anybody, I'll be sure to let you know... Sure... God bless you, too... Sally, stop worrying! You know Train's heart. He would rather die himself than see Tom hurt or in any kind of trouble... Yes... Yes. O.K. I will. Bye now."

Pastor Wickham put down the phone. "That was Sally Bracken, Tom's wife," he said to the distinguished-looking man sitting across from him in front of his leather-covered desk. "She hadn't heard from Tom and... well, you must have heard what I said."

The man smiled condescendingly, but somewhat pleasantly, addressing the triviality of someone else's problems. Sam Thompson, a very successful restaurant franchise owner, was in no mood to hear about anyone else at this time. He was about to insist that no more embarrassing incidents such as the one that happened the previous night should ever take place in "his" church again.

"One more petty, controlling power play," Pastor Wickham thought, while staring at the intricate pattern of his silk designer tie.  But then, he was a large contributor, so his weekly visits and constant letter writing needed to be endured.

"Why do I have to put up with this, Lord?" he mused to himself, listening halfheartedly to the ramblings of the busybody across from his desk.  Every conversation with Sam ended in the same manner.

"OK, Sam, we'll try not to let it happen again and we'll look into that other concern," he said, ushering the recently and very temporarily contented man to the door.  "Have a good day," he said politely.  "I'm sure," he thought.

Returning to his desk, he looked out his office study window at the beautifully sculptured, scrupulously manicured landscape.  "Morgan Wickham," he thought to himself. "Pastor Morgan Wickham."  He had gotten pretty used to the sound of that in the last twenty-two years.  "Could it be that long ago?  Twenty-two years!"  Fresh out of seminary and on fire for the Lord, he came to His Holiness Christian Fellowship.  He remembered many long, but beautiful nights of prayer and communion, seeking the Lord on behalf of his people.  It was much smaller then - a budding, little church in a growing community outside a major city.

"Who would have dreamed it would come to this?" he mused, as he looked admiringly at his vast, paneled, four room office complex with private bath.  After randomly touching and lovingly remembering the contents that matched the titles of books in his library of floor-to-ceiling shelves and centered reference table, he proceeded to the private chamber he used for rest during those particularly rough times.  He then went through the immaculate kitchen, past his full bath with shower, and headed back to his office.

"God sure has been good," he thought.  Somehow, though, he missed the times when in desperate need, he would close himself in with his Lord to intercede for his little fellowship of friends.  When did all that change?  When did the mechanics of

110

the wisdom received in board meetings replace the steps of faith received in prayer? "About the same time the miracles stopped," he said out loud. Then, shaking the thought and the melancholy, he pressed the intercom.

"Mary, would you get Jim Wilson on the phone for me?"

"Yes, Pastor," came the immediate response. "He's waiting for your return call."

After several moments, the intercom phone sprang to life. "This is Jim Wilson."

"Jim, Morgan Wickham here. What can I do for you?"

"Morgan, thanks for calling so soon," the black and chrome box returned. "I've been thinking, Morgan... well, more than thinking. In fact, Charlie Bates, Bill Smithers and Bruce Harrison and I felt we should do something for this Train fellow. He looked pretty ragged and harried the other night and we thought he must be in real need. So we each threw in a thousand dollars to...you know, help him out. If you would like to open up the offer to help out to the rest of the congregation, we could do that."

"That's very generous, Jim. I will do that. We could invite him here Sunday night and present it to him."

"Good idea," Jim said. "Let's do it. We'll make the arrangements with Mary and let's go for it. She can contact him." With that, the intercom went silent.

"So easy," Pastor Wickham mused. "Four thousand dollars, just like that, to someone who is almost a stranger. I wonder if they would have taken it to him in the inner city?" He was almost embarrassed to think that of such good, caring people. "Of course, they would...wouldn't they?"

*Do not despair or lose heart when I am taking you through a hard time. Do not despise or turn away from Me, but rather run to Me with open arms. Run into My open arms and know that I will hold you close to Me. In such times as these, do know My purpose for you and My plans for you. I know the plans I have for you, declares the Lord. Plans to prosper you and not to harm you. Plans to give you a hope and a future. (Jer. 29:11.)*

*Just learn to trust in Me. Depend on Me. Rest in Me and know that I am in control of every situation of your life. There is nothing that happens in your life that I don't know about first (Matt. 10:29-31.) Put your trust fully in Me and not in the things of this world.*

*Draw close to Me. Spend time with Me. Get to really know Me.*

# CHAPTER THIRTEEN

*"So if when you are offering your gift at the altar you there remember that your brother has any [grievance] against you, leave your gift at the altar and go. First make peace with your brother, and then come back and present your gift."*

*Matthew 5:23-24 Amp*

"Mama, don'ta worry. It'sa gonna be O.K.," Joe said lovingly to his bride of forty-six years. "God, He always take good care His'a kids. He never not'a be there before, right? He gonna help us now, you justa watch. He gonna do somet'ing real special like in the movies, only we gonna be the stars. You en me mamma, we gonna be the stars in God's movie. You keepa pray, I keepa pray and God, He keepa being God, O.K?"

With those words, Joe tenderly kissed his lovely Maria on the cheek, observed only by the silent, invisible warrior that had overseen the "incidentals" needed to accomplish the answering of the prayers of his two greatly loved charges. For sixty-seven years without fail, this "guardian angel" had done his Master's bidding on behalf of Joe Ingrelli and his wife.

For many years, Joe and Maria, more comfortably known as "Papa and Mama Joe," prayed and gave and served and lived all in the name of their beloved Savior. They received a meager, but adequate income from their small, corner grocery store. In their worldly poverty and trials, they became rich in their Lord and Redeemer.

Their store was less a means of income for them and more a way that they could contribute to the needs of those they knew. Often, the out-of-work neighbor was able to provide food for his family even though he had no money. Some would take it upon themselves to repay such generosity, but more often than not, Papa and Mama never saw the money. There were those few who would take advantage, but most honestly would never have enough to be able to repay. To the loving couple, the debt became non-existent, even a welcome opportunity to give a gift unto their Lord. For over forty-five years, they gave as they saw need. The neighborhood was much more than customers. It meant good friends, warm times and giving and sharing opportunities.

Within the recent years, however, things had changed around them. The neighborhood had become rough. Friends moved away to safer, more comfortable areas. Others took their business to the more modern, better-stocked supermarket on Elm Street.

The most grievous of all the changes around them was the deterioration of the values they themselves held as most important, especially in the young. All too often they had to watch helplessly as boys and girls they knew as smiling, happy youngsters became poisoned and hardened by the street. Some of those they had helped as children, later as teens, returned to rob them and vandalize their small store.

As Papa and Mama Joe got older, it was all they could do to make ends meet. Still, they held on to their deep love for each other, their neighbors, and their God. They represented their Lord as they knew He would desire. They forgave those who stole from them, prayed for those who spitefully used them and blessed those who laughed at them in their weakness.

Now, in their twilight years with failing health and weakening bodies, the mounting medical bills for Maria tested them both. Mutual love for each other and their combined love for the Lord were their only hope. It sustained them and allowed them to complete each day with the knowledge that He would provide for tomorrow. He had before; He would again. They had no other source.

"Are we just going to walk in on them, tell them you were the ones who took it and then leave?" Tom asked, betraying his nervousness.

"I don't know," Steely said. "I just go. What happens, happens."

"I should have guessed 'what happens, happens'," Tom thought.

As the tiny bell - that had for so many years announced the arrival of everyone who opened the door - once again beckoned Papa or Mama from their endless tasks, the trio stepped into a bygone era of sights, smells and simple pleasures. Tom was overwhelmed.

In the time it took for Papa's greeting from somewhere behind one of the four rows of sparsely stocked shelves to come to them, it was all Tom could do to hold his boyish delight.

"My Dad used to tell me about going to places like this when he was a boy," he whispered to Mic, who was reading a faded poster thumbtacked to the wall.

"Incredible," Tom found himself saying several times as he visually explored the small, quaint surroundings. Glass bulk candy jars, wooden bins, concrete crocks and ancient barrels that held everything from peanuts to pickles, a thin ladder that rolled along the wall of shelves behind the counter that held the most beautiful brass-filigreed cash register Tom had ever seen - it all enthralled him. It brought to life all of his Dad's reminiscing bedtime tales. Tom smiled to himself as he turned to look out the front window, almost expecting to see a hitching rail and horses. Instead, he found only the drab street, momentarily bringing him back to reality.

Seeing Papa Joe took Tom back to his sentimental journey. A small man, looking very much like Gepetto of the fairytale Pinnochio, Papa emerged from his task of scrubbing the wooden plank floor at the rear of the store. Stiff from kneeling, and walking somewhat bent over at first, he wiped his hands on his freshly starched, white grocer's apron. He greeted his waiting guests.

"Can I helpa you?" he said.

"Perfect," Tom thought as he saw and heard the white-haired man with his thick Italian accent. "Just like in the movies," he marveled, almost feeling the elderly man somewhat over-acted his Italian grocer role.

"You boys need somet'ing?" Papa Joe continued warmly, walking to his position behind the register.

Tom noticed the well-worn curtains that probably covered the entrance to the couple's living quarters. They moved aside just enough to reveal a small, silver-haired woman, warily observing the situation.

"I know you boys," Papa spoke, looking over the top of his square, wire-rimmed glasses that grasped the very end of his nose. "Ain't you guys the ones..." he started again and then hesitated. A remembrance showed visibly on his reddening face.

"Aw, boys, we got not'ing left," he said pathetically, now fully recognizing his former assailants. "How many times you gotta come here before you quit? Please, don't do this today," he continued, as he helplessly opened the cash register in full surrender, ready to withdraw its meager contents.

"No, no," Mic cried urgently. "Papa Joe, you got it all wrong. We didn't come here to rip you off. Look into our eyes. See, we're different. We're like you now! We come to give - see?"

Mic looked at Steely who pulled the folded money from his pocket and held it out in front for all to see. Papa Joe stood immobilized. Finally, Mic walked over and took the money from Steely, placing it in Papa Joe's hands. For several moments, no one said a word. The trio just stood there grinning like school kids.

Papa looked at the money in his hands, then at the trio, meeting each man's eyes in wonder, then back at the money; then he looked at the men again, who by this time were uncomfortably happy.

"Mama," he began quietly, almost to himself. He turned to his left, money laying in his open, outstretched hands and again, this time with more volume, exclaimed "Mama!"

All looked in the direction of the emerging woman, with hands clasped over her mouth and tears of joy streaming down her cheeks. Tom looked at Mic and Steely, who were teary eyed and shifting from one foot to another like a couple of school boys who had just given an apple to their favorite teacher.

"Mama, look," Papa said softly, as he presented his gift to his precious wife. "Look, Mama," he said again in wonder as she gently put her hands under his, eyes wide with joy.

"Bless the Lord," Mama said quietly. "And bless you," she continued, looking into the eyes of the three men.

"Why you boys do this?" Mama queried, wiping the tears from her eyes as she moved to the front of the counter so she could hear better.

Tom looked at her wellworn, but neatly pressed housedress and pocketed apron. Her attire truly completed the overall picture painted before his eyes. What he hadn't noticed before was the badly swollen leg and ankle that looked very painful. As she walked to the men, she leaned heavily on the counter to steady herself.

The couple stood quietly and in awe as Mic and Steely explained the events leading to the presentation of their gift. Tom could only wonder why God does things the way He does. Did God allow these good people, people that most of this world would consider foolish failures in life, to suffer and lack all of these years just so this moment could happen? Why was he now privileged to be a participant in this moment?

Where was it all leading? His mind soaked up all that was happening, and at the same time, raced with wonder and questions.

Mama reached up and each man bent obediently to receive a warm kiss on the cheek and a loving embrace. As she hugged Mic and Steely, Tom was anxiously preparing himself to accept his share. When his time came, he tenderly received. Tom's own mother never hugged him, so this gesture was very special to him.

Papa, who was still somewhat dazed by the whole event, tearfully, without a word, held the hand of each man for a moment and simply patted each one's chest affectionately, gently signifying his grateful acceptance.

Before they left, Mama, who had slipped into the back room while Papa was thanking everyone, came out with arms loaded with goodies. To each man, she presented her gifts of thanks. Mic received a tray of warm, homemade, oozing with caramel and cinnamon nut bakery. Steely received one of the largest garlic summer sausages they had ever seen. Tom was presented with warm, fresh rolls. They could have received more from the grateful couple who kept offering, but they knew they shouldn't.

"Boy, that was fun," Tom giggled, holding his jaw with his free hand and moving it from side to side. "My cheeks hurt from smiling for so long," he continued. The others nodded in agreement. Their expressions, as they performed facial gymnastics, must have been quite a sight to passersby.

The trio continued to walk silently for a few blocks, booty in hand, grinning and reflecting on the joy of what just happened. Then almost in unison, they stopped and looked at each other, at their gifts and then back at each other. "Let's eat," they said together, hurriedly moving over to the steps of the building nearest them.

"If only we had a kni-" Tom started to say as Mic whipped a shiny switchblade from his back pocket and opened it in one fluid motion with a pronounced click. Tom couldn't take his eyes from the knife, as memories of the first meeting under the street lamp flooded his mind.

"You say something, Preacher Man?" Mic said nonchalantly as he cut a large slice of sausage and placed it in the roll Steely had broken open with his fingers.

"No, just remembering," Tom said, receiving the sandwich from Steely. "Just remembering," he said again as he perched on the first step.

As the men sat and ate and spoke joyously, Tom marveled to himself at what this day had already held for him. "Could it get any better?" he thought to himself. "Could I feel more alive than this?" he mused, trying to remember if he had ever felt this good before.

As they finished their food, and were still licking the gooey caramel from their fingers, the men headed back to Train's place. Tom walked a little behind Mic and Steely, who were playfully rubbing their fingers on each other's shirts. Tom was not a part of their playfulness and it gave him time once more to try and sort out all that was happening. "Almost unbelievable, somewhat unreal," he thought as he looked a little more closely at his companions. "Do these guys know something about living for Jesus that I don't? I really want to find out, Lord; help me."

"You comin,' Preacher Man?" Steely quipped, turning to Tom who had fallen several steps behind. "We'd hate to have you too far behind us in this dangerous neighborhood," he continued.

"Yeah, you got the rolls," Mic laughed, "and we might need another sandwich."

All three enjoyed the rest of the walk, laughing, joking and praising their God. "Thank You for everything, Lord," Tom said quietly to himself. "Thank You for today."

Holiness, denial of self, sacrifice, and the crucified life. Why do you not seek them? They are the true path to happiness.

You fight to protect those things you hold tight and call it My work. You walk without power because you have not made Me your source of power. You are ineffective by My standards, but your search to fulfill your personal needs blinds you from seeing how barren your life really is. In doing your work and calling it Mine, you have become angry, fearful and in need of changing your world. How foolish. How vain.

I am seeking those who cherish holiness unto Me. I will use those who turn from this world and its ways. Despise those things which stop you from giving up your life completely to Me.

# CHAPTER FOURTEEN

*"Is not this the kind of fasting I have chosen: to loose the chains of injustice and untie the cords of the yoke, to set the oppressed free and break every yoke? Is it not to share your food with the hungry and to provide the poor wanderer with shelter--when you see the naked, to clothe him, and not to turn away from your own flesh and blood?"*

*Isaiah 58:6-7 NIV*

The rest of that Friday and all day Saturday, Tom had the continued privilege of seeing the true church of Jesus Christ in action. With constant joy, spontaneous prayer, and thanksgiving, people who had little delightfully gave to those who had less. Love was more important than pride; integrity before the Lord drove out the stench of serving self, while the gratefulness of what Jesus had done for them directed all their activities.

Selfless giving, such as Red Carlson selling all he had to buy three buses so that children could be transported to "Christian School" through dangerous neighborhoods, seemed to be the norm. To see Red and others faithfully pick up and deliver well over five hundred kids per week in numerous shifts - kids who never would have otherwise known of Jesus' love - brought conviction to Tom's hardened heart.

Taylor Washington, a local contractor, decided to remodel and make safe the homes of those who either didn't know how to or couldn't afford to do it themselves. His imprint and the Lord's were evident wherever he went. A special glow remained in and around each home he touched.

Andy and Ceil Bobrowitz of "Ceil's Home Restaurant" opened their doors early to provide a healthy breakfast for children who may otherwise never have gotten anything to eat that day.  Each child was sent to school full in stomach and carrying a brown paper bag containing more nourishment for lunch.  Volunteers even took time to seek out and assist any youngster who desired help with his homework assignments. More often than could be counted, grateful parents would stop in to see if their child's glowing stories of love were true, only to see and hear the gospel in action and willingly surrender to the Jesus who loved as these people did.

On and on, in story after testimony after personal observation, people gave and loved and lived as Jesus did. With selfless hearts desiring only to please their Lord, the humble served the needy and each other.  As God blessed with signs and wonders, grace and mercy, and love and open involvement in the lives of those who served Him, He joyously provided Himself to those He loved.

When there was need, He provided the proper manna. From the upraised hands of praise to the bent knees of petition or the open hearts of submission, the King of All Creation freely responded as only He could.  There was always enough. Somehow, someway those living for Him had what was necessary to accomplish any and every given task.  God had restored His true church and was daily preparing His bride.  A sense of holiness unto the Lord, a priority of serving Him and selfless giving permeated every facet of the lives of those involved.  It was truly like walking back in time to the days of the Bible writings.

Everywhere Tom turned, he saw Jesus Himself lived out in the people around him.  More questions flooded his mind. Could this be the beginning of the outpouring of the Holy Spirit that precedes the return of our Lord for His bride?  Could it be?   In this generation?  Could he be witnessing the beginnings of that time frame?

Tom recollected the undercurrents that seemed to follow him most of his lifetime.  They spoke of the importance of the times and the seasons. Often, he would hear about some preacher or read some article that commented on how the news of the day was fulfilling prophecy precisely. Many talked about the endtime church that would be raised up by God Himself in the last days to walk in unselfish love and unyielding devotion to God alone. Those kinds of stories had always been around, hadn't they? Even the apostles thought that Jesus would return in their lifetimes.

But Tom remembered hearing of this kind of life being raised up in little pockets in random cities. Even if it wasn't the end times, Tom knew that His life was far from the kind of life that these people exhibited each day. In comparison to the kind of life that he realized was attainable, his life was an embarrassment.

In the quiet of Train's apartment, Tom petitioned his Father to change him. His life - his selfish life, his walk with Jesus, as cold as it now seemed - was distasteful, even disgusting to him.

"I am so ashamed, my Father," Tom cried in silence. "What I have seen makes me know how wrongly I have lived - how I have missed, even taken for granted, Your great gifts to me. I have consumed what You have given me upon myself, thinking it was O.K. I'm sorry, my Lord. Forgive me, for I have sinned deeply against You and against all those You have put in my life who needed to see Jesus in me. I don't know what to do from here, but I surrender to You to change me."

With that silent prayer, Tom Bracken drifted into a sound sleep. The winds of change had begun to blow on his life - change that would alter his life forever. These were only the beginning breezes that would lead to hurricane forces that would impact, and sometimes uncomfortably disrupt, those lives he would touch.

## The Knock

Jesus comes to all of us in individual fashion. The most important thing is that we accept Him when He does knock on the door of our life. Many of us do not acknowledge Him right away.

Our Lord, being the merciful God that He is, will continue to give us a chance for salvation. He may come to us directly or through someone who is a witness in his or her daily Christian walk. Whatever the means, He does call all of us... All we need do is ANSWER!!

# CHAPTER FIFTEEN

*"The wicked have set a snare for me, but I have not strayed from your precepts. Your statutes are my heritage forever; they are the joy of my heart. My heart is set on keeping your decrees to the very end."*
                                    *Psalm 119:110-112 NIV*

She didn't know why, but Crystal had spent most of the day preparing herself for this meeting. Even though hospital regulations strictly forbade visitors after hours, she made some calls, pulled some strings; and eventually got her way. But then, she always did. That's what made life so boring. Everything came her way eventually. There was no challenge in anything; nothing was of any real value. Crystal Hollingsworth got what she wanted no matter what it took to get it. Using whatever means available - deceit, her ample charms, pressure, money - she was a master of manipulation. It was almost like a game to her. She knew that everything and everyone had a price. It was just a matter of finding out what that price was; and once that was determined, the rest was simple.

Her favorite sport was using people to provide diversion. She enjoyed pitting women against one another; and she watched expectantly as true personalities came to light, most of the time to the ruin of reputation. Men were also great sport for her. Long ago, she had determined that long-lasting relationships produced no gain. Many failed ones had proven that, so each new encounter was simply used to temporarily meet whatever her need was at the time. An endless trail of broken, crippled and shattered people - both men and women - were simply trophies to Crystal. After all, when a person is good enough or talented enough to win at something, they receive a trophy, right? Why shouldn't she?

In the corners of her mind, she had long ago built a special trophy case in which she placed all her human trophies. Whenever she felt threatened, she would gaze upon these symbols of victory and reassure herself of her imperviousness and superiority. As far as she was concerned, her mental trophy case provided the prime reason for the existence of others.

This latest potential prize - this pile of dumb rocks, as she recalled referring to him - seemed a special challenge. After her anger had subsided and she could think clearly, she realized that he had almost fooled her. "Quite a trick," she conceded, "playing that innocent, farmboy role," and then getting her off-balance by naming a ghost from her past that triggered long-suppressed emotions and fears. She hadn't quite figured out his game yet - probably money or some other favors - but that's what made it interesting. In fact, she hadn't felt this challenged in a long time.

So far, the groundwork had been easy. She made simple inquiries as to whom he came to see, found out his name, asked some locals how to find him and...bingo...he's on his way. Now for the fun part!

"Let's see, this should do it," she thought as she pulled her most revealing negligee from her case. She smiled to herself as she felt the flush of the chase rise up within her. Too bad that feeling had to leave. It always did, and then everything was so boring again. What a shame.

"Anyway, let's see," she plotted, bringing her thoughts back to the present. "Act...hmm, what will push his button? Demure, innocent...no, he's already seen that I'm not that. Sexy, street tough. Yeah, that's what he's probably used to. I'll throw in a whole lot of vulnerability for insurance. Good, good! Crystal, you are so good at this," she congratulated herself, a confident smile crossing her face. "O.K., Big Boy, let's see how long you last. You started this, now we'll see what you're really made of!"

******************************

Other than this visit to his friend, Tiny, in the hospital, Train had spent most of the last two days in prayer. Even though his days with Tom and his family were wonderful, the experience of seeing Christians function so much like the rest of the world was extremely unsettling to him. When he came to understand that there really was a Savior of the world and that someone could have hope in this lifetime, he saw no option but to serve Him completely. To see anyone who knew of Jesus and functioned differently drove him back to his Father for answers. In the warmth and safety of fellowship with the One he loved the most, he had again found assurance and peace.

Everything was clear again. What he had learned was right. There was no reason, nor place, to doubt anything the Word or the Spirit had to say. As far as he was concerned, the plumb line had been drawn; His name was Jesus and everything else was compared to that ideal. Time was of no consequence to God, nor did it take its toll on His ways. Truth always remained truth, no matter how long ago it was written. He could trust and function in that.

He regretted that he had not been able to see much of Tom since they came back from the church service at His Holiness. Mic and Steely had assured him that everything was fine, and that it was possibly even better that he had stayed away, so that Tom could experience their world for himself. Consequently, Train was at peace.

Train had chosen to walk to the hospital instead of taking one of the orange and black city buses. As he found himself enjoying the familiar sights, sounds and smells of the neighborhood, he knew he had made the right decision. The distractions on the bus would not have allowed him to quietly think while he rode.

About two blocks from the entrance, Train felt an overwhelming desire to stop and sit on a large boulder next to the sidewalk. A feeling of great anticipation began to well up in his spirit. He had become very familiar over the last year with what he was feeling and knew his Lord was about to tell him something very important and extremely valuable. For a few moments, Train heard nothing. Then, he heard his Father speak.

*"It is the beginning of the end of time as you know it. You, and others who will listen, will soon see My hand in action to change My church. My son, your ways of knowing Me are just the beginning. I am about to change My church so that all who come will see Me as you do; as I have intended for My people from the beginning. It is about to happen all over the world as My plans go forth. Be ready. Be prepared. It will happen soon and speedily. I have begun and no one will change what I have set in motion."*

After a time of quiet thanksgiving and praise, Train stood and headed for the main entrance of the hospital. The impact of what he heard rested fully in his spirit, without turmoil or resistance of any kind. In his simple faith, he knew that as important as the message was, his only place was to trust in his Lord - which he did. At hand was this next hospital visit; and somehow he knew that it all fit into his Father's plan, so he was at peace. He entered the lobby with great anticipation, knowing that he was where he was supposed to be at that very moment. It didn't matter what tomorrow would bring.

Wealth, power, fame, all fall pale next to My glory. Begin to see My glory as something tangible and real in your life, not simply a word, an entity beyond reach for you. My glory is coming back to My people.

Surrender fully to what I am doing in your life and you will be a part of what I am doing in the end times. Your only hope is My presence.

The world and all of its wisdom is soon to pass away. Do not be distracted by how powerful it seems. It is all a lie. All is moving toward an end I have determined.

Do not be fooled. Only in Me is there peace. Only in Me is there the power to overcome. Submit to what I am doing and you will be safe.

# CHAPTER SIXTEEN

*"Turn away my eyes from beholding vanity (idols and idolatry); and restore me to vigorous life and health in Your ways."*                                    **Psalm 119:37 Amp**

*"Do not conform any longer to the pattern of this world, but be transformed by the renewing of your mind."*
                                                        **Romans 12:2 NIV**

Sally Bracken busied herself, tidying up the loose ends of the day.  At least she had heard from Tom, she thought, as she deposited one of Becky's new outfits on a hanger and tried to make room for it in her already bursting-at-the-seams walk-in closet.  Shopping was always good therapy for her; and with the uncertainty of Tom's wellbeing, even though Pastor Wickham felt all was well, she needed to buy something.  It made her feel better.  Whether she needed to buy all that she did was another matter, but it did make the day go faster.  And now, Tom's recent phone call put her mind totally at ease.

"Something was different about him though," her spirit quietly prompted as she went about her business.  Brewing a cup of herb tea and stirring it mindlessly, she began to reflect on the events of her life.  Maybe recalling some fond memories would relieve this unusual feeling in her spirit.    Why did she have this sense of melancholy all of a sudden?  What made her decide to take an accounting of who she had become?

The steaming bath water from the gold, dolphin-shaped faucet rushed down the side of the large, marble tub and formed pools of reflecting color as it joined the bath oils.  Sally sat pensively on the satin, upholstered dressing chair.  Moving to the mirrored wall above the matching marble vanity, she looked at herself, wondering if she really knew the person looking back at her. Who was she - really? Wife of an extremely successful architect, very successful and sought after fashion designer, honor student, the head cheerleader who married the quarterback, someone from a wealthy upbringing, president of the local Parents For Better Education, participant and chairperson of most Missionaries for the Preservation of Morality events, still quite pretty, (even if she did say so herself,) good, involved mŏther. Yes - all that was true.

"But is this who God's really purposed me to be?" she asked herself as she submerged up to her neck in bubbly, perfumed reverie. If she could do it all over, would she do it the same way? Better still, if each move in her life were absent of any personal motive - pure in its intent, holy in content - would she be where she was now?

A strong feeling of shame came over her as she compared the elegance of her existence to the harshness of the slivered cross born by her Savior. She and Tom were good stewards of what God had given them. They gave their ten percent to the church and gave to others, praying before they did so that their money wasn't misused. Surely, He didn't expect everyone to live exactly as He did, giving everything away, did He? I mean, He lived in another day, another time, when there was no choice, right? But then again, could she defend her style of living, all of her actions, if Jesus was with her every day?

Suddenly, Sally realized that during the time Train had stayed with them, she had spent most of her time apologizing for having so much in comparison to him. She asked him not to be uncomfortable and even made sure he knew that she had not paid too much for anything he saw. She had done her homework and had gotten good deals on each item.

Why was she so defensive? Why did she always feel a need to justify their wealth and how much they owned in front of this humble man of God? He didn't seem to do or say anything that warranted that kind of behavior. In fact, he was most cordial and appreciative of even the least gesture of hospitality. Why did she feel as if she were being exposed in front of some great light, somewhat embarrassed by what was revealed? Sally began to realize that she had gotten into the pattern of looking past needs when they came her way. "I can't be responsible for everyone," she told herself.

"Lord, what are You trying to show me?" she said out loud as she dressed for bed. "If You are trying to get through to me, help me to see what it is."

Knowing her mind was simply too alert to allow her to sleep, Sally went into the library to find a good book to read. "That's unusual," she thought, as she picked up a book that was lying in the middle of the floor, directly in front of the door. "In His Steps: An Experiment in How Jesus Would Walk if He Were Here Today," she read.

"Boy, what a coincidence," was her thought as she turned back toward her bedroom and settled in to read. Her unseen protectors glanced knowingly at one another, signifying "mission accomplished" as they silently transported themselves back to their positions to await further orders.

I know that this is hard for you to comprehend at times, but your sins no longer exist as far as I'm concerned, if you've turned them over to Me through Jesus. Any failure you've had, any wrong you've done or do is no longer on heaven's register, if you repent to Me.

My desire is for you to walk in the liberty that has been bought at great cost for you. Do not be weighed down by worldly cares. You cannot see Me clearly through guilt and fear. I am a loving God. You are My child.

Why do you resist My love? Even if I am taking you through a trial, it is for your good. I know best. Please know that I am with you through it; as a father protects the first steps of an infant, I shield you. Just trust Me.

The power of My love can make a way.

# CHAPTER SEVENTEEN

*"...Choose you this day whom ye will serve."*
**Joshua 24:15 KJV**

No one had stopped him in the lower lobby, but recently it seemed as though he was able to go pretty much where he wanted. "Let's see...1122...Oh, yeah, just down the hall from Tiny's room," Train remembered, pushing the button with the number eleven on it. "Hmm... They're not really buttons, just little recesses with lights in them; but when I put my finger in one of them the door closed, so it must work," he thought to himself. "I wonder what makes it work? It must be the heat from your finger," Train mused, knowing that if he had a pen or something cold on him he would try to see if that worked, too.

"Oh well! Not enough time," he realized as the bell, announcing his arrival on the eleventh floor, halted his search for a pen. All he could produce was a stick of Juicy Fruit gum that tasted like a combination of coat leather and sweet juice. He stepped from the elevator and said a silent prayer to his Father for wisdom and power.

Crystal had become somewhat annoyed at the tardiness of this plowboy. She had strategically arranged everything in the room in its proper place for added impact and optimum effect on her unsuspecting prey. Even flowers - lots of flowers - that she herself had sent added that special touch of vulnerability and needed atmosphere to the stark hospital room.

Positioning herself comfortably upright in bed, allowing the covers to be lowered just enough to more than interest any normal, functioning human male, and allowing a tuft of her long red hair to hide a small portion of her barely concealed flesh, she waited. The large bandages on both of her wrists -

137

bandages that could have been removed by now and replaced with smaller ones - were the only evidence of a reason for her hospital stay. She knew they would invoke sympathy and she was not about to miss any opportunity to be in control.

1120, 1121, 1122. Train entered the room and immediately turned around and left just as Crystal was about to issue her honey-like greeting. "What the ---," she said out loud. "Where are you going?"

Moments later, Nurse Thelma Matlinger walked through the door. Thelma noticed with disgust – as had the other nurses - the preparations Crystal had been making; and she seemed extremely delighted to give her a message from Train.

"Mr. Winslow has asked me to tell you that when you are decent he will come back into the room." Triumphantly, she turned about-face and proceeded to walk out the door, pausing only long enough to grab a cotton, hospital housecoat and throw it in Crystal's direction. Then, defiantly commenting over her shoulder, as if to add insult to injury to the now off-balance, pouting child, "He also wants me to be in the room all the time he is here. If you agree to that, you can buzz us when you're ready. If not, he needs to be leaving."

"That felt really good!" Thelma chuckled to the quietly cheering nurses at the station. "I've wanted to do something like that ever since that spoiled brat came in here. I think she has her hands full."

Train had quietly taken a chair over in the corner, neither noticing nor caring about the admiring looks sent in his direction by Thelma and her night crew. He was grieving in his heart, as he knew his Lord was, for someone so lost and needy of God's love and forgiveness.

"Who does that guy think he is? As if I would stoop so low as to do what he thought I was doing. Why, I've got a mind to..." she paused.

*"...You've been caught. Now get ready and listen to what this man has to say,"* came a very unfamiliar voice - a voice some people might consider a conscience - a voice that Crystal long ago had stopped listening to, but for some reason knew she should heed at this time.

After approximately ten minutes, the light for Room 1122 indicated that Crystal had agreed to the terms set forth by Train through Thelma.

"Would you have Mr. Winslow come in now?" came the somewhat timid, very uncharacteristic voice through the intercom. "I'm ready."

Thelma, followed by Train, entered Crystal's room. Crystal had put on the very unfeminine hospital robe and steeled herself to regain control of the situation. As is always the case, the man of God's glowing warriors had preceded him and prepared the way for God's work to be done. Looking through spiritual eyes, one would see a bright, glowing hedge of protection around the perimeter of the room locked in position and ready, available and very willing to totally eliminate any ignorant, dark foe attempting to return to his willing host and familiar prey. Now that the premises were secured, the man of God was given permission to speak by the Holy Spirit.

"I have a message for you," Train began before Crystal was able to say anything.

"What is it?" was Crystal's off-balance response that surprised even her.

"Your life is a vile taste in the mouth of the Living God," Train began in a voice almost too quiet to hear, but one that carried the presence and power of the Holy Spirit to obliterate any opposition. "You have three times now been saved from committing yourself to eternal damnation by your Father in heaven because He has called you to much more than you know. You have consumed all that He has given you upon

139

your own selfish desires and your actions are a stench in His nostrils. 'This day,' says the Lord, 'you must make a choice. Choose life or choose death.'"

Wide-eyed, and looking very much like a cornered rabbit frantically searching for but finding no place to hide, Crystal sat in fearful silence as the final, astounding revelation was given to her.

"That night outside your parents' room when you and 'Boofer,' your teddy bear..."

Crystal jerked as if given an electric shock that stiffened her joints.

"...The night you heard them say that they hated you and wished you had never been born - Jesus was there also and now removes the hurt you've carried for all these years."

Pools of unfamiliar tears, tears Crystal had sworn she would never shed again, were stifled out of habit and sheer tenacity.

"How did he know? No one knew! I was there alone and never told anyone. How did this man know?"

"Jesus would again say to you, 'Johnny Lassiter's death was not your fault. The ropes were old and you couldn't have known about the pitchfork.'"

Once more, Crystal pressed tighter into her pillows as the word of knowledge from the Holy Spirit through this mortal man impacted her inner being with force enough to hold her immobile. She could think of nothing to say; but the memories- those hidden, fearful, dark memories that had been covered by every available distraction - played vividly, lifelike in her mind.

She saw this little girl and her riding mates in the barn loft of the riding academy. She saw herself taunting Johnny Lassiter to tears, chiding him mercilessly to get on the barrel, which was rigged with ropes attached to the barn corners and saddled to provide a bucking bronc ride when the ropes were pulled. She saw, as if in instant replay, the little girl, with malice and hatred in her heart for this weakling of a boy, pull and pull, harder and harder, with strength beyond her years until the bronc was violent with movement.

She saw...she couldn't look at it again...no, she saw the rope break and Johnny flying into the hay, landing face down, not moving. She saw the four blood-coated, metal fork tines protrude through his small back as he spasmed grotesquely and then went silent forever. And she knew he was dead because she had wanted him to die. Nobody ever said it, but she knew; and she lived every day with that hole inside of her - the hole that was left when Johnny died.

Crystal looked pleadingly into the eyes of her large assailant with an unspoken request to please, please make it go away - make the pain go away.

"I speak healing to your wounded spirit and life - God's life - into your broken heart."

For several brief moments Train stood quietly, his head lowered, waiting to see if he should say any more. Then, tenderly and gently, he took Crystal's hand and covered it with his other massive hand. Looking into the blue eyes of this quieted foe, he began.

"You need to know that even though your life seems to have been a waste up until this moment, there is still time to change. God loves you and it is no mistake that you were born." A reassuring smile covered his handsome face as he spoke, affirming all that had taken place.

With that, Train turned and quietly walked from the room, leaving Thelma, who thought she had already seen "just about everything," standing wide-eyed with her mouth open. Train walked past the nurses' station to the elevator, leaving the five nurses who had been listening on the intercom dumb with wonder. Silently following him with their eyes, they looked like five matching white doves moving their heads in unison.

141

They stood silently, looking at the elevator long after the doors had closed to carry its cherished cargo to the lobby floor; and only after candy striper, Connie McFarland, rounded the corner with her noisy, flower-laden cart and bubbly greeting, were they shaken back to their duties.

Thelma and Crystal briefly stared at one another, not knowing what else to do. Then, Thelma moved toward the quietly sobbing child in the bed in front of her and embraced her. Crystal embraced her back, and for the first time in as long as she could remember, she submitted to the feelings she had deliberately stifled at such a young age - and she cried. Floods of tears and gut-wrenching groans of released hurt flowed painfully as Thelma held her. Sure, she was in the arms of a stranger - not her momma or her daddy whom she needed so badly - but for now these arms would do.

Thelma looked out the window at the painted sky, lit by the lights of the city, as she held her past foe and soon-to-be friend, promising herself she would call her own daughter to tell her how much she loved her. Throughout that quiet night, numerous phone calls were made from the nurses' station to parents and children and loved ones just to say "hi" and "I love you" to groggy recipients awakened from a sound sleep.

There is precious little time - but it is enough! There will soon come upon churches a mighty and sovereign move of the Holy Ghost. At first, you will not believe your boldness nor the power available to you! But you will remember My visit, and you will know that the Word of God is mighty and beyond your understanding. You will finally comprehend the spiritual weaponry that has always been yours.

In this final hour, the winning of souls is all that will matter. The power of God entrusted to the church is not for consumption - it is for battle. The fires of hell will never be quenched, and the people all around you steadily march in its direction. You must turn them back. Trust Me, obey My Word, use My Name often and you will turn many to righteousness.

Carefully mark your time - there is not much remaining. Do not be shaken by what will soon come upon the earth. Remember how you felt in My presence, and how I have already told you that I would never leave you nor forsake you.

# CHAPTER EIGHTEEN

*"...I saw also the Lord sitting upon a throne, high and lifted up, and his train filled the temple. Above it stood the seraphims...And one cried unto another and said, Holy, holy, holy, is the Lord of hosts: the whole earth is full of his glory. Then said I, Woe is me! for I am undone; because I am a man of unclean lips, and I dwell in the midst of a people of unclean lips: for mine eyes have seen the King, the Lord of hosts."*

*Isaiah 6:1,2a,3,5 KJV*

With nothing to hinder them and led only by the Holy Spirit and the Word of God, Train's "church" was a continuous praise, petition, repentance and prayer event. It did not start at any specific time nor did it end with formulated accuracy.

"Sunday Church," an event that admittedly was a little more purposeful in attendance for the benefit of neighbors and newcomers, actually began when the first person arrived and ended when the last person left. That was the best way of explaining it. As a matter of fact, a more concentrated mass of people began arriving around 11:30 p.m. Saturday night and most of the participants dispersed sometime late Sunday afternoon or early evening. The building was rarely empty and sometimes "more full" from Sunday to Sunday depending on the moving of the Spirit upon the hearts of obedient lovers of the Lord. During these times, those persons not led to stay and pray would make sure some form of food was always available so that those "in close with the Lord" could keep up their strength.

Church, in other words, had little to do with a building. The building may have been used to bring the real church together in one place, but that is where the identification ended.

God's people - wherein was tabernacled the Risen Christ - were the living, breathing, world-affecting organism called the church. Always functioning, never sleeping, some portion of the body of Jesus Christ was moving to affect someone who needed to hear and see and receive the Good News of salvation. This Sunday was no exception.

About thirty people - men, women and children, including Train who had decided to pray instead of going home - had been at church since about midnight. By 8:00 a.m., when Tom Bracken arrived, well over three hundred people were involved in various stages of praise and worship. Having no plan other than God's plan, they moved in the Spirit and only in the Spirit throughout the "service." An eight-year-old boy was closing his prophetic word as Tom found his place in the back corner of the vast room.

The church was a converted warehouse, and Tom was somewhat taken aback at the starkness and simplicity of his surroundings. There were no frills, no trappings that would indicate that this was a church. From the exposed rafters high above the bare concrete floor to the block walls with industrial windows vented at an angle for air movement, the building looked more ready for the beehive activity of a working shop than a place of worship. Plain, sturdy benches made from heavy lumber were in orderly position as furrows would be in a plowed field. Everything was scrupulously cleaned and maintained, however, and all was presented as a gift offering to God.

"It truly must be pleasing in His sight," Tom thought as he sat on one of the benches polished from wear.

As Tom surveyed the fellowship, something peculiar was happening. Something almost frightening was taking place. If he hadn't seen his new friends' honesty and integrity before God in the last few days, he would have immediately judged what he saw as mindless emotionalism at best, or fanaticism at its peak.

Those who had been there the longest seemed to be most involved, but others who came later became involved in stages. It was amazing. A wind - no, a glow - would hover over individuals or groups of individuals almost as a flame would dance on a log in his fireplace at home. It seemed to be more intense in the front of the church where the thirty initiators of this meeting were, but it would periodically stretch to newcomers at random, always widening in area. As it did, the people would drop under the benches or kneel or fall prostrate, groaning and weeping, or simply sit in reverent silence. Slowly, but surely, the area affected by these "tongues"- that's what they were, tongues like fire - became larger and larger.

Mesmerized by the combination of joy, weeping, praising and sweet abandonment, Tom didn't realize that the fire had grown to involve those on benches directly in front of him and was sweeping in his direction.

"Unclean! Unclean! Unclean!" Tom heard himself cry out as he lay prostrate before holiness beyond description. Whether under his bench or kneeling in surrender, he did not know, but his spirit was exposed before the Creator and Lord of all mankind. Light purer than crystal and penetrating every fleshly corner, every unconfessed sin, every secret thought, sapped the strength from his being.

"Oh! Oh! Oh! How filthy! Oh! Forgive me, Lord! Oh! I can't stand Your presence. I'll be consumed," he thought as the light, heat and holiness became unbearable. "Even cast me away - I am unclean - I am but dirt. Please come no closer, my Lord. I cannot stand it - You are so holy, so pure. Ohhhhh!"

The presence of God involved Tom Bracken's every cell, separating the flesh man from the spirit man just as wax would become instantly non-existent if thrown into a raging inferno. "Please, please, come no closer," Tom found himself

147

screaming inside as the Living Christ in all of His splendor emerged from the flame. Radiant beyond description, clothed in the glory of the Father, and awesome in power, Jesus, the Light Himself, reached out to touch Tom.

Tom knew he would cease to exist. He understood now. He saw himself compared to the Living Christ and he now knew that if he were thrown into the pit of hell forever it would be what he deserved. He also knew, now that he had caught a glimpse of the Lord of All, that he would praise Him forever, even if he were in the torment of hell. It was all he could do, for Jesus is worthy of praise - not for any other reason than for who He is.

*"Come, My son,"* were the words that instilled enough strength in Tom to slightly raise his head. *"You have been cleansed and called, so now come."*

More hope - enough to glance at the nail-scarred feet. "Oh, my Lord, I have been so wrong, so selfish. I'm ashamed."

*"It's over now. Today we will talk and now you will be completely Mine. I love you, Tom Bracken. A time is coming and is now here when My people will feel the wrath of their sin and neglect of Me. For too long, they have been blemished by the world and its ways.*

*"Watch as My Word goes forth to purge and to purify. What looks to the unskilled in My Word as persecution by the enemy is really My hand upon them to cleanse their lives. Too many have called themselves Mine but chose to stay in the world.*

*"Walk above anything that resembles the ways that seem right to man for its end is death. Holiness unto the Lord is the only heart that will prevail. Boldness coming from purity will allow My people to survive. Faith coming from fellowship with Me will be the answer to all the needs of those who walk with Me.*

148

*"I will be Lord, and now the world will see Me through those who are purified by the coming fire. For eternity, We will explore the wonders of what has been provided for you, but now there is work for you to do. There are many who need to see Me in you - many who have not heard. I long for them to come. You go and tell them. You tell them, Tom Bracken. Tell them of My love.*

*My church is about to be purified. All that is about to happen is for your good and for My Word to go forth. Do not be surprised by what is about to happen. Do not fear, for I will be with you. What I am doing now is the beginning of great changes. The world will again see My kind of love, My kind of strength, My kind of power. Do not be afraid, Tom Bracken, for I am with you."*

With that, Jesus touched Tom's head. New strength empowered him to stand. Tom was lifted to look directly into the eyes of his resurrected Lord, eyes so full of compassion that only the Lord's strength flowing in Tom stopped him from being consumed.

*"You tell them for Me."*

"Holy! Holy! Holy! Holy!" was all that could be said. "Holy Lord. Worthy of honor, power and praise. Holy! Holy! Holy!" Tom's words joined with eternal choruses and celestial choirs and became part of the living testimony to the Lord of All. Never would he stop. Never would he leave.

"Tom… Tom." He felt a hand on his shoulder.

It was Train. Once again, becoming aware of the physical world and looking around trying to regain his bearings, Tom surveyed the room - empty except for a few people here and there. He stared blankly at his large friend.

"He touched you, didn't He?" Train said, with a knowing smile. Tom nodded, not finding any words. "The Holy Spirit shows us Jesus often. Did He tell you what was about to take place?" Tom nodded again. "It's the same message we're all

149

getting. I believe something big is about to happen and it looks like we're a part of it," he continued. "Now do you understand why I was so confused and heartbroken at the empty goings-on at your church? I have only known this," he said, sweeping his hand in a descriptive motion.

"And I have never known this," Tom responded woefully. "But I know I can never go back to any other way. Did you see those eyes?" he said pointedly to Train, after gathering himself together.

"Yes, I know." Train shared a covenant smile that said volumes to eliminate any doubt that might occur in Tom in the future.

"It's not about us, is it?" Tom stated. "It's about Jesus," he continued. "Everything - our lives, our families, where we live, what we do - it's all about Jesus and what He's done for those who can't see yet, isn't it? All this," Tom looked around, gesturing with his hand to mean the whole world and God's plan for it, "all this and its events mean only what God has done to reconcile man to Himself. No matter what happens, it doesn't matter, does it? It's not about us and what happens to us. It's all about Jesus and those who haven't heard yet."

Tom sat in awe of what God was revealing as Train obediently remained silent. He realized for the first time that the only real reason for being born is to eventually make a choice as to whether or not you will accept God's plan through His Son, Jesus.

"What time is it?" Tom questioned after many quiet moments, as if awakened from a restful sleep.

Looking at his watch and immediately double-checking with Train's to confirm his amazement, Tom read 5:27 on both of them. It felt like he had walked into the room only moments ago when, in reality, it was nine hours and twenty-seven minutes that he had spent with his Lord. Suddenly, eternity took on a new perspective. The two friends walked to the door at the rear of the building, which now had a glow about it because of the praises of the saints of God.

Unnoticed by them, in a corner under a chair, lying motionless except for the movement needed to quietly cry to her newfound Lord, was a young lady. Except for some small bandages on her wrists, she was no different than any other child of God in that room. Several saints of God had chosen to stay with her as she was cleansed, healed, restored and taught of love. They would be there for a little more than three days, but that was O.K. There was nothing they could think of that was more of a delight to them. Crystal had finally come home.

The brightness in your eyes will soon reflect the perfected work on the cross by My Son in you.

Your spirit of joyous praise will soon quiet the blasphemous words that defy Me to be the God that I Am.

Your holy presence will make anyone who will not acknowledge Jesus as the only Lord too uncomfortable to remain where they are physically or spiritually.

Who will be able to remain where they are when they see the Living Christ as a plumb line in you, My people? Choices must be made; it will be life or death. There will be no middle road once My work is fulfilled in you so that they can see Me and choose.

Do you see how important it is that you surrender fully to Me? Do you see how important it is to set aside doctrines of man, those that have an appearance of godliness, but deny the power of the Living God?

The only way anyone can really see the power I have created by the cross is to see the change in you. As you walk in holiness, in purity, while remaining in your weak vessel, they will know that such power cannot come from within, but by the One who lives within you. Draw close now. Many lives depend on you becoming what I desire of you.

# CHAPTER NINETEEN

*"For what will it profit a man if he gains the whole world
and forfeits his life [his blessed life in the kingdom of God]?"*
**Matthew 16:26a Amp**

"How come we gotta go to church in the morning and at night?" Tommy Bracken asked as he walked past the room, never once breaking his stride or looking up from his battery-operated, handheld computer game.

"Because tonight's a very special night," Sally said, brushing Becky's long, flowing hair.

"Ouch, that hurt, Mom!" Becky reached for her head, giving Sally an angry look through her mother's vanity mirror in front of her. Both children had spent most of the day whining, complaining, and generally expressing their disapproval or unhappiness at most events in their midst.

Sally, herself, was more than distracted. After spending almost the entire night reading, "What would Jesus do in this situation?" was a question she kept asking herself. In fact, she was inwardly feeling new stirrings of dissatisfaction, almost embarrassment, at how well she lived in the light of the life her Lord and Savior had lived.

Somehow, though, she knew it would be resolved. It seemed that what had been all right yesterday would no longer be acceptable tomorrow. Seedlings of changes for the better were being planted deep within her spirit. Her Lord was not angry with her - He was simply instructing her to begin to listen to His new direction. How she knew things were about to change or what that change would be, she couldn't say. She just knew; and it was time. It was also exciting!

"I wonder..."

"Ouch, Mom. That hurts!" Becky cried again. "You're pulling."

Sally realized she wasn't really concentrating on what she was doing. "I'm sorry, honey. There. We're done. You and Tommy put your things away. We'll need to leave in about fifteen minutes," she said, gently smoothing her daughter's hair. "I'll be right down." With that, the two fled the room to get a couple more minutes of TV in before they left.

Sally slowly walked to the window. Sliding the sheer drapes aside and holding them gently with her fingers, she serenely stared at the manicured grounds, the terraced garden, and the large pool with its surrounding outbuildings.

"Could I give all this up?" she thought, surprising herself that she might even consider such an idea. "We've worked so hard to come this far. Could I give it up?" The thought came stronger this time and was a real question that required a real answer. A peaceful smile brightened her beautiful face. Somehow, she knew that deep down, way down in her inner being, she already had. "Yes, Lord," she said as she turned from the window. "Yes," she said out loud as a statement of obedience and confirmation to Him rather than as an answer to her own thoughts.

As she surrendered, a unique freedom - a freedom she hadn't felt for years, more years than she could remember - filled her entire being. Sally put the finishing touches of makeup on her face. As she did, she noticed a new brightness in her eyes - an almost childlike sparkle that she remembered only being there when she was about to embark on a challenging adventure. "That hasn't been there for quite some time, Sally Bracken," she teased herself. Embarking on a peace mission, she started down to the television room where Tommy and Becky had again, out of boredom, decided to disturb each other. On her way down the stairs she commented, "Tom Bracken, are you in for a surprise!"

When did I ever say that ease and comfort would be your lot? Look into My Word. Those that I called My own, those I held dear to My heart at times had no place to live. Even My own Son had no comforts of this world. You seek to satisfy your own needs and call it My will for you. I prosper you and you use it to pad your rest areas.

Do you not see that I cannot use you with a heart that has grown cold? The weight of your possessions and lusts and fears of loss have nullified your testimony. You look no different than the world.

Change your hearts now. Turn from seeking Me for your own gain. The selfless life is the life to which I have called you. You gave Me everything. Why do you take it back?

I want to use you for My purposes, but you are too busy serving your own needs. The people perish all around you and you don't even look up from your toil. You praise Me with your lips, but your hearts are far, far from Me. Return now that I might use you.

# CHAPTER TWENTY

*"Be careful not to do your 'acts of righteousness' before men, to be seen by them. If you do, you will have no reward from your Father in heaven. So when you give to the needy, do not announce it with trumpets, as the hypocrites do in the synagogues and on the streets, to be honored by men."*

*Matthew 6:1-2a NIV*

"You invited that big guy back, didn't you?" the chrome and black box on Reverend Wickham's desk squeaked. "I'm warning you, Morgan. If this guy causes any kind of disturbance like he did on Thursday, you're gonna hear about it. I've already talked to some of the people around here who don't go along with this whole thing, and they aren't about to put up with any of his - or your, for that matter - shenanigans. You had better be in control tonight or you're gonna hear about it. That's all I have to say." With a loud click, the box went silent.

"You're going to hear about it," Morgan Wickham said, mocking the shrill voice and "old maid, busybody" attitude of Sam Thompson, his most recent caller. Normally very reserved, even stuffy some might say, he had to laugh at himself as he said it again to ease the pressure and discouragement he was feeling. "What a gleep!" he exclaimed, startling himself and looking around to make sure no one was within hearing distance.

Pastor Wickham moved aside some papers on his desk in a mindless show of straightening up a little bit. He adjusted his matching pens at the front and moved the pencil box to the right about an inch, centering it as he did. Then, he tapped that evening's sermon notes on end, and decided to go through them one more time before the service.

157

"Why am I so restless, Lord? I feel as though I'm a farmer and I'm standing here looking at a whopper of a storm brewing off in the distance. I know the machinery is safe inside, the wife and kids are safe and I've done all I can do to prepare; but this season's crop, my complete provision for this year, is in the field exposed and there is nothing more I can do to protect it. If this coming storm is a squall or has hail or hurricane winds in it, I'm in deep trouble. I could lose everything I've worked so hard for. Still, all I can do is ride it out and let what is about to happen, happen. Everything I own is in Your hands, Lord."

"Anybody home?" From the outer office, Jim Wilson announced his arrival for their scheduled pre-service meeting.

"Come in, Jim," Morgan greeted him warmly, extending his hand as he walked toward his head deacon.

As Jim walked to one of the maroon, leather, tufted chairs in the conference area, he began speaking even before they were both seated. "Boy, is this guy going to be in for a shocker. I'll bet this is more money than he's seen in a lifetime," he said, handing the check made out to Horace Winslow to Pastor Wickham.

Pastor Wickham opened the folded piece of paper and exclaimed at the amount, "Seventeen thousand dollars! We're going to give him seventeen thousand dollars!?"

"Yeah, isn't it great!" Jim said, leaning back in his chair with a confident smile on his face that hinted of the pride he felt, as if he had his hand in a very successful business venture. Then again, that's why he was head deacon. He knew how to put things together - things that needed to be put together - for the success of the church.

"I just made some calls here, pulled some strings there, pushed a couple of the right buttons and 'voila'," he exclaimed, as he swept his arms wide as if unfolding a bounty on the table before him. "Look, these people won't even feel it. There could have been double that amount if we'dve had more time, but that'll do for now. If we ever want to help him out again, we can. Let's see what he does with this, first. We'll keep an eye on him and how he spends it," Jim said, rising from his chair and walking toward the door. "We had better be good stewards, you know. This is God's money. We'll watch him closely."

Morgan followed him to the door in the outer office, and after shaking hands, watched Jim as he greeted the first people about to enter the sanctuary for the evening service.

"Boy, is Train ever going to be surprised," he thought to himself, as he closed his private office door for prayer before the events of the evening.

"Does this have anything to do with that storm, Lord?" He just couldn't help feeling that it did. Somehow, something just didn't feel right. He went to the padded kneeler in the corner of his office. "Please protect the crops, Lord. I've worked long and hard. It would be rough to start all over. I'm asking you to please protect the crops."

*Holiness is freedom for you. When Jesus was with you on earth, He never set His mind on the things of the earth. My purposes and My goals were always His goals. As He kept His heart on things above, He walked through all earthly circumstances untouched. Even on the cross, He was untouched. There was no earthly power that put Him there. Schemes and dreams of mere men were of no effect, for He was not moved by them.*

*That same freedom is yours if you trust in Me. You need not be touched by that which is around you. Surrender fully to Me. Seek My purposes rather than your own. Learn of Me and My ways. Submit to My Spirit that you might be free. The work that I plan for you is for your best interest. Submit to it. You, too, can be untouchable if you keep your eyes on Me.*

# CHAPTER TWENTY-ONE

*"Do not love the world or anything in the world. The world and its desires pass away, but the man who does the will of God lives forever.*       *1 John 2:15a, 17 NIV*

Tom took a deep breath and released it slowly, almost sighing resolutely as he pulled into the newly paved parking lot. He and his imposing friend had come directly from the city, stopping only for a quick, drive-through hamburger; and now, they sat looking at the gleaming, massive stone and steel monument called His Holiness Christian Fellowship.

The church was teeming with activity, making last minute preparations for the 6:15 service. The duo had driven in silence, eaten in relative silence, except for some comments on how good the food tasted; and now sat in silence, hoping to hold on just a few moments more to the experiences of the day.

The beautiful grounds, the fresh air, the flowers - Tom especially noticed the flowers. He realized he hadn't seen any for days. All was so new and bright. Still, it seemed so cold, so void of reality, the reality with which he had recently become acquainted. He felt as if he no longer belonged.

How could that be? He did belong, didn't he? He had been here most of his born again days. This was his church; these were his friends. How then, did he feel closer to the now very somber friend in the seat next to him, and for that matter Mic and Steely, than he did to anyone here? Could he have changed so much in such a short time? He didn't belong to the street, but he didn't belong here any more either.

"I'm just gonna go and sit by the swings for a minute," Train said, looking at Tom helplessly. "I gotta get quiet for a couple minutes or get away or something. I'll be right in, O.K.?"

Train unencumbered himself from the front seat, and as Tom watched him walk down the flower-lined, stone walk to the play area, he said a prayer for his covenant friend. "Be with him tonight in a special way, my Lord. This is pretty rough on him. He sees with Your eyes now. Let him not be discouraged by what he sees."

As Tom finished praying, a bunch of kids, who had spotted their big friend and staunch ally, ran over to gleefully greet him. Grabbing his gigantic hands, sitting on his shoe tops to "ride" as he walked and jumping with anticipation to be the next one to be picked up, they ministered once again to his temporarily morose spirit. Train looked back at Tom, smiling as if to say, "It's gonna be fine."

Tom felt it, too. "With You, Lord, no matter what happens tonight or anytime from now on, it's gonna be more than fine."

"Daddy! Daddy!" Tom was roused from his thoughts by two voices he hadn't heard in several days.

Stepping from the car just in time to catch the two treasures as they jumped to embrace him, he exclaimed, "Boy, I missed you guys!" He really hadn't had too much time to think about them with all that had happened; but now that they were here, he realized how much they really meant to him.

"Hi, honey," Sally said, arriving just as Tom was setting Becky down.

"Boy, you look great," was all Tom could say as he embraced his love. They kissed in a way they had not kissed for a long time; probably somewhat inappropriate and extended for a church parking lot, but that didn't matter to either of them. New life, God's life, had rekindled some feelings and emotions covered for years with the routine of daily existence, and they were delighted about it. They walked into the church, hand in hand, oblivious to the people around them, including the make-believe gagging noises of Becky and Tommy.

I have sent My Son, Jesus Christ, to die; and I have raised Him from the dead that the world might again be brought into fellowship with Me. I have sent My Holy Spirit to indwell each one that will believe and submit wholly to Him. He is to exhibit to a world, dying and out of real answers, the only answer - the life of Jesus - and it is to be done through those who believe.

By His life in you, the believer, others are to see how Jesus loved, lived and died so that they might not perish. Your life is to be so empowered by My Holy Spirit that the blind might look at it and recognize the life of Jesus and be brought to Him for their salvation.

Instead of them seeing who My Son really is, they see weak, pitiful, empty ramblings of moral finger pointing and self-righteous, self-serving religious bigotry. The name of My glorious Son has been brought to such low esteem in the eyes of your world because of your cold, fruitless religion, that they laugh and mock Him instead of calling Him Lord.

When will you hear what I have been telling you? When will you stop your foolish, powerless activity and lock yourself up with Me that you might really exhibit the life of My Son, empowered by My Holy Spirit? Repent, turn, stop now! I am waiting for you.

# CHAPTER TWENTY-TWO

*"Stop bringing meaningless offerings!"*

*Isaiah 1:13 NIV*

*"Oh, that one of you would shut the temple doors, so that you would not light useless fires on my altar! I am not pleased with you," says the Lord Almighty, "and I will accept no offering from your hands."*        *Malachi 1:10 NIV*

Tom and Train sat in quiet, personal praise to the Lord as the evening announcements were being read by Jerry Ferringer. Jerry had an uncanny way of making the most exciting event seem boring. But then, Jerry was boring. That was not a judgment, but a factual statement. Jerry Ferringer was bored with everything, so he had no life to give to anyone else. He was interested in no one but himself, and had no interests other than making money for himself, so he simply expressed boredom to everyone he met.

Sally, Tommy and Becky sat between the two quiet men - Sally in thought about her last day; Becky and Tommy adjusting their "space" and making sure the other didn't violate it. Each secretly began to plot how they would encroach on the established boundaries; but then, that was understood and part of the fun.

Tom wondered how Train was doing and glanced toward him, unable to read his expression as the usual testimonies were given. Tina Weatherspoon, a very large lady in a bold, flowered dress, was grateful to God for helping her overcome her temper in recent days, especially in light of the fact that she had hit her husband over the head with a frying pan the week before. "And Jesus worked on my doctor's heart to allow me to not be so restricted on my diet for a couple of weeks," she rejoiced. "It's been almost unbearable. I could hardly eat anything." Several others nodded their heads knowingly as she finally sat down.

Matt and Martha Smithers announced they were pregnant. "Martha, that is!" Matt stumbled, red-faced at his faux pas.

Tom and Rita Justford praised God for putting their marriage back together and several others thanked the Lord for unspoken answers to their prayers. It wasn't until Betty Hagerty, the town gossip, praised the Lord for His giving credence to her latest tidbit that I saw Train grimace and put his head down in silent prayer for her.

"And now, before we go any further," Pastor Wickham said with excitement, "we have a very special announcement. As most of you already know, we again have a very special visitor with us this evening. We have invited him back so that we might show him some of the love we have here at His Holiness. Train," he continued, looking at the now visibly uncomfortable man sitting next to Becky at the end of the pew, "I know this is a surprise to you, but we would like to give you a little..." He glanced in the direction of Jim Wilson, who outwardly exhibited most of the pride he felt at that moment. "...well, a not so little gift. Would you come to the platform, please?"

Train sat immobile for an instant; then, with a quiet sigh of resignation, he submitted to the pastor's request.

"We would like to present to you this check," Pastor continued once Train was standing next to him, dwarfing him by comparison, "just to show you our love. Normally, I wouldn't mention the amount, but in this case I feel we owe it to these people because of their generosity. Train, please accept this check in the amount of $17,000 on behalf of all of us at His Holiness. It's for your work in the inner city. A much needed work, I might add." A quiet, sporadic applause, mingled with expressions of wonder, emphasized the moment.

With that, he handed the folded check to Train who took it and held it, unopened. For moments, he stared at his hands. The congregation, assuming that he was overwhelmed and feeling quite proud of their more than generous gesture to someone they knew very little about, waited in silence. The moment was pregnant with anticipation. Quietly, Train raised his head and looked with loving eyes at the people.

"My Father in heaven has revealed to me...to us," he said, looking at Tom, and meaning to include him and Mic and Steely and all of the others, "that He's about to do a great and mighty work in His people to purify them for the soon coming of Jesus Christ. It started on a smaller scale even before the ripplings of war touched our own soil. For some time now, there has been a great stirring in the heavens and a heralding of His people to draw close to Him as never before. He has called His people to an intimacy with Him, to make <u>Him</u> their priority, and to surrender completely.

The calling is getting more sure, and in recent weeks, even days, His Spirit has poured out to those who will come in a manner that hasn't happened since soon after Jesus walked this earth. God is looking for a pure and spotless bride, alive to Him and Him alone - dead to the deceitful riches of the world." Then, with the love and compassion of Jesus in his eyes, Train continued. "Let me explain to you why I can't accept this check."

The stunned audience sat in increasingly agitated silence. Soon, small murmurings began in groupings across the vast sanctuary and open disbelief at the audacity of this invader became apparent. Jim Wilson and some others sat poised, eagerly waiting to hear the next offense that would come from the mouth of one so ungrateful.

"I understand what you are trying to do tonight, and for that I am grateful," he said. "But if I were to accept this check, I would be allowing you to remain in your sin." He looked in

167

Jim Wilson's direction, making him somewhat uneasy, like a child caught in the act. Then he continued.

"God is not looking only for your money. He is not interested in anything that allows you or me to remain cold, uncaring and unneedful of Him.

"The Lord would say to you, as He is saying to all of His people all around the world so that they might prosper and be used for the great harvest that is about to take place: *'I know your record of works and what you are doing. You are neither cold nor hot. I desire you to be cold or hot! Because you are lukewarm, neither cold nor hot, I will spew you out of My mouth. For you say, I am rich; I have prospered and grown wealthy, and I am in need of nothing; and you do not realize that you are wretched, pitiable, poor, blind and naked. Therefore I counsel you to purchase from Me gold refined and tested by fire, that you may be truly wealthy, and white clothes to clothe you and to keep the shame of your nudity from being seen, and salve to put on your eyes that you may see.'"*

He began to prophesy: *"There is time, but not so much as you might think; time to be conformed to the requirements of My Word. My Word was given to you simply and clearly. You have made it confusing and difficult by constantly attempting to make it suitable for your purposes. Does not My Word declare that it is sent to accomplish My purposes? 'All is Mine- everything belongs to Me.' The principle of first fruits, the tithe, is not so much a heavenly tax on what has been, but rather a sowing into what will be. Many have robbed Me of My tithe and think I haven't noticed. I know what will shortly come upon the earth. Then, you will see that My Word works better for you than your own devices. To the faithful, remain faithful; only you will stand. Only you will see My rewards in life to come. Remember what a few loaves and fishes turned into when willingly placed into My hands. That is but a shadow of the return on what is sent ahead and stored up.*

"Search My Word. One day it will search you. On that day you will be before Me. Only what My Word says will matter then. My Word is your only standard for holiness, faithfulness, obedience, love and all other issues. My Word reveals to you what I love, what I hate, and what I require. There's still time.

"I encourage you, My people, to humble yourselves before the Lord and allow My Spirit to make your hearts tender. Settle the issue of obedience forever. Seek Me right now. My blood still covers. My grace still avails. My love never ceases to call out to you."

Train stopped for a moment, head bowed, waiting for the plumb line that had been drawn by the Word and prophecy to do its work. Within seconds, the dividing sword revealed pockets of open rebellion, lethargy and conviction. Before this moment, all gathered may have been of one congregation, sitting in one room; but now, the real heart motives of those who had said "Lord, Lord," were being exposed.

He continued, "Many of you have been entrusted with much to be used for God's work during your short life here. You have, however, consumed most of what you have been given - whether that be money, talent, influence, education or any other gifting - upon your own lusts. Your gifts are not really gifts, as you suppose, but simply the returning to God of what was never yours. All was rightfully His in the first place. You have been put in charge, as hired shepherds of sheep would be, but you have sold God's property for your own gain. You have been found out and now are being called to account. This day you must make a choice: serve the Lord Jesus Christ alone and be part of the great harvest, or serve the world and its materialism."

An eerie, uncomfortable silence remained in the room. People full of pride and not used to being called to account for anything – especially what they did with their money - were

169

stunned, but restrained by a force much stronger than they. Mighty hands with blazing swords in heavenly realms constricted the working of dark powers in individuals guided by those powers. God's warriors were implementing an orchestration of complete control until the Word was allowed to accomplish its work. Only as glowing warriors, upon command, allowed their captives to whisper to their familiar host would the silence be broken.

A small hand was timidly raised near the rear of the sanctuary. Nancy Offheiser, a frail, ashen-complexioned lady who never smiled, stood to her feet and began to speak. Nancy continually needed prayer for many unspoken needs. Whenever a group of Christians gathered, she was there like a little puppy. Most of the time, the gatherings she attended were sidetracked to focus on her and her tribulations.

"I don't know how you can say we are consuming God's property upon our own lusts," she began defensively. "Some of us here have nothing." She motioned pitifully and continued, "We don't live in big houses, or drive fancy cars. We simply make it from day to day. I think you are a little out of line." Many heads nodded in agreement as the warriors loosed their hold on their foes for a moment; then retightened their grip, leaving them immobile and ineffective.

Looking steadfastly through Nancy to the spirit of self-pity and pride that had been directing her all these years, Train began in the Spirit. *"Nancy, you have consumed upon yourself the Word of God, His grace and the stewardship of His mighty power which is for the express purpose of overcoming all obstacles through Jesus and to bring salvation to the lost. You have chosen to stay broken and not believe God's healing Word, all so that you might bring attention to yourself. I now bind false pride and self-pity and command them to leave you, never to return, by the power of the Holy Spirit in the Name of Jesus Christ."*

To the astonishment of all gathered, Nancy flew backwards against her pew as if struck under the chin by a large fist and fell in the middle of the aisle under the power of the Holy Spirit. Immediately, her complexion began to take on a lifelike appearance as she laid perfectly still.

"Do you not understand?" Train again began addressing the crowd in general. "This is not a game. You are not in control of your lives any longer, the Holy Spirit is; and all that you see here is being done in the Name of Jesus Christ. This is the beginning stage of God's plan for His creation in the end of the end times. Nothing other than God's will and God's way will be done in His Name. He is once again visibly taking charge and we simply have a choice to either submit to His will as we have professed we've done all along or be set aside, looking on helplessly during the coming peril. Tonight, which do you choose?"

There was no anger in Train's voice. He had not raised it, but simply spoke at a volume that all could hear. God was anointing the words of His trusted servant with power to accomplish what was needed during this time.

Having been released, the meddling, religious spirit in Sam Thompson began to speak through its long time host. "You have no right to come into my - " he corrected himself hurriedly, "our church and offend these children of God like this."

Again, Train moved in the Name of His Savior. *"Sam Thompson, tonight the Lord of Hosts is requesting that you serve Him and Him alone, not yourself and your controlling greed. Choose now whom you will serve or this night your own words will consume you as you have enjoyed their harsh effect upon others all of these years ."*

"How dare you," Sam - now livid with rage, his face turning red with anger - began. "I have a mind to call the police and have you thrown out of here you...you undesirable, you.

"See, I told you this was not a good thing to do, Morgan," Sam screamed in the pastor's direction, shaking a finger, and becoming more vehement each moment. "Tomorrow, I'm calling some of those here to petition to have you removed."

Now bright red and visibly out-of-control, Sam began almost foaming with anger, "I'll not be held responsible..." he stopped in mid-sentence, grasping his throat - he was choking. There he stood, eyes bulging from lack of oxygen. Some froze in amazement, not knowing what to do. Shaking grotesquely, he dropped to the floor with a sickening thud.

A frantic effort at CPR by Mike Coffer, a local gym teacher, was to no avail. Using his handkerchief to cover Sam's face, he announced to the shocked observers, "He's dead."

The congregation was too stunned to move. Showing no emotion, but feeling deep sorrow for someone who chose to continue in his sin rather than turn; Train, who had not stirred from his position on the minister's platform, spoke again.

"The Father Creator extends His loving grace to all of you during this time. He asks you, as He is asking all those who are called by His Name around the world, to choose this day whom you will serve. Each of you has been hearing His call to you for many months, and even years. Some of you have applied it to your lives in differing degrees. You have understood the signs all around you and discerned the times and have made the decision to lay your lives down before the Lord for His total work in you. Tonight, you shall be sealed by His Spirit in your inner being.

"Others here have not chosen to recognize the times and seasons and you have remained in service to yourselves, doing even self-motivated good works, supposedly in God's name.

You will be given ample opportunity to repent, but will not be part of the outpouring of the Holy Spirit.

"Tonight, the Lord would say to you, *'You have for too long called for My anointing to fall upon you without submitting your lives to a walk of purity. It will no longer be. Only the pure in heart will be entrusted with My power. Only those holy unto Me will be entrusted with My rhema Word. Only those dead to the world will see the manifestation of My grace in their lives. I have called and few have heard. I have warned and few have heeded. I have exhorted and still My people go about their own business and call it Mine.*

" *'Soon that will end. No more,' says the Lord. 'No More. My gifts are without repentance, yes; but My presence must accompany those gifts or they will fall to the ground. You will now see who will serve and who is not pure in heart. Watch. Watch and be amazed at what I am about to do in the church. It will no longer resemble the church of the world when I am finished purifying it. It will be holy. It will be pure. It will serve no other gods. Now it is full of whoredoms, but soon it will be My bride.'*

"Do not be mistaken," Train continued, "You will be called to account for disloyal, wavering hearts, your divided interests and your spiritual adultery. I counsel you, as in James, to grieve, even weep, over your disloyalty. Let your laughter be turned to grief and your mirth to brokenness and heartfelt shame for your sins. Humble yourselves, feeling very insignificant in the presence of the Lord and He will exalt you, He will lift you up and make your lives significant."

With that, Train again bowed his head in prayer. The Father was finished talking; so Train, in learned obedience, could not, nor would he, say any more.

In the spirit world, the heavenly host released their captive, dark forces. These ugly forces, in turn, began to inflict their desires on their willing listeners.

Pandemonium broke out. Some stood screaming abuses and shaking their fists toward the altar. Others simply stormed from the premises, taking their questioning children with them. Some carried Sam Thompson from the sanctuary, vowing to return with the police to arrest this murderer.

God was allowing heavenly separation to take place. Many others had heard what was said and had received it with welcome hearts. In silence, oblivious to the clamor of those leaving, young and old, rich and poor, waited before their God with surrendered hearts.

Their wait was not in vain. As He had done to Tom, Train and the small body of believers that morning; as He was doing to fellowships similar to His Holiness Christian Fellowship all over the world that very moment; and as He would do to remnants of believers in the coming months, the Holy Spirit moved. With the presence of the Living God in their midst, surrendered vessels were cleansed, healed and taught of the work to be done and introduced to their portion in that work. The doors remained unlocked and the lights stayed on at His Holiness, (and, for that matter, at many other churches around the world,) as time again had no place nor bearing on the matters of God when He was communing with His children.

One of the many wonders the God of Heaven performed that evening was done in Carrie Hutchinson's life. For seventeen years, Carrie had been a quadriplegic bound to a wheelchair. Born a beautiful, very active, little girl, Carrie's back was broken at the age of five when her father, an alcoholic, lost control of his car on wet pavement and struck a utility pole. The incident caused Robert Hutchinson, in his brokenness and remorse, to surrender his life to Jesus.

In subsequent years, his wife, Emily, and their three children, Sadie, Joshua, and Carrie, were also saved. The family was a testimony of God's mercy and grace, and functioned for His will to be done in their lives. Carrie's joy,

174

despite her circumstances, was a witness to everyone she met. Never seeming concerned for herself or her needs, she continually showed deep caring for others who were hurting.

This night, when the presence of God fell on those available to Him, Carrie was thrown about ten feet in front of her chair. Immobile themselves because of God's power on them, the family did nothing. As Jesus presented Himself to Carrie, He blessed her for the testimony her young life had been thus far and assured her that He would use her in a more powerful way than ever before. When the Healer of all mankind lifted her to Himself, Carrie was totally healed. Atrophied muscles were made strong, brittle bones became whole and a body that had been useless tissue was instantly restored to vitality. When the family again became aware of their physical surroundings, they were presented with the additional gift of Carrie - restored and beautiful, standing before the Lord only she could still see, arms raised in praise, tears flowing freely.

When Carrie became aware of her physical surroundings, she realized that what Jesus had done to her in the Spirit was manifested in the flesh. Jubilance and unabashed praise would be the most descriptive, but wholly inadequate, words to describe the hugging, crying and laughing that resounded around the Hutchinson family. Robert Hutchinson, too weak and grateful to even move, huddled against the end of the pew and sobbed quietly, his head hung in wondrous abandon to the Lord for the mercy shown his daughter. Pent up sorrow, masked emotions and years of almost unbearable guilt were released in tides of restorative tears as Carrie knelt beside her father and softly spoke these healing words: "Daddy, look at what Jesus did. Now we're both free."

Tom and his family, Pastor Wickham, Train and many others spent time long into the next day and even longer with their very present Lord. It was definitely not "church as usual" at His Holiness Christian Fellowship that night.

Under a pew in the third row of the middle section of His Holiness Christian Fellowship was Carlyle Henderson, Tom's employer, wholeheartedly enjoying His Lord and Savior Jesus Christ. After having been in the presence of the Lord's consuming fire; he, too, was being formed for service and gladly receiving the beginning volumes of his personal instructions from the Lord in regard to the changes the world was about to experience.

*It is the close of a season. I am marshaling My forces. I am preparing hearts to be part of the great army of the body of Christ.*

*Do you see how bold the enemy has become? Do you see how he has attempted to disfigure the children that are called by My Name?*

*A turning point is at hand. A new awakening is in this land and it must start with you. Take hold of what you are in Me. Begin to realize that all My promises are for you. Understand though, they are not for self and flesh or your worldly needs. I do desire that you have life more abundantly - yes! Use that life to rise above - look to the provisions I have given you to be used for a greater need.*

*As I gather My army, your part will become increasingly clear. Drop all preconceived notions as to what you felt were the uses for My provisions, and submit to Me with an open mind. I have prepared you for a specific purpose.*

*The time is now - you can be the one. Do not limit Me for I have chosen you.*

# CHAPTER TWENTY-THREE

*"And he who does not take up his cross and follow Me [cleave steadfastly to Me, conforming wholly to My example in living and, if need be, in dying also] is not worthy of Me. Whoever finds his [lower] life will lose it [the higher life], and whoever loses his [lower] life on My account will find it [the higher life]."*

*Matthew 10:38-39 Amp*

*"And anyone and everyone who has left houses or brothers or sisters or father or mother or children or lands for My name's sake will receive many [even a hundred] times more and will inherit eternal life."*          *Matthew 19:29 Amp*

And so, the preparation of the bride for the return of her Groom, Jesus, began in earnest all over the world. The heavenly hosts, charged with the anticipation of something wonderful about to take place, moved to carry out their now increasing activity with a wonder of it all. The heavens resounded with a symphony of endeavors that would crescendo with all the hosts bursting forth in praise as the Lord would soon appear for His own.

A momentary brightness, a window of grace, a season of harvest would be released upon the earth before the coming purging which all preceded the coming of the Lord for His people. The earth, in response to the Lord's command, groaned and strained as if in childbirth, as a warning to those who had eyes to see or ears to hear. Natural disasters such as unparalleled storms, earthquakes, and flooding would leave many helpless and without hope. Manmade disasters such as fires, riots, rampant terrorism and unbridled crime made citizens demand something be done for the safety of the majority. Although all was, in His mercy, a fulfillment of God's promises to reveal to mankind its helplessness without Him, and to allow those who would hear the opportunity to repent, many would scoff at the thought that He had a hand in it at all. More police, more organization, more law, more money, would become the cry. Instead of turning to God, most would turn their backs on Him all the more, with ever hardening hearts.

Those who would respond to the call to holiness and to full submission would walk in intimate fellowship with their Savior. If they chose to move selflessly and reverently with crucifixion power, they would see the wonder of God in their daily activities. An irresistible wooing, except to the most hardened heart, would become visible to the church first, and then to the ripe fields ready to produce their crop in abundance.

*******************************

Surrounded by rejoicing heavenly hosts and accompanied by Train, the Bracken family drove in silence deep into the inner city despite the warnings over the radio of continual bomb threats. No amount of coaxing affected Train's decision to go home. It was late Monday evening by the time Train was delivered to his door. The events and intensity of the last days had taken their toll, and the exhausted family hugged one of their own in a loving farewell before returning home.

Both Sally and Tom rode in silence almost the entire drive to Elmfield. Words were not needed to convey what the knowing smiles and loving glances they had for each other said so completely. Sally blushed, a little embarrassed at her thoughts of wishing that the BMW didn't have bucket seats, so she could slide next to Tom as she had done so many years ago.

As they turned into the driveway, the headlights scanned the beautiful yard and swept across the front of their home in what seemed like slow motion, almost as if to point out each beautiful detail of the imposing structure.

"Are we home?" Tommy questioned groggily, rubbing his eyes. Both he and Becky had fallen asleep almost immediately after embarking on their return trip home.

"Yes, dear," Sally said quietly, as the garage door rose in response to the button being pushed on the visor mechanism. "Wake your sister. It's time for bed."

"I'll just carry her upstairs," Tom whispered, opening the back door of the car and picking Becky up gently, taking her to her room. Becky never stirred and Tommy was fast asleep even before the bedroom light was out.

"What are you thinking, darling?" Sally said, as she began to dress for bed.

"I don't really know how to answer that," Tom said, as he sat on the side of the bed, absentmindedly toying with the cuff of his shirt and looking at the carpet. "So much has been happening. I've got so many thoughts, so many feelings and at the same time, I..." he paused. "At the same time, I don't feel the same about so many other things. It's as if I began to live, really feel alive in some areas and very much dead in others. Does that make any sense?"

Sally sat down next to Tom and reached for his hand. "I know exactly what you mean, honey. When we turned into the driveway a few moments ago and the headlights flashed on the house, I felt as if I were saying good-bye to something. I don't know how to explain it; but after being with Jesus and hearing what He had to say, this..." she looked around the room, "...this could be used for God's work and help so many hurting people."

Tom and Sally lay next to each other in silence, reflecting on the thoughts, the feelings, the events of recent days before drifting into a peaceful sleep.

\*\*\*\*\*\*\*\*\*\*\*\*\*\*\*\*\*\*\*\*\*\*\*\*\*\*\*\*\*\*\*\*\*\*

"Would you call Tom Bracken in here for me, Miss Jones?" Carlyle Henderson said, speaking into the intercom.

"Yes, Mr. Henderson," the voice responded, as it had done countless times before. "In fact," Miss Jones continued, "Tom just moments ago asked if he might have a moment of your time. He said he would like to see you."

The click of the intercom assured Carlyle that his request would be fulfilled as expeditiously as possible. Miss Jones had been a faithful employee for many years. She had, in fact, dedicated her life's work to organizing, directing, and protecting him from the endless details that surrounded his business life. She was the well-oiled hub of the Henderson Architectural Firm; and through her talent, dedication and tenacity, it ran very smoothly.

From his tenth floor window, Carlyle had a wonderful view. When he and Tom had designed the building, they made sure that he could see in every direction. The unique floor plan of his office and the panoramic placement of windows had accomplished all that he desired for a very favorable work environment. He felt safe high above the din of the city below.

One of his favorite features was the small, raised area to the left of his balcony patio door that had a glazed ceiling. This area provided hours of relaxation on the many nights that he would stay late to work on a special project. Many projects took a lot of development; and during their gestation period in his mind, he would look at the stars through his brass telescope, a treasured gift from his deceased wife, wondering what they were all about and where they really came from. "I know now," he said to himself, as he looked at the skyline to his left, while remembering those times. As Carlyle looked through the window, the reflected light allowed him to see Tom in the mirror before he entered the office.

"Come in, Tom," he said, turning and moving to greet his new friend. A friendship bond, the likes of which Carlyle Henderson had never known before, had been placed in his heart for the body of Christ; and especially, for the man before him. He had been given new eyes now and a new heart that replaced his uncaring, hardened heart. "Come in, my friend," he said, as they grasped hands warmly.

"I understand we both want to see each other this morning," Tom began with a smile, as Carlyle motioned him to sit in a soft chair in a corner grouping. Immediately, both men felt the bond that Christ had placed between them. They talked, not as employer and employee, but as two brothers that had been separated for a long time and needed to catch up on much. The formality of "Mr. Henderson" or "Carlyle" that was part of the office policy, and part of the authority that was needed before, was dropped as heart conversation ensued.

Time passed quickly, as Carl had many questions about his brand new faith. In fact, the majority of the conversation focused on Carl's needs, and Tom sensed they were more important than the reasons he had for wanting to see his boss.

Carl spoke freely and candidly about his innermost feelings and his newfound life and all that pertained to it with youthful enthusiasm. Suddenly, however, the joy on his face faded and he became very serious, almost solemn. Somewhat uneasily, he got up and walked to the wet bar in the recessed cove in the south wall of his office. As he toyed with the empty mixing container, he began to speak again, keeping his back to his new friend.

"Tom," he began, "as you know, I'm a voracious reader." He turned to face Tom directly and leaned against the bar.

183

"Since I met the Lord, I've read everything I could get my hands on. The Bible is my priority, of course; but books on prophecy and how this is all going to end have been my constant diet. Tom, I don't even do work anymore," Carl said in mid-stride, as he came back to sit directly across from Tom, who was beginning to feel that he was about to be told something very important.

"Don't get me wrong; I'm delighted about it. I've never been happier. I've finally found the peace I've been looking for all my life. Jesus not only saved me, but He gave me answers to all of the questions that have haunted me most of my adult life."

Again, Carl got up, walked toward the window and stood silently for a few heartbeats with his hands in his pockets, looking at the scenes with which he'd become so familiar. Then, without moving, Carl began very slowly. "Tom, you know very little about me. I know we've worked on many designs together and..." he paused briefly, "and before Clara died, you and Sally were two of the people we felt comfortable enough to spend even a small amount of time with. But you know nothing of who I really am."

Tom watched as Carl stood motionless, just staring through the window. Then slowly, he turned to Tom and said, "I'm going to show you something only two other people in the world know exists."

He hesitated, choosing his words carefully. He began slowly. It was evident to Tom that what was about to be shared was hard for Carl because of the way each sentence was thoughtfully composed.

"Remember when I sent you and Sally to Europe for a month, just after we built this building?" he began. "And when you came back I had redone my office to make more space for this private spa? Well, there were reasons you never saw the plans. You see, I needed to make sure this wasn't known by anyone." With that, Carl moved to the wet bar at the entrance to the spa. Reaching down, he pressed a button that was concealed under the toe space at the very bottom of one of the bar cabinets. The panel, to the right of the mirror that hung on the back wall, moved left to expose a hidden doorway to a room about the size of a large walk-in closet.

As Carl walked into the room, Tom rose from where he had been sitting and mechanically followed him. Tom noticed immediately upon entering that sound was deadened. The layout was quite simple. Along one wall, there was a desk module with a computer, a model which Tom had never seen before. In fact, it was a foreign model with unrecognizable lettering. There was also a fax machine, two telephones and a built-in file cabinet. Tom noticed that one of the phones had no push buttons and reasoned that it must be for incoming calls only.

"Are we in some kind of intrigue movie, Mr. Bond?" Tom spoke to break the tension he was beginning to feel.

"You have no idea," was the response from Carl as he typed a series of passwords into the computer after it sprang to life with power supplied by a remote switch concealed to the left of the upper cabinet. "I'd never try any of this if I were you," he stated flatly, as he continued typing. After the typing stopped, he motioned to Tom to come next to him.

"Take a look," he said, as Tom moved to his right. Much to his surprise, Tom saw his picture on the computer screen with his name and vital statistics next to it. As Carl advanced the information, Tom was astounded to see everything about himself, from the time he was born to the present. Each organization he had belonged to, each time he left the country, where he went, even the exact amount he had in his bank account at the present time were displayed. As Carl scrolled down the page, Tom saw designations and a rating system of some sort. He was about to ask what they meant when Carl interrupted his thoughts.

"I have access to it all," Carl said as the screen went blank.

"What do you mean, 'to it all?'" Tom said in wonderment, still staring at the screen as Carl got up to leave the room.

"Everything on everyone, everywhere, given enough time," he continued, as they both moved back to the corner grouping in the office. Once they left, the panel closed silently in place to again conceal the room. Tom was too dumbfounded to even ask a question. Actually, there were so many questions spinning in Tom's head that he didn't know what to ask first. Tom was much relieved when Carl broke the silence.

"My friend, why don't you just listen and let me explain." As he poured each of them a diet soda, Carl began. "For as long as I can remember, I have been deeply concerned about this world and its growing global problems, as my father was before me and his father before him. I sat many long hours at my father's knee as he explained the "special" people and organizations and plans that really ran this world. They orchestrated the rise and fall of governments, implemented wars and skirmishes; and, in general, did what was necessary to bring forth their overall agenda for a peaceful society.

"When I became old enough and was allowed to join these organizations, I gratefully did; knowing that they had the answers to the world's needs: a unified world, a "New World Order" with one democratic government, one people, one plan, and one common good, all controlled from one place and policed by one police force. It would be a utopian society, where only peace and safety exist for those who desire it. The plans were not being carried out by one organization, however; but by thousands of organizations - many, many levels of operation that knowingly or unknowingly were fulfilling that ultimate goal." Carl gestured toward the panel they had just walked through. "This is one small section of many such locations, all in place to do the required work when called upon."

Carl took Tom's glass and refilled it without asking Tom if he wanted any more. It didn't matter, however, for Tom was too interested in what Carl was saying to even notice. He again sat across from Tom and continued.

"I thought no one knew about this plan. For as long as I can remember, I was taught never to share anything I knew about our work. Sure, there were always remote articles written, and periodically, someone would uncover some plan or another talking about the secret societies; but they would be discredited or disappear or something and it would all be over. Great pains had been taken to hide all of this," Carl stated, again pointing to the paneled wall. Then quietly, he began again, looking directly into Tom's eyes.

"Can you imagine my astonishment when I began reading the Bible? What I had been a part of almost all my life, thinking we had this revolutionary idea for the final good of all mankind, hating God or at least thinking we were doing it without God - if there really was one - had been foretold by Him from the beginning. We are scheming our way right into what God predicted all along that mankind would do. What an awesome God!" Tom smiled as Carl marveled at the ingenuity of His God, Lord and Friend, and then continued.

"He even predicted how it is all going to happen, right down to the details developed by the people I used to admire. God said that there's going to be a world leader. He tells us of a "mark" that people must take in order to function in times to come." Carl pointed to the back of his right hand. "It's a computer chip! It is so amazing I can hardly control myself!" Carl slapped his knees and threw his hands upward in praise. "What a wondrous God!"

After Carl and Tom took a break to reflect on the wonders of God, Carl again became very serious. He rose from his chair, went to look out the window once more, then turned back to Tom and said, "Tom, it's all about to come to pass."

"What do you mean, 'come to pass'?" Tom inquired, speaking for the first time in quite awhile.

"I mean, it is all about to take place. Centuries of planning are all leading up to a time in the very near future when people will cry for solutions to the dangers and needs at hand. Responding to that very real danger created by the natural hatred in mankind for one another, plans are in place to accommodate us with peacekeeping troops, martial law, and anything else needed to allow "peace" to remain.

"Unknowingly, each "helpful" step is one step closer to a goal of complete global unity and New World control. All of the necessary technology is in place to have complete control of everyone, everywhere. No one will be able to "slip through the cracks," so to speak. I'm certainly not one of those on the top level of all of this, but I understand enough to know that plans are now being implemented to move in quantum leaps to the fulfillment of all we've worked for. As the breakdown of this life as we know it occurs because of man's sin, we will be moving on to the next phase, and then on to the next, and so on, just as God said we would. My people take advantage of all situations and use them to further their goals.

"On the world level, you've got the economies, remote military interventions, the peace and environmental movements, the Euro currency, UN forces being established, the peace pacts. Locally, it's the racial issue, racial riots, computer glitches, people ending up in prison and children being removed from their parents because of false accusations, and so much more. The escalating threat of worldwide terrorism with all of its horrors will be the opportunity to install restraints that will eventually bring on total world control.

"Remember the story about being able to easily boil a live frog in water if you start him out in a pan of cold water and slowly increase the heat? He just succumbs to the process. All that you read and see on the news has the same effect. Little by little we become familiar with and accepting of escalating events, like bombings, terrorist acts, and incidents of biochemically caused deaths. So soon, and I mean very soon, things are going to escalate and change drastically and it will just be a matter of course.

"The unparalleled rise in the economy, and the soon to come economic crash - which will render even the people in the highest levels of society in need of our solutions – will work to benefit those in the know as people call out to the government for help. Even in the spiritual arena, the predominant theme that we all serve the same God and you can choose whatever path you desire to reach Him will have a reverse effect upon those who hold beliefs other than those of the New World Order. You can see that it's all in place, can't you, Tom? The next..." Carl paused and turned back to the window.

"It's really quite ironic," he began again, as if he were thinking out loud. "About the only people who can never accept and agree to all that is planned are..." he turned again with a half smile that expressed the irony of his life. "About the only people who will not embrace our plans and humanism with its manmade religion are those one of whom I've joyously become.

" For years the plans to discredit their beliefs have been established. Christians ignorant of the Lord's real plan for their lives have played right into our hands through their selfish motives to maintain their freedoms. As they fought to keep what they had, laws were formed to remove those freedoms and now I know that *all* was moving exactly where God said it would. Now everything is in place. It's just a matter of time."

189

Carl held his hands against his chest for a quiet moment as tears formed in his eyes. "You see, I now follow Jesus," he said as he smiled wryly again through tears, "and I will eventually be removed through plans that I once applauded as being for the good of all. Isn't that enough to derail your thinking?

"Tom, prayers are being offered for the cleansing of the world of all those who don't agree with and submit to the dictates that will soon be implemented. I didn't know at that time that God said He was going to take His people away just before the end. We played right into His hands. Everything we were doing lines up with the plans of God, even the coming of the one world ruler; I know that now.

"I also believe that through the difficult times ahead we will be prepared for the coming of the Lord for His bride - it's all part of the refining process. Persecution will prepare the church for bridehood. I know that few really understand that, but I need to say it out loud. These times will separate the true, holy bride from those who are following Jesus for their own good.

"This time, however, will be more difficult than we could ever imagine. As Christians, we are never to fight against the government. We are to comply with all of the laws as Jesus did- even laws meant to harm us. Our privilege is to endure for the sake of our Lord and one more soul. Hell on earth is the price for anyone who will not accept the way that will be provided by those in charge. After reading the Bible, I now know how it will all end; but in the meantime, it's going to be pretty rough for those who believe in the real truth, the truth of Jesus Christ. I know it's for our own good, but that won't make it any easier. Yet as hard as it may get, it's somehow exciting to know that God has purpose for my life."

Both men sat again in silence. Tom's mind was racing, reflecting, remembering. He had done some studying on the

190

endtime scenario. He had heard of clandestine organizations moving toward and orchestrating world peace, and in his mind he knew that somehow it all had to come to pass because God said it would.

All nations had to unite in the endtime generation to set the platform for the coming of Christ and the rule of the Antichrist leader. There would have to be a breaking down of all cultures so that everyone would call for a blanket peace and safety. He could handle all of that. He had even thought through the possibility that it was happening in his lifetime; and had, in general, accepted that.

He read the daily headlines and saw the quickness with which nations would rise, fall, and rise again. Change upon change upon change. Overnight the best plans of the wisest men needed modification because of some incident that would shift the focus of the world, leaving individual plans of no consequence. He even marveled at the "coincidences" of earthquakes, fires, floods, riots and terrorist attacks, all increasing in frequency and intensity and seemingly bringing everything to some sort of unavoidable crisis with no hope for a solution except for one – a one world leader.

"There did come that day when Jesus' feet actually touched the Jordan River, ya know. And things happened pretty fast after that," Carl said, breaking into Tom's thought pattern almost as if he were reading his mind.

"What do you mean?" Tom responded, already knowing what Carl was about to say.

"I mean, I believe that all that I know - all that I've read and everything I hear - points to one undeniable conclusion." He moved closer to his friend. "This is the time, Tom. And we..." he paused, "you and I and all those waiting for His return are the people who will see the coming of the Lord first hand. Everything points to it."

Carl paused again, then settled back in his chair. "Look, in my former world, the plans were set in motion a long time ago. Those who believe, and are privy to the orchestration of the times and seasons, already know who the new world leader will be, and they worship him regularly. Doesn't that tell you something?

"On this end, I mean in the spiritual realm, you must agree that God is doing something mighty big all over the world, right? Just what we've experienced in our own little corner is enough to make you stop and think that something pretty spectacular is happening. The world is crying out for peace and safety. People are seeing the need for a world leader to help them. At the same time, believers are being called to prepare for the return of Jesus. The two elements coincide perfectly.

"From what I've been able to gather, it's not just us; it's happening all over the world. God is doing something everywhere with His people. In thousands of ways - whether it's movies, books, through prophets or actual visitations similar to what we've experienced, He has been showing us that the time is near. I think He's preparing us for what will soon come to pass. We may have thought that we were making the plans, but God is way ahead of all of us."

Carl sat forward in his chair, waiting for Tom's response. This time, Tom got up and walked over to the window, looking at nothing in particular. Finally, without turning around, he spoke.

"So, you're saying that this day, in our lives, Jesus' feet have touched the Jordan again, as it were." His thoughts went back to the people of that time. Four thousand years of promises, prophecies and teachings were being fulfilled before the eyes of everyday, ordinary people just like him. That particular day was uneventful for those who were not looking for their Messiah or those who thought His coming could never happen in their lifetime. To them it was just another ordinary day, even while the long awaited promise was being realized in their midst.

What had happened, though, was irreversible. The plans of God intervened in the minds and hearts of that generation and all they could do was respond, whether they liked it or not, were ready for it or even desired it. It was happening in their midst and they had no power to change it. The Messiah had come and nothing would ever be the same. God's plan was set in motion.

"And now, in the same way..." Tom waited to let the impact of what he was about to say settle in his heart, "...in the same way, this time, we are in the beginning of the very end of our time. It has begun. It is happening now, right before our eyes. What we've seen and heard recently, all of the changes to our individual worlds, the escalation of wars all over the world are simply a covenant-keeping God telling His people to prepare. Things are now set in motion again."

A peace settled on both men as they felt the confirmation of the Holy Spirit to the truth of what was said. Tom turned to Carl; and as calmly as he would choose a site for a new building, spoke these words: "Then we have some decisions to make, don't we?"

Both men smiled warmly at each other, and then Tom asked: "What are you going to do first? I would imagine that you'll soon be in a great deal of trouble," he said, motioning toward the concealed room.

"I don't know for sure," Carl replied. "The people I know have no rules to play by, only outcome-based programs. They will not be stopped and I know pretty much. I've been praying a lot and I have a peace in my heart. I was willing to die for a good cause before; now, I am surely willing to do anything for the cause of Christ, my Lord, no matter what the cost.

"At the same time, I am convinced that the Lord has plans to refine and use me during this time. I don't want to waste a minute looking out for my own good. I need to learn how to serve others for their good. I need to learn to live like Jesus did. Time is too short."

With that, they knew that enough had been said. It was time for them to pray. Tom and Carl knelt in front of their respective chairs and presented themselves to their God for His wisdom and power in order that they would be able to do what He called them to do in the future, so that He might be honored.

Both knew that they would truly need their God in a very real way because of what was coming. Both men also knew that their God - the One, True, Living God, who knew the beginning from the end and knew of, loved and cared for them- could be trusted. They had faith in Him, and knew beyond a shadow of a doubt that His purposes were good no matter what the outcome looked like to them. So they continued to pray, thank Him and praise Him for the privilege of taking part in His plans, which were continually unfolding before them.

When I pour out My Spirit, it shall be as never before. This world will know those that follow Me for they shall be set apart; no longer a laughing stock, but a wonder.

But deceit will still abound and those stiff-necked ones will find a way to justify their sins and be hardened to even the largest move on My part. Understand that it must be so. Free will is a most misused gift, but it must be so.

Delight in Me for I am about to move in your life. Much has been promised in the short time you have known Me and all will come to pass. I am pleased, but seek My face as never before. Do not worry about what is or is not happening, for I am proud to orchestrate your life.

Learn to submit to My voice, for you will need to know for sure when I am talking and move instinctively. For My Spirit is as a breeze and then gone, so know when it is My Spirit.

# CHAPTER TWENTY-FOUR

*"About midnight Paul and Silas were praying and singing hymns to God, and the other prisoners were listening to them. Suddenly there was such a violent earthquake that the foundations of the prison were shaken. At once all the prison doors flew open, and everybody's chains came loose."*

*Acts 16:25-26 NIV*

Great upheaval beginning in the heavenlies was played out on the earth with violence. Many laws, lawmakers and complete systems throughout the land turned reprobate in thought and action. Good and right were at times heralded as evil and restrictive; while pockets of evil seemed to prosper unchecked. In some instances, malicious rulers took advantage of the desperate times and justice became a nebulous concept simply deteriorating into a means to achieve any given agenda for their side of the "law."

On community and national levels, unparalelled violence erupted throughout the land. Laws were required to control unwanted elements and provide safety for citizens. Nations were at war internally. While most Christians began to realize that their lives were not really in order and sought God's mercy, those who could not or would not submit to what God was doing became unknowing agents for change.

Foolish, unloving behavior by some in the church caused all in the church to come under society's judgment as a detrimental influence. Anything religious was viewed with skepticism.

Most of the church simply didn't want to change or didn't realize they needed to change their ways, scoffing at those who could see the handwriting on the wall. They continuously tried to maintain the status quo. Even though the Lord had called and warned, those who wanted God's best and the world's best were shown for what they were. While thinking they were fighting for the rights of all, they were, in fact, being used to escalate prejudice against Christians and to help develop the image of bigotry. Looking and sounding like all other intolerant religious zealots, they became what those who hated God always said they were – hypocrites.

Words like "fundamentalist" and "conservative," which once described a loving, caring people, now became synonymous with those involved in terrorism and other ungodly, life-threatening acts. Consequently, definitions of terrorism became "progressive" and loosely interpreted by local officials, abetting the achievement of a God-free society.

Not distinguishing between believers on their quest for bridehood and those concerned about their temporal situation, some courts had a free hand to do whatever happened to please the most powerful. This, at times, became an open door of opportunity to stand as Jesus did before Pilate - accused, yet never defending himself. This challenged even the most faithful believer.

*******************************

Mic and Steely were falsely accused of a horrendous, drug-related mutilation and murder of a local restaurant owner. Their work with drug addicts and pushers since they came to Jesus had put quite a dent in the income of that illegal, but highly profitable, local industry. Each time a main player would come to Jesus and clean up, it meant thousands of dollars per day to many people. The two men simply needed to be removed from the streets.

Judge Michael McDermott was notorious for misdealings, using the courts to further his own agendas. A chief player in the drug industry himself, he held a kangaroo court in which his people hired most of the witnesses and the jury. The tampering was so evident to God's elect that they offered no defense and entrusted the outcome of the "trial" to the Lord's hands. The judge, desiring to get them out of his hair for good, sentenced them to life imprisonment without the availability of parole.

However, in God's Kingdom, what is evident is not always what it appears to be. In God's economy, His plan for his two trusted, surrendered servants was to bring His strong Light into the darkest of places. Understanding that this life was "not about them," and walking in the power of the prophets of old, Mic and Steely - "The Preachers," as they were called - wreaked havoc upon Satan's behind-bars strongholds among prisoners and guards alike. Strongholds of sin, lust, greed, murder and hatred gave way to the predominant spirits of prayer, praise, love and peace.

As a continuous taunt to the judge and his henchmen, and as a witness that no prison can hold God's people when God desires otherwise; both Mic and Steely often found themselves transported supernaturally by God outside their walls. Once their "mission" was completed - whether it took hours, days or weeks - the front door guards became accustomed to opening up to let them back into the prison. Even with the punishment inflicted upon them after their return, they rejoiced for having been chosen for God's use. Their light brought many to understand the sovereignty of God.

"They're gone again, Captain!" John Mason, the Chief of Guards in cellblock 113 exclaimed, his voice almost shrill from frustration and fear.

"You idiot!" replied Captain Slodsue, not knowing who else to blame. "The warden is going to have our tails this time. 'One more time,' he told us and we're sent to guard the hole. What's going on around here anyway?"

Judge Michael McDermott emerged from his private restroom adjacent to his chambers, adjusting his robe and readying himself for his next court session. Closing the door behind him and looking up, his face turned pale as he spotted his two guests.

"What the...? How the...?" he stammered, mentally calculating to see if he could make it to the gun he kept in his top desk drawer before either Mic - who was sitting comfortably in the chair in the corner - or Steely, who was standing by the door, could stop him. Still in prison garb and knowing their record, he would have no trouble defending his actions. "I would be a hero," he thought. It was worth a try.

Surprised that neither man made an attempt to stop him, he pulled the loaded gun out from under some papers that were kept in the drawer. "You fools," he stated coldly, holding the gun so he could fire if either of them moved. "Don't you know that this will cost you your lives? I could kill you now and many would rejoice."

The pair remained silent and retained their positions, exhibiting a calmness that began to unravel the agitated judge.

"What would possess you to come back here and why did you allow me to reach this?" he queried, looking momentarily at the shaking weapon he held in his hand.

"First of all, you do not now, nor have you ever had any power over us that was not given to you by our Lord Jesus Christ. Secondly, we have been sent to give you a message," Mic said, not moving from his position while he talked.

"Yeah," Steely chimed in with uncharacteristic brightness in light of the seriousness of the situation. "And you had better listen."

They both began to move toward the judge. Because Mic moved first, the now livid judge pointed the gun at him and pulled the trigger several times. Mic never flinched, but kept coming in his direction. An unseen guest had placed his heavenly finger over the firing pin of the gun as the two men of God continued toward the judge until they were standing right in front of him. Too frightened to do anything, he simply looked up into the eyes of his assailants, who remained calmly before him.

"You have violated every principle of honesty and integrity possible and the Lord Jesus has, at this moment, called you to account for your pitiful life," Mic said. To impact his words and to assure the judge of their heavenly source, Mic continued calmly. He slowly explained to the judge the consequences of his life and his misuse of the position and privileges God had given him. The judge stood mesmerized as Mic explained events that no one, not even his most trusted ally, knew about – events which, if publicized, could destroy his reputation. He also calmly explained that if repentance - a turning from his sin- did not take place, the judge would be given over by God to the same helplessness that most of the people who stood before him felt when he denied the facts presented; and for his own gain, unfairly destroyed their lives.

Prophetically, Mic continued. "From this moment, you shall be unable to see until you repent. If you do not repent, what has been stated will befall you."

Immediately, something like scales covered the judge's eyes. As the heavenly host removed his finger from the gun, the judge, in shock and uncontrolled fear, began firing in the direction of the two men. Within seconds, the courtroom guards burst into the room, now empty except for the blind judge who was groping for a place to sit down.

Weeks later, the headlines in the local paper read: "Judge Michael McDermott committed to St. Thomas Hospital." The story told of how the judge, now blind and subject to fits of drooling rage, was deemed mentally incompetent by one of his fellow judges. It related information on a court case in which evidence in favor of Judge McDermott was deemed "inadmissable" for technical reasons. It seemed that no matter what defense the judge presented, the court threw it out. All he could do was stand helpless and defenseless before his former friends and associates. When the sentence was handed down, McDermott became uncontrollable, demanding "justice." Below the article was a picture of him in a straight jacket being taken to the waiting ambulance.

"The judge decided not to repent," Mic stated, wiping the tears from his eyes as he put the local newspaper on the small table in the corner of his cell.

"Yeah," said Steely. "Some just won't hear."

They both dropped to their knees in prayer to request that more would hear before it was too late.

Do not fear the giants in the land. The largest and biggest giant in your eyes is simple and small in Mine.

The most powerful people with the loudest voices are only a ruptured vessel or stopped heart from being silenced. All is at My control, even though it looks like I have lost control.

I don't move through worldly, visible power. I don't move through logic and reason. I move as I see fit for My purposes to be accomplished. My weapons are not and have never been those the world understands. Fire, wind, cold, earth movements cause change and are warnings. Weakness, humility, forgiveness and love are My way of doing much good.

Be sure to see through the plans of man, and remember the plans that I have ordained from the beginning. As they unfold in My perfect timing, do not be surprised by the blindness of this generation - even My people.

Those who have not heard, will not hear. Those who would not see, will not be able to see. Surrender fully to My will and My Word. It is the only safe place to find sure steps in the coming times.

# CHAPTER TWENTY-FIVE

*"Let each of you esteem and look upon and be concerned for not [merely] his own interests, but also each for the interests of others. Let this same attitude and purpose and [humble] mind be in you which was in Christ Jesus: [Let Him be your example in humility:]"*

*Philippians 2:4-5 Amp*

*"Whoever says he abides in Him ought [as a personal debt] to walk and conduct himself in the same way in which He walked and conducted Himself."*

*1 John 2:6 Amp*

"I knew we'd be moving, but I didn't think it would be like this," Sally said lightheartedly, as she stepped up into the truck Tom had borrowed, which contained all of their remaining belongings.

"You know, darling," she said, as she moved next to Tom and snuggled tight to his side, "I wouldn't have it any other way. I don't think that I have ever been happier." She took the small package that Becky handed to her while Tommy helped his sister into the cab and then climbed in himself. After a final check to make sure they had everything, a final look at the cold-looking, empty structure that had been their home for all of these years, and a final nod of agreement to each other, it was time to go. Tom put the large truck in gear and the Bracken family proceeded, jerking forward a bit as Tom released the clutch prematurely. The truck lunged unceremoniously a few times, but forward they went, giggling with family joy.

As Tom turned the corner onto the main highway, he began to reflect on the last eight months and the incredible changes that had occurred in so many people. The youth group, from which he had recently resigned, had been transformed by the power of God from a bunch of non-caring, scared kids into mighty warriors desiring to take their schools for Jesus while addressing their country's needs in any way they could.

Remembering what these young lives used to be and what controlled their passions before, Tom could only marvel at their renewed sense of patriotism and their love for those in need. When he first started with the youth group, all they could think about was relationships, how they looked, the latest fashions, and how not to act like their parents in any situation. Now Jesus had gotten hold of their lives.

Knowing that the Bible says that we are "in the world but not of it," they understood their responsibility as citizens. Led by adult advisors who also saw their responsibility as members of society, the youth reached out to others all over the world, focusing on their own age group whenever possible; but gladly being used where needed. In countries where mass destruction was taking place, they would raise up relief efforts, or coordinate with established government programs designed specifically for people their own age. If a city anywhere in the nation would come under siege of any kind, this group and many like them would do what it took to help, sometimes physically going to the torn area for weeks at a time, cleaning up debris or helping with food programs.

Their lives had taken on an honorable nature as the life of Jesus poured out to anyone who needed them. Many everyday heroes were formed out of ordinary people as the life of Christ in them continually spurred them to dig deeper and go farther.

The most wonderful thought for Tom, though, was what had happened in his own life and in the individual and collective lives of his family. Tom took his eyes from the road for a moment to glance at the precious cargo that sat with him in the cab. He silently thanked God for all that had happened to them: how they had been drawn together as a family, and how they each had been touched and changed by His ever-present Spirit.

Tom glanced to his right again at Tommy and Becky, who were helping each other memorize Bible verses. Their encounter with God had eliminated all strife between them and bonded them as never before. Even more evident was the change in their daily walk and desires. Although both of them had given their hearts to Jesus long before, it wasn't until the Pentecost-like experience "that night" that they walked continuously in Jesus' love.

Tom reflected back two months to the time when he'd heard sounds coming from Tommy's room late one night. He went to investigate and found Tommy kneeling beside his bed, sobbing on behalf of those who would be lost for eternity; and requesting that even though he was young, he would be used to present the gospel so that people would be saved. Becky showed great concern for the elderly and infirm. On weekends and after school, she could be found at Community Memorial Hospital on Lake Street, helping those too weak to help themselves.

So, here they were. A family. More than that, they were a family dedicated to the Lord with a newfound love for Him and for each other; a family who, after much prayer and dinner conversation, found that all the world's goods and their present lifestyle held nothing for any of them any longer. They collectively decided to sell "everything that wouldn't help them to help others," and use the money to be vessels of service wherever the Lord opened the door. Most of their neighbors and friends thought they had gone off the deep end, but they said little. They were quite happy to see the "fanatics" leave before they infected them with their foolish religion.

Tom could still remember the confirming light in each of their eyes when they found out that a vacant building about three blocks from where Train lived could be converted into a "clinic and care" building for just about the same amount for which their house and belongings were sold. They would be available for any crisis that might arise due to the threat of terrorist activity throughout the land. War had often been threatened, but had never actually been waged on home soil before, so those who loved deeply were required to make drastic lifestyle changes.

There was no question in any of their hearts as to whether or not it was the will of God for them to go. Their God and their nation needed them and to do anything other than obey would have been unthinkable. It was their offering to God for a land in turmoil. Not only could they help physically, but their recent recommitment to the Lord added an unparalleled dimension to their offering.

Once the decision was made and confirmed in prayer, the family found themselves on weekends and every other spare moment, fixing the building and supplying it with needed equipment. Through the love of the church - Train, Crystal and many more - the most unfamiliar and frightening parts of the city became loved and cared for as home.

"I've never lived on the third floor before," Becky said, looking at her Mom, who had just folded a city map and put it into the glove compartment.

Sally smiled and put her arm around Becky and said, "It's going to be quite an experience for all of us, isn't it?" The family nodded their heads in unison, which made them laugh as they caught themselves.

"One good thing," Tom said, "is that we know Jesus lives here, too!"

"Yeah," Tommy agreed. "He better or we're not gonna make it." They nodded again, each knowing that even though they had no idea what the future held, Jesus did and that was all that really mattered.

There will come a time when My anointed will walk in freedom, having no bonds or entanglements with the world. It will be a time when those devoted to Me and Me alone will rise above all of the restrictions and sin that have held My bride captive.

Those who have chosen to scoff at the things which I hold dear will no longer be able to do so. They will see with their own eyes, a people that make My world come alive; living testimonies of the true gospel. Choices will need to be made by all people; either they will submit to the truth of My Word and become part of My true church or they will deny Me in those who are before their very eyes.

When My anointing falls on My bride - those who have sold out to Me during this time of testing - there will be no doubt as to who belongs to Me. Purity, holiness, devotion, mercy, power: all of My fruits and gifts in fullness will be manifest in and through the humble, the meek, the lowly in spirit. My Word will pierce the hungry soul as My people live and move and have their being in Me.

I have told you of a salvation to be revealed in the last time. I have told you of a great harvest. Now I am about to equip those whom I can trust. Be part of My bride. Give everything to Me. Devote yourself to My ways and My desires. Respond to this call, My beloved. Do not turn away and be left outside. I love you and would love for you to be equipped to help bring forth the harvest. Choose to be completely Mine now. The time is short.

# CHAPTER TWENTY-SIX

*"In his pride the wicked does not seek him; in all his thoughts there is no room for God."*     **Psalm 10:4 NIV**

*"Then the kingdom of heaven shall be likened to ten virgins who took their lamps and went to meet the bridegroom.*
*Five of them were foolish (thoughtless, without forethought) and five were wise (sensible, intelligent, and prudent)."*                    **Matthew 25:1-2 Amp**

As the time grew nearer for the Lord Jesus to step from His throne to come for His bride, a final call was given to those who hadn't received life from on high.  In contrast to the anticipation, joy and wondrous order in the heavenlies, strife, upheaval and total chaos encompassed the earth and its inhabitants.

Mixed with seasons of relative peace and temporary security, wars, rumors and threats to every kind of freedom were rampant. Economies of single nations would topple overnight, causing devastation to the staggering world economy.  While U.S. troops were sent to fight never-ending wars around the world and foreign troops practiced locally, terrorist activity, administered by those hating for the sake of hating, caused feelings of absolute safety to be a thing only remembered in stories told to help calm fearful children into falling asleep.  People clamored for the government to do something, not knowing that their cry meant losing more of their freedoms a little at a time.  Governments responded with more laws and restrictions, furthering a totally controlled society.

A vicious pounding almost broke the thin office door of Pastor Wickham, shaking him from his prayer time. Wiping tears of repentance from his eyes, he stood to answer the door as the incessant pounding continued.

Morgan Wickham, having been "requested" to resign from his duties at His Holiness Christian Fellowship, started a small gathering of remnant believers in a warehouse two miles from his former congregation. Lacking all of the glamour of his former position; but abounding in the grace, love and life of God, he was able to be the true shepherd of the flock the Lord entrusted to him. Sold out and uncompromising, Pastor Wickham had embraced the moving of God's Spirit in his heart and walked in the power of a crucified life.

As he opened the door, he was surprised to see his former head deacon, Jim Wilson - wild-eyed and visibly shaken - staring at him, anxious for an audience. Jim had been the initiator and aggressor in the move for the resignation of his former pastor. Morgan had forgiven him and all of the others who had signed the petition. He even understood that the accusations, false stories and condemning words of some of his former flock were not the words of the people themselves, but of the spirit behind them which drove them to say and do such malicious, ungodly things.

"It's crashed! I'm ruined!" Jim exclaimed, almost shouting as he pushed his way into the small, single-room office.

"Now calm down, Jim," Pastor said quietly. "Here, let me get you a glass of water," he added, as he started toward the water cooler in the corner. The water gurgled and a large, lone bubble belched its way to the top of the see-through, plastic jug as the water filled the tiny paper cone.

Taking the water without thanks, and gulping it down in one swallow, Jim continued as he crumpled the paper cone. "You don't understand. The stock market has crashed!

Everything I had was invested in stocks. I even re-mortgaged my house last week to buy Zandar Chemical - a sure thing - and now, it's all gone! What am I going to do?"

"Well," Pastor began, raising his hand to Jim's shoulder in an attempt at consolation, "We had better seek the Lord..."

"I know," Jim interrupted, pushing the pastor's hand aside. "Maybe Mike Pettingsworth over at the bank could extend the note. Maybe he could help me. I gotta go see him." Jim again pushed past his former confidant as he rushed to the door, mumbling to himself. He charged out without saying good-bye.

Pastor Wickham went back to his prayer time and held the confused, panic-stricken man before the Lord. In his heart, though, he knew that Jim had not trusted nor believed in the work that God was doing.

After a short time of prayer, there was another knock on the door. This time, the knock was slow and almost solemn. The voice on the other side quietly called, almost whispered, his name. "Pastor Wickham, are you there? May I talk to you?"

Morgan Wickham again rose from his kneeling position in the corner of his very modest room. The single room served as office, kitchen and bedroom. He spent most of his quiet times by the couch in the corner, either kneeling in front of it to pray or sitting on it to read. Its secondary purpose provided a temporary bed for a needy man.

On the way to the door, he caught a glimpse of himself in the mirror. Because he had been in prayer most of the night and hadn't had time to prepare prior to Jim Wilson's disturbing visit, he was still in his pajamas and robe.

"This is sure going to impress whoever that is," he said to himself as he continued toward the door. "Eleven o'clock in the morning," he mused, "and here I am looking like I've given up on myself. I sure hope it's someone who will understand."

Morgan opened the door to the full extent of the short security chain. Peeking through the opening provided, he observed a well-dressed man in his twenties. As soon as the door opened, the man's eyes brightened and he immediately thrust his extended hand through the opening. Before Pastor Wickham could move aside, the man's hand poked him in the stomach, causing him to react and hit the door with his head, inadvertently closing it tightly on the man's hand.

"I'm sorry," the man said, grimacing through the smaller opening. "My name is Mark Deider. I guess I so wanted to meet you and shake your hand that I got a little carried away. May I talk to you?"

"What is it about?" Morgan responded, while eyeing the man and determining by his countenance that this was a meeting of friendship.

"May I come in?" Mark queried somewhat hesitantly, while trying to extract his now bright, reddening hand from the door.

"Yes, I'm sorry," Morgan replied. He pulled the door back to free Mark's hand, closed it to undo the security chain; and then opened it again to usher in his latest visitor.

"How can I help you?" he said, motioning with one hand for Mark to come in and rubbing his head and stomach with the other. Mark walked to the center of the room, turned and faced Pastor Wickham.

"I need to talk to you about something very important to me. I..." he hesitated. "I need some answers, some real truth; and I think you can help me."

"I'll do what I can," Morgan said, "but would you mind if I got dressed first? It'll only take a few minutes, and you can begin to talk while I'm changing. The door on this walk-in closet is quite thin and I'll be able to hear you perfectly. One of the advantages of cheap rent," he added with a grin that seemed to break the tension that Mark was obviously feeling.

214

With that comment, he motioned for Mark to sit on the couch as he walked to the closet. He pulled the light chain, closed the door to the closet and began putting on his jogging suit. "This will be comfortable enough," he thought, "until the meeting is over and I can dress for the day."

"Pastor Wickham," Mark began.

"Call me Morgan," said the voice from behind the closed door.

"Morgan," Mark started again, receiving the openness and friendship that had been given to him. "I've been in great confusion for many months now and I need your help. I thought I knew what it meant to be a Christian and subsequently, how I should act; but now as I observe what is happening all around me, I'm not so sure. I was hoping you could help me."

Mark went on to tell Pastor about parts of his life: his association with Stephen MacDougal and God's People for the Restoration of Morality; his last meeting with Stephen; and most specifically, their last conversation about "Katie's Naughty Toys." He told of the deep confusion he was feeling, especially after his search for her came to nothing. All that he was able to find out was that she had decided to go live somewhere in New Mexico. The friends Mark was able to contact in his search for her had little to say, except that she cried a lot and cursed "those self-righteous bigots," as she called them. She left angry and empty, "to go rest for awhile" was the report.

Mark had settled most of that in his heart with the understanding that only the Holy Spirit can change people. His job was to love and serve to a greater degree so that others could see in him the kind of love that took Jesus to the cross. His concern at present was the open warfare played out on the streets of every city.

215

"How do I live for the Lord in the face of such change?" he said quietly, expressing his heart to the man on the other side of the closet door.

Morgan reappeared from the dressing closet, combing his hair and adjusting his jogging suit. "It makes you wonder, doesn't it?" he quietly spoke, as he walked to the chair next to the couch and sat down. "Would you like some coffee?" he remembered to ask after he sat down. Mark gave a silent "no thank you" with his hands, signifying that talk was more important than cordialities this morning.

Morgan toyed with the pages of his well-worn Bible in momentary silence to gather his thoughts. "I don't know whether I have everything in order myself, Mark," he began slowly. "But I do know that the Holy Spirit is sending out a call: He's requiring a depth of commitment - a total death to all that I used to hold dear. It has made me re-evaluate all that I thought I knew before.

"I heard about that," Mark responded, leaning forward attentively, poised to hear what would come next. "That's why I came to see you. It looks like I may have to make some major decisions in my life – like fighting for my country which I know I should do, dealing with someone who might take my last piece of food, or coming face to face with someone who wants to take my life or the lives of those around me. I don't know that I have what it takes to make those kinds of decisions."

As Mark spoke, Morgan took a quick look out the window, then continued. "Mark, I gave my life to Jesus a long time ago. Since then, I've tried my best to represent Him to others in accordance with my understanding of His Word. I thought I was filled with the Holy Spirit. I even spoke in other tongues. I believed and led many to Jesus. In all of those years, I had no idea how far I was from Him."

216

Mark stirred, a little uneasy, thinking that Morgan had missed the point of his visit. "Recently, however," Morgan continued, "something has happened." Morgan's face began to take on a childlike radiance, as in adoration of one who is very dear. His voice drifted as if reliving some wondrous event. "The only way I could describe what happened would be to compare it to what I think the event of Pentecost must have been like. Remember, I already thought I was filled with His Spirit. That was a wonderful experience, but this...this was incomparable."

He continued looking directly at Mark. "By the way, I've contacted many of my pastor friends and people that I know and trust; this is far from an isolated incident. It's as if Jesus, through the Holy Spirit, is visiting His people to change them."

Mark stared at Morgan, so entranced with what he was saying, that there was a long pause before he spoke. "What do you mean, visiting His people to change them?"

"Well, for some time there had been a stirring, like a call in the hearts of many to draw close. It began with a questioning in my heart, a desire for more of Jesus, very much like the one it sounds as though you are experiencing through your need for answers," Morgan said, putting his hand on Mark's shoulder for reassurance. "This led me to seek Him for more of Him, like a wooing of some sort. With my seeking Him for Himself- not for answers - a newness, almost a rekindling of first love rose up in me. Then..." Morgan paused, remembering. "Then He came...Jesus showed up and everything was changed. Now He's always here."

"What do you mean, Jesus 'showed up?'" Mark asked quietly, putting aside his immediate needs, trying not to disturb the seeming reverence of the moment. He hadn't really thought of the importance of being equipped in his spirit for the times ahead.

"Mark, good people do die. Many times in the past, there were very difficult circumstances and life became unbearably hard. Without a special kind of power, which presently we know little about, the people in those difficult circumstances would have died cursing those who came against them, thereby nullifying the work of the cross. I am convinced that Jesus is equipping us with Himself for the days ahead.

"From what I've learned," Morgan said, "it is not the same for everyone. Some actually see Him." Mark was wide-eyed and unable to speak. "Some simply sense their sin and lack of ability to handle situations as Jesus would. Others only feel a peace and a presence beyond anything they have ever felt, but the outcome is always the same. Everyone is changed instantly."

"What do you think it means?" Mark questioned somewhat fearfully, not understanding completely.

"I think Jesus is preparing and equipping His bride. I think He is revealing Himself to those who have open hearts to receive Him and Him alone, so that they might do His work during what lies ahead- before He comes to take us with Him. It's happening all over the world in large churches, Bible studies, small groups, and private prayer closets. It's happening to brand-new Christians and to those of us who have been Christians for some time now. He's coming to those who desire holiness and separation, those who recognize the times and seasons and choose only the pursuit of Him and His agenda of loving others more than themselves.

But more than that," Morgan paused retrospectively, "at times, He's coming to little children and to those with hardened hearts like Saul of old to make them His instantly. It's the most remarkable time since the first-century church. There's a plumb line being drawn; it seems to run almost down the middle of all mankind and…" he hesitated, "and down the middle of His church, too. We're all given a choice as to which side of the line we embrace, and when that choice is clearly made, He visits those who choose Him... He just shows up."

Morgan stretched out his hands in a gesture of wonderment, then continued. "The whole purpose of God becomes clear. It's not about nations, peace pacts, rights, persecutions, or any of the distractions before us, even though we are required to respond to the daily trials until we no longer live on this earth. This is all about God, His kind of love and His plans and purposes for mankind, our acceptance of His Son, Jesus Christ; and the Christ-like character developed in each of us, just so that others might also see and accept Him. All for His honor.

"For a long time, the church has not come alongside those who have been told to walk by faith. They had something most of us didn't. It's nothing to their credit. They just had the opportunity to go there first, a lot of times not understanding what was happening. Now with this renewed visitation, those who have walked as best they could, trusting only in Jesus, can lead the rest of us who now see His true ways."

Mark and Morgan sat in silence to allow the impact of those thoughts to have access to their hearts. Mark moved to speak, but Morgan began again in reflex response to an inner urging.

"I think the generation that sees the coming of the Lord will witness the kind of literal hell that is breaking loose all around us, due to man's pride and rejection of God. I believe the fullness of the sin nature is being exposed and all society is plummeting to a depth of depravity in order to expose our absolute need for God and our true character without Him. As always, Satan attempts to discredit the real heart of God by raising up fanatics who kill and destroy in the name of God.

"At the same time," Morgan continued with clarity of thought, "He is raising up a remnant that is truly His. They are being cloaked in His power and enveloped in His love, having eyes for Him alone, all for the purpose of gathering in the endtime harvest before His return. What the world has to offer no longer affects them." Then, staring piercingly into Mark's eyes, he said, "And we are that people and that is what is happening. It's the salvation to be revealed in the end times, as stated in I Peter 1:5."

Mark remained quiet for a moment to soak in Morgan's last statement. "What about those who love God, but aren't responding? I mean, I know many who don't see it as you do. They haven't heard what you are talking about. I know they love God, but they are out there fighting for their lives daily. They can only see their needs and would think you are mad."

"I don't know for sure," Morgan began pensively. "The closest I have come to an explanation is that there must be a difference between the bride of Christ and the body of Christ. The Lord keeps leading me back to Matthew 25:1, the parable of the wise and foolish virgins, each time I ask Him about that kind of separation. In a time when you would think we as a church should be coming closer together, there seems to be a division or separation occurring.

"Mark," Morgan moved forward on his chair, his hands outstretched, "they were all virgins, you know. All were pure. For the purpose of this discussion, they all had a relationship with Jesus, were looking for the coming of the Bridegroom; but only half went into the wedding banquet. I don't believe it has to do with the salvation of the remaining five or anything like that, but it sure does seem that distinctions are being made. I think that it has something to do with the oil of the Holy Spirit and how much we are pressing in to Jesus, looking for His coming with proper motives in our hearts."

Morgan stopped for a reflective moment and then said, "I guess the only thing I can be sure of is that I and all those who have been drawn so far have no desire other than being in intimate fellowship with Jesus and the Father, and in telling others about His incredible love. The worst possible thing that could happen is that I would dishonor Him in any way. The trappings of the world have become as nothing. In all the years I've served Him, that has never been the case with me. I've also noticed that even people very new in the Lord instantly walk in a Christ-like purity - with intimacy, understanding and obedience far beyond many who have known Jesus for years."

Mark closed his eyes to concentrate on what he'd just heard. Then he opened them quickly, a myriad of questions flooding his mind. "Do you think that's what's happening to me? Do you think I'm part of what God is doing?"

"Only God knows," Morgan responded, "but it sure seems like part of that wooing I was telling you about. It looks like you are being given some choices. What I would do if I were you would be to eliminate everything in your life that stops you from serving Him. I don't mean go live in the hills or anything like that. The Father may use you right where you are, serving your country when needed, doing it with His heart.

"I know I'm supposed to be here near the people I've discipled all these years to show them the way. We're working with the Red Cross in disaster zones. If I were you, I'd sell out to God. Buy your extra oil now, before He comes," Morgan urged, referring again to the wise and foolish virgins. "Make Him your priority and wait for Him to move. It's still the answer to all of your questions, even if we're not in the end of the end times."

Mark sat silently for a moment, looking at the floor. " So I live each day loving deeper and serving others with fervency. You're telling me to basically invest in the right things with Christ's motives in my heart and everything will be all right?"

"Mark, it really is no different than what transpired in the first century churches; why should it be so foreign to us? They had it rough. They did die because they were hated for their kind of love; but while they lived, the love of God was shown to all around them. Could it be that we are so far from what we should be? Could the world and all of its ways have become more important to us than the One we say we serve?"

"What about joining the army, or going to war to help my country and being ordered to kill someone? What am I supposed to do in those situations? What would Jesus do?" Mark's eyes teared from intensity.

"I can't answer all of those questions for you Mark, but God can and will answer them when the time comes. If you make it your priority to sell out to Him, the answers will come as each situation presents itself. He will be so much of a presence in you that they will come freely. You just determine to love God, people and your nation with all of your heart and move how and when He tells you to. He may have you serve as a medic or find some other way to help if you're not supposed to fight, but you must serve."

Mark stood, hands in his pockets, eyes absent-mindedly focused on the recurrent pattern in the rug. There really wasn't much left to say. He did have more peace. He was so deep in thought that he found himself opening the door without saying good-by. Turning around once he'd walked down the steps to the sidewalk, he gave Morgan a relieved smile of thanks.

Morgan closed the door and chose to continue in prayer with his Lord. He prayed for Mark and anyone else he could think of, that they might answer the love call of the Bridegroom

A few days later, the Elmfield Chronicle announced that Jim Wilson, the Chairman of the Board of Directors of His Holiness Christian Fellowship, was found hanged in his garage. The overturned stool at his feet assured the police that the death was a suicide.

My wrath is soon to break forth upon your land. There will be no place to hide for those who have not heard My call to holiness.

But fear not! Those who know Me, who have learned to be locked up with Me, will rise above the darkest places. I will have My bride. The world will see and notice the redemptive power of the cross. They will be astonished as I bring forth the beauty of life from the ashes.

My Word will go forth. My plans will be accomplished. My people will be vessels of honor to Me. Be of great courage. Be steadfast. Lock yourselves up with Me and live.

# CHAPTER TWENTY-SEVEN

*"Greater love has no one than this, that he lay down his life for his friends."*　　　　　　　　　**John 15:13 NIV**

It was a rainy day in the city. Tommy Bracken sat in the window seat of "Red" Carlson's bus, watching the rain pelt against the window on the way to his first day of school at Thomas Jefferson Middle School on Melvina Street. Red had been led of the Lord to sell his home in order to buy several buses in which to transport children back and forth through rough neighborhoods, so they wouldn't be hurt on their way to school. Originally, Red was transporting to and from a Christian school, but the Lord "saw fit" to expand his ministry.

As Red would say it, with that everpresent gleam in his eye: "Kids who ain't Christians need to see someone who cares. When I pick 'em up for free - no strings - they and their parents see Jesus. And you know what...?" he said, as a mischievous grin crossed his freckled face. "To them, Jesus looks just like me. I might be His only representative in their lives. Wow! What an honor."

Tom and Sally furnished the upper floors of the building which they had purchased as a "safe place" for people who wanted to be delivered from alcohol or drugs or bondages of any kind. On the first and second floors, a free walk-in clinic was established for anyone who had need. The purchase and operation of it exhausted the money they had acquired from the sale of their home and personal effects.

Carl Henderson, Tom's former employer, had decided to sell his business and donated the profits to Tom and Sally to use wisely. Within weeks of the sale, he had disappeared; and no one had heard from him since. The money purchased and renovated the abandoned hospital two blocks away. Love, care, hope, and especially answers in Jesus, were part of every prescription. And there was always an open door for the Healer of Mankind to perform His wonders on those deemed medically hopeless. Many bodies were supernaturally restored to continue to testify of the power of the cross and its effect on believers. If and when the Lord chose to intervene, many believers were able to continue their missions unaffected or miraculously healed when exposed to chemical and germ warfare. Deadly poisons simply didn't have any adverse effect as God protected them.

As the family - now somewhat acclimated to their new surroundings - began finding their ministry base, Becky followed a desire to work in the clinics and hospital while Tommy felt he should concentrate his ministry in the schools, to work with the street gangs so prevalent in the area. The social programs, political rhetoric, and even local government and law enforcement were no match for the pressure put on the young by local gang mentality. Too often, the motto of the Rebels, "Join or Die," became a reality in the life of someone who attempted to stand alone. Through the Holy Spirit, Tommy saw through the exterior of gang toughs into their souls and saw the need only Jesus could fill.

As the bus pulled into the school, Tommy said a silent prayer: "Lord, I remember You told me that if I would go, You would be with me and make my life significant. Here I am, Lord. Use me."

"Well, lookee here...a brand new pile of dog _____ just got off the bus," a voice came from the side as Tommy's foot touched the pavement. As Tommy turned in the direction of the voice, a pain overcame him; an excruciating pain just before things got fuzzy. Tommy found himself flat on his back near the front wheel of the bus, blood spurting from his nose all over his shirt. Instantly, Red Carlson bounded from the driver's seat and lunged at Waco - the kid who threw the punch- and pulled him into the now-empty bus, closing the door behind them, and leaving Tommy and the startled gang members outside.

As Tommy realized what was happening and recovered enough to get to his feet, he could see through the bus door windows that Waco was on the floor with Red's knee on his chest holding him down. Everyone was so surprised at the unusual turn of events, that for an instant, Waco's gang members, the rest of the kids on the playground; and even Waco, Red and Tommy stayed frozen in their positions in utter silence.

Finally, Tommy said the first words. "Come on, Red. Open the doors. He's just trying to be tough. Let him go."

With a kindly grin, Red removed his knee from Waco's chest. Before he was completely set free, Waco was stopped by the doors that were still held shut by his captor. Quietly, Red spoke to his agitated, unwilling audience; and his words greatly impacted the spirit of his startled captive.

"Young man, should anything like this happen again to Tommy Bracken, this bus, me or any of Tommy's friends, I will pray that the powers of heaven come against you to bring you to your knees. I'd suggest you make it your life's work to protect that young man," he said, nodding toward Tommy, "or your life won't be worth the twenty-seven cents you have in your pocket. Do you understand what I mean?"

"Yes, Sir," was all that would come out of Waco's mouth.

"One other thing..." Red added, "...within that boy," again nodding in Tommy's direction, "is more power than you've ever dreamed of in your entire life. I'd find out what it is if I were you." Having said that, he opened the bus doors.

Waco bounded from the bus and walked past Tommy without even looking in his direction. His gang, the Rebels, followed obediently behind him. Waco's only response to their questioning of what should be done was, "Leave 'em alone. We've got better things to do."

Without anyone realizing it, the Lord, through the heavenly warriors in the bus and on the playground, had established Tommy as a quiet leader in the school. Waco thought that he ran the school and had attempted to establish that authority the instant Tommy stepped from the bus. But God had other plans for the souls of His precious children held in the bondage of fear.

Tommy was to be found faithful as a strong, bright light, testifying of Jesus. He was given the grace gift of agape love for his fellow man. Motivated by it and caring only for others, he allowed them to see Christ. He loved the unlovable and always had the time to help the hurting. He then discipled them until they themselves were able to show that same Jesus to others. Most newcomers would try to infiltrate the most popular group of kids in the school, but not so with Tommy. He sought out the lonely, the outcast, or the helpless and befriended them.

One instance of the miracle power of love was visible in Larry Stern. Larry was born without the full use of his left side. His left arm was dwarfed to appear approximately half the size of his right arm. He always had pain in his left leg, so he favored it. As he would walk, he gave the appearance of a crippled bird. The kids, in their evil ignorance and need for importance, gave Larry the name "Bird Claw" and would taunt him unmercifully at any opportunity.

One afternoon lunch period, when the games had run out and boredom had set in, most of the class had congregated in the corner next to the school steps. The guys were demonstrating their bravado by arm wrestling, and the girls were standing around ogling, posing, and spurring them on.

Larry and Tommy had been catching up on some homework in the rear of the school, and upon completing their assignments, they walked to the stairs to wait for the bell to call them back to class. Often, in times like these, they would discuss the things of God and their purpose for being born. Larry had given his life to Jesus several months before, and had been healed of all the anger and hurt caused by the ridicule he had faced throughout his life. For hours on end, they would discuss the life of Jesus and how He glorified the Father with every action He took and how they could adapt it to everyday life. Often, Larry would pray to be like Jesus to those who needed to see a strength they didn't have themselves.

Tommy and Larry would make up situations, and then study and pray as to how to best represent Jesus. Their watchword together was, "What would Jesus do given the same situation?" In fact, as either one would come upon a given situation, and would call out "check it out;" it would mean that the other one would have to determine what Jesus would do, and prove it through the Bible.

The pair had just seated themselves on the steps when Tony, the most insecure - and therefore, the loudest of the group - noticed that they had arrived. "Hey, Larry," Tony jeered in their direction. Some of the crowd tried to quiet him, but hate and need for approval compelled him to continue.

"Hey, Bird Claw, I'm talkin' to you," he began again, walking over to the steps. Larry and Tommy began to pray silently. "Since you been hangin' around with 'Loco' over here, you've gotten even uglier than you were before." Tony turned in Waco's direction and received a nod of approval, which gave him more confidence. "What do you say, you and the Cripple do a little arm wrestlin'? You got one good arm, and he may not have any legs that work; but he must be good for something - why don't the two of you go at it?"

The Cripple was Nicky White. Nicky had been a very active gang member before a bullet severed his spinal column and left him paralyzed from the waist down. Because of his anger and festering hatred, and because the rest of the gang just tolerated him unless they could somehow use him; he was the most dangerous. He really belonged nowhere, and hovered at the perimeter of everything. This last taunt made him furious. To be classed with the Bird Claw was the highest insult Tony had ever paid him. "I ain't gonna fight him. He's freaky," Nicky spat in Tony's direction.

"Why not?" Tony goaded him. "You guys could be the fight of the century." The laughter of the crowd gave Tony more bravado.

"What about you, Claw?" he continued, turning to Larry, who was calmly observing all that was developing.

The two children of God had waited in prayer for everything to unfold. Too often they had seen the heart of a hero rise up in very ordinary people when empowered by God. They were not going to miss this opportunity by taking anything on in their own strength. Larry, taking his eyes off Tony, looked at Tommy, who was grinning seemingly inappropriately for the circumstances. Both knew what that meant, and simultaneously said, "Check it out!"

Larry hobbled over to Nicky, who was fuming at the embarrassment of the situation, hatred toward "the Claw" literally oozing from every pore. As Larry approached him, he growled in a low, determined voice, "I ain't gonna fight no freak."

"I know." Larry said, with a smile. "You couldn't gain anything by beating me, because anyone could beat me. However, there is a war that has already been won for you on a cross over two thousand years ago. So… in the name of Jesus of Nazareth, rise up and walk!" With that, Larry extended his good arm to Nicky, who stared at him for a moment in disbelief.

Slowly, Nicky reached out to grasp the extended arm. As soon as he did, the strength he needed to stand was released. A collective gasp from the crowd broke the silence as Nicky arose from the wheelchair. He simply stood and stared, questioningly, into Larry's eyes.

"Go ahead - walk," Larry encouraged him.

So, he did. Nicky walked and within days was running and jumping and completely whole. Over the weeks, Nicky inquired about the power that healed him. In doing so, Larry had the opportunity to show him his best friend Jesus. The new heart that came with his salvation would soon lead him to lay his life down while attempting to rescue a small child from a burning building. He was running in for the third time when an explosion rained debris into him, killing him instantly.

Larry never experienced that kind of healing miracle in his own life. He may not have been healed physically, but he did have the miracle of new life and friendship. Because of God's love through Tommy, seeds of greater love would grow and be given to many. Through Tommy, at times even the most hardened heart saw the love that took Jesus to the cross and surrendered to it.

On Thursday, Waco's gang, the Rebels, decided to settle the long and bitter battle for the Third Street turf once and for all. The Falcons were determined to hold on, even though most of the time, the turf was occupied by the Rebels. As hostilities grew, everyone knew that it was just a matter of time before it would come to this.

The time had been set for 6:00 PM. Each side had laid out its strategy. The rules were simple. There were none. The only guidelines were that it was going to be face-to-face, no hiding, no cars, simple weapons, head on, until one gang backed off and ran.

Tommy, seeing the stupidity of all of this, tried to talk to Waco, even days before the fight. "You're loco," Waco responded to his pleas. "You and yer Jesus can go to hell. Leave me alone." Tommy spent most of Wednesday night

231

praying for God to intervene somehow. Hours at a time, he wept for the souls of the boys on both sides. "Somehow, let them see You, Jesus, before it's too late for them," Tommy cried.

"It's an ambush," Sara Felding said, with tears in her eyes. "Tommy, it's an ambush to waste Waco. They're gonna kill him and then there won't be any fights no more. Dick Bellows told me. You gotta do something."

With that, Tommy took off in a dead run across the open field that led to the vacant lot on the corner of Third and White Oak. The site had been chosen so that all who lived there could witness who won, and there would be no more dispute. He headed for the alley behind Cooley's Groceries, where the Rebels were meeting before going to the fight.

Tommy arrived at the same time Waco did. When he saw Tommy, his anger flared. "What are you doing here, you_____? Get out of my face before I kill you myself!" Waco foamed. He picked up a piece of iron that was lying near the step that led to the back door of the store. "I said, get out of here, freak. Prayin' ain't gonna do..."

Tommy, noticing a speeding car rounding the corner behind Waco, ran straight toward the intended victim. A gunshot was heard at the precise moment that Waco was pushed to the side. The bullet ripped into Tommy's chest, throwing him heavily against the wall of the building. Waco turned and saw the car speeding away. Mesmerized for a moment, he could only stare as blood gushed from Tommy's chest, soaking his shirt.

By the time Waco came to his senses, one of the Rebels had already taken Tommy into his arms and was sitting with him against the building. "Why'd you do it, you stupid idiot? That was for me. Why'd you do it?" he said, screaming, with tears in his eyes.

Tommy looked up weakly at the person who had hated him, blood now coming from his nose and the side of his mouth. "Because, if you die now," he said, choking on his own blood, "if you die now, you'll burn in hell for eternity, and Jesus doesn't want that."

Tommy coughed and then went silent - forever. Waco gaped at his still, bloodied body. The pipe he was going to use on this "freak" was still in his hand. As he became aware again of what he was holding, he let the pipe fall to the ground and walked away.

*************************

The sun was bright and the morning mist had just dissipated in the old cemetery yard. Quiet conversation could be heard between sobs as the medium-sized, wooden casket was gently lowered into the ground. The Brackens - aching at their loss but knowing that Tommy was simply on loan from God - bathed in a quiet, inner peace and hung on to the fact that they would one day be reunited.

Behind a tombstone, in the far corner, sat Waco. He had been there all night, needing answers to questions he had never asked before. In Tommy, Waco had seen a strength that he had never experienced before. The weakness of that kind of love had always made him angry for some reason. "How could weakness be so strong?" he asked himself over and over. It all made him sick to his stomach.

Prior to everyone's arrival for Tommy's burial, a lone, old man came out of the morning shadows. He walked right up to the startled youth and spoke gently. "The answer is Jesus. Tommy has gone to be with Him, but you are here to do the work that is left. Go to Jesus - He loves and forgives you."

With that, the man turned and walked back into the shadows. Waco dropped his head between his knees and called out to the One who Tommy loved most.  In future weeks, the love of God would spread hotter than the hate of the street and stronger than any war through Waco.  Jesus had been glorified through Tommy and many would know of a love far more valuable than any turf could ever be.

*The lusts of the flesh and the pride of life allow the enemy to gain access to you. They make you vulnerable to attack by opening the door to every form of fear and oppression.*

*You <u>must</u> overcome them. There is hidden sin in your heart. Remove it by repenting of it to Me. Let the light of My Holy Spirit shine on it. Confess it as sin and turn from all entertainment of thoughts, sights or habits. Renew your mind daily with My Word, My thoughts, and My presence; and you will be set free. You turn away from sin and I will be there for you; but you must turn away. Each time a thought is noticeable, cast it down. Stop looking in the direction of sin. Stop holding it dear for it has no place in you. You are Mine and I want you spotless. I am jealous for that area of your heart.*

*Come to Me and be holy. In My holy fire, any presence of evil will be consumed. I am your safety, your strong tower, your haven. I am your consuming fire. I require you this day - return to your first love - your consuming love for Me, the desire for My Word and the power that is Mine.*

*You know Me. Now begin to believe again. Flee from fear. It no longer has a hold on you. I have cut its cord, so turn from it. You are Mine and nothing will take you from Me. Be intense for My presence and My presence alone.*

# CHAPTER TWENTY-EIGHT

*"For the god of this world has blinded the unbelievers' minds [that they should not discern the truth], preventing them from seeing the illuminating light of the Gospel of the glory of Christ (the Messiah), Who is the Image and Likeness of God."*

*2 Corinthians 4:4 Amp*

The very unlikely couple waiting for their luggage at the baggage claim drew the incredulous stares of many passers-by. She - a diminutive, red-haired, strikingly beautiful woman with kind eyes and a peaceful smile; and he - well, he was beyond description. Massive in size and street-rugged in stature, his quiet demeanor belied his immensity. People had all they could do to restrain themselves from finding any excuse to talk to Crystal and Train. Their spirits were so open and alive. Children flocked to them; and they, in turn, shared each moment necessary to satisfy their youthful needs.

After Crystal found her Lord, Savior and Healer that Sunday, she was held close by people who could really guide and direct her to wholeness. Women entrusted with the love of God and His Word, ministered life and testimony to the empty vessel. As her heart was filled with God's love, she was able to pour that love into others. She found satisfaction and purpose in ministering at the clinic and hospital established by Tom and Sally. Working tirelessly, she met the physical and spiritual needs of the unwashed, the vile and the hopeless. With her new life and submission to the Lord, Crystal had found her reason for living. All her money, power and social contacts had left her empty. Now, her Lord had filled her full. His life and desires became hers, and she was truly at peace.

With her new eyes, the "pile of dumb rocks," as she had once called Train, had now become a mountain of precious jewels to her. She had found worth in Jesus and He entrusted one of His men of honor to her care. The match that seemed very unlikely on earth was truly made in heaven. A holy alliance, which had been appointed from the beginning of time, was formed before the eyes of loving friends. They moved and lived and had their being in Jesus Christ, their Lord. From that relationship, love and undergirding flowed forth to one another and to the world around them. They were truly a series of inconsistencies, molded and formed until they were equipped and anointed to present the Pearl of Great Price to the world.

"I'm so sorry we missed Tommy's funeral," Crystal said, looking up at Train as he picked up the last bag. "That young man was much older than his age."

The two couldn't attend the funeral because Train had been deputized and sent by the police to work with some of the gangs in another city. There was scuttle that some group had intended on using chemical warfare to harm a great portion of the population and that police needed some information from the street world, so they sent for Train to find out what the real situation was.

He knew the street and was known for his integrity among gang members, so he had access to places where few others could go without being badly hurt. He had also proven the changes in his life many times over, so law enforcement trusted him, too. The combination was perfect and he had found incredible satisfaction helping in this unique fashion. It was God's plan for his life.

This time, the rumor was correct and a plan to hit the city with biochemicals was thwarted before it ever got off the ground. The information that Train received from his contacts was solid evidence that helped to destroy key players in a ring of terrorists that had eluded the FBI for many months.

Waiting for Train to finalize the luggage inspection, Crystal started to reflect on life in general – questions like why are we born, why this particular time frame, why this part of the country? She now understood that God does not make mistakes. He ordains our lives to impact our world for His purposes. Most of the time, we waste that life - or at least many years of it - in wandering confusion, thinking that we are doing good things and that we know what truth is.

The truth had become so distorted by confused people who wanted to harm others, supposedly in the name of God, that it made Crystal want to scream. If everything we do is not directed by God through seeking Him, it usually has little real impact as far as His plans are concerned and quite often has the opposite effect than what He intended.

"God is real," she said quietly. "He does direct all of our lives, but never to harm anyone. There is an overall plan and we are part of it," Crystal stomped her foot to emphasize her convictions. Train, knowing Crystal and her habit of saying her thoughts out loud, looked up from his conversation with the security guard - who was questioning Train's gun permit - when he heard her shoe slap the floor. She smiled sheepishly at him as he waved.

Crystal took a couple of steps to the side to take a good look at her husband and reflect on how dramatically he had changed in a very short time. He started out as a homeless, frightened little kid who learned to survive on the street with a mind so clouded by fear and hate that all he could muster from life was minimal at best. At worst, there were times when he was nothing more than a cold body lying in some dark alley, having no positive, lasting effect on anyone or anything.

Then he met his Lord. Now look at him! Clear-headed and truly understanding his purpose for living, he was a catalyst for positive changes everywhere he went.

"Boy, Lord, I sure do love that man!" she commented to herself, yet loud enough for a female passer-by to give her a knowing grin and a thumbs up. Train turned again to acknowledge her presence, radiating a joy that came from deep within.

Crystal recounted the many valuable people she had the privilege of knowing since she found her peace with the Lord. How exciting and full they were in comparison to those who lived only for themselves, the way she had done for so many years.

Tommy Bracken...Wow, what an incredible part he played! So much life packed into such a short time. Mic and Steely...They had unstoppable power to do good rather than waste away without direction on some nameless street. Tom, and Sally, who repented of calling themselves Christians while living a life of hedonism, and Becky... They were her best friends. What a change to go from standing in the shadows of life to becoming totally immersed in it. Red Carlson, Pastor Wickham... The list got so long that Crystal felt praises of thanks rise up within her.

"These people are my personal heroes," she said out loud.

"You're doing it again."

Crystal jumped. She hadn't seen Train walk up behind her. She turned and gave his arm a good shaking.

"Don't do that!" she said in feigned annoyance, grinning and somewhat embarrassed. Both laughed as Crystal buried her head in his chest.

As the two walked to the cab that would take them home, Train asked Crystal what she'd been doing while he squared things away with their luggage.

"I was just going over in my mind how wonderful it is to be alive, even in times like these. I know that most of us want to live without heavy challenges all around us; but when I had everything, I had everything but purpose."

240

Train opened the cab door and Crystal seated herself in the middle of the back seat. Train got in next to her after the cabby closed the trunk.

"I mean," Crystal continued as the cab pulled from the curb, "for so long I thought the American dream was to get as much for myself as often as I could. I had everything, or so it looked that way to others; but I was dying inside. That's where it matters. For me, the American dream is loving God, loving others, having integrity and having your life mean something."

Crystal looked at Train, who was trying to find room in the back seat for his feet.

"*Stuff* doesn't matter, ya know," she told him playfully.

Getting serious again, she continued. "Living for the Lord is exciting. Helping people is exciting. Being an asset to your country is exciting. It's exciting to find out why you've had the privilege of being born, even when..." she stopped to correct herself. "Especially when times require you to dig deep and do what it takes for the good of all - wherever the Lord plants you."

Train gave Crystal a squeeze. "You're incredible," he said with a smile. His thoughts drifted to the first time he had met the wonderful lady who was now his wife and how the power of the cross of Christ had changed her from being hollow to being whole.

"Wow!" he said out loud after a few seconds.

"Now you're doing it," Crystal remarked. "Come on, Big Boy. Let me in on what's going on inside that head of yours."

Train's expression suddenly turned very serious.

"Stop the car!" he yelled, scaring Crystal and the driver. "I said, stop it!"

Before the vehicle could even come to a complete stop, Train grabbed Crystal's hand, opened the door and dove onto the pavement, pulling Crystal on top of himself to cushion her

241

fall. The two rolled into a drainage ditch and Train unceremoniously pushed Crystal's head to the ground just as bullets - from what must have been several automatic weapons- flew a few inches over their bodies. The screeching tires of a high-speed car could be heard rounding the previous corner.

"You O.K.?" Train asked, moving back to the road as Crystal nodded uncertainly.

She stood up, dusted herself off and then ran back to the street where Train had already determined that the cab driver was dead. He was on his way to help an older woman who was hit in the leg and shoulder. Halfway there, Train switched directions and ran to the cab, forcefully yanked the dead man to the pavement and snatched the keys from the ignition.

"Get down!" he yelled to everyone in the vicinity as he popped the trunk lid and removed his gun from its case. People scattered in all directions, wherever they could find some kind of protection from whatever was about to take place. Fortunately there were a lot of businesses located in this area, so most people scrambled into the nearest unlocked doorway.

As Train readied his weapon, the sound of squealing tires could again be heard a block away and the speeding car headed back toward them from the opposite direction.

Crystal leaped into the ditch, taking a small bleeding child with her as Train positioned himself at the right rear corner of the cab, his elbow propped on the now closed trunk. He took aim and as the car approached, Train waited for the precise moment and fired two shots into the passenger side front and rear tires. The car caromed off several cars before it jumped the curb and slammed straight into an old, abandoned building, exploding in a ball of flames. Train dove into the ditch as debris from the explosion landed all around them.

"That was Dirk and some of the Kings," Train said to Crystal as he hurried to see who else was hurt.

The Kings, a large gang with a reputation for extreme violence, had been looking for years for the opportunity to eliminate Train even before he left his life on the street. In fact, Train was on his way to settle with them for wasting his friend, "Boney," when he first met Tom and then met Jesus.

Since the start of the war and all the terrorist activity, the Kings had decided to take the opportunity to make a lot of money doing what they already loved to do for free. They had no allegiance to anyone or anything except themselves, and were known to be involved in several local bombings. Because they knew every square inch of their territory, no one could find them.

Crystal turned to the child in her arms. In her hurry to bring her to safety, she hadn't noticed the bullet hole in the little girl's neck. She was dead before they'd even hit the ditch. Looking at the lifeless body she cradled, Crystal couldn't help but think of the uselessness of all of this. Hatred had claimed another, possibly several other lives judging by the crying she heard on the street above her. Hatred for the sake of hating. No matter how hard she tried, she could make no sense of it.

Placing the little girl gently on the ground, Crystal went back to the road where she discovered several lifeless bodies and another four victims who were writhing in pain and in desperate need of help. Train and a few others who escaped the torrent of bullets were tending to the victims, doing what little they could until some form of help arrived. Most likely whatever assistance was offered would come from passers-by. The medical community was already overworked all over the city because of this type of incident.

Six hours later, two bloodied and very tired people unlocked the door of their apartment. The water in the building had not been available for several days, so they cleaned up a little with some moistened rags that were given to them by their neighbors. Train and Crystal dropped heavily into bed. Both of them fell asleep immediately.

The incredible incident that the two of them had been involved in went unnoticed except for those who lost someone or those who were hurt. Occurrences such as this were so commonplace that the evening news shelved this report to cover more volatile issues elsewhere.

Train didn't talk much about what transpired. He had to find peace with His Lord for taking the lives of others – even if it occurred indirectly and wasn't his intent. Sure, he saved many by taking action; but still, it caused people to die – people he had once known.

In one of his previous encounters with them, could he have shown them his Lord somehow? Provided the opportunity for them to receive Jesus and be changed? Could something he might've done then prevented what happened yesterday?

Sure, his friends on the police force heartily commended him, and many people would be spared the brutality that would've come their way if these men had lived; but he still agonized that their lives did not belong to the Lord before they left this earth. That hurt him deep inside. In subsequent, quiet moments with his Lord, the peace he longed for returned through the mercy of God.

My children who thrive on and desire only intimacy with Me are about to be empowered with My presence. Those who have turned away from their useless flurry of activity to change the world are about to enter into a spiritual understanding that will allow them to again represent My Son, Jesus, to their world. People will recognize My Son through their lives. They will see Him and have to choose between life or death because of the convicting power of a wholly surrendered vessel of honor that contains My Holy Spirit.

Who can deny what has been done for all mankind when it becomes visible through the lowly, the weak, the surrendered, the children?

I will not use the dead, the empty and the proud. I never have and will not start now. Whitewashed containers full of dead men's bones have no place in the economy of spiritual power. I have called you. Now I am about to empower those who have come.

# CHAPTER TWENTY-NINE

*"Death has been swallowed up in victory. Where, O death, is your victory? Where, O death, is your sting?"*
                                                        *1 Corinthians 15:54b,55 NIV*

As time passed, the heavenly realms stood poised for the completion of all things before the coming of the Holy One of God for His bride. On the earth, the beginning of the very end of things looked chaotic at best. Turmoil and upheaval were so commonplace that any semblance of peace was a thing of the past.

Martial law - with its accompanying assault troop movements, black helicopters, wire barriers, and checkpoints to monitor and question movement - enacted to help quell looting and rioting that erupted because of terrorist activities, became a lifestyle that inhibited the ability of the ordinary citizen to plan for daily business and personal travel. The Federal Emergency and Management Agency (FEMA) also used military troops, both foreign and domestic, as police forces in locales where upheavals were prominent or suspected.

Whole families, some extremely wealthy one day and devastated the next because of failing economies, were moved to emergency shelters. People of high position, finding themselves devoid of all ability to survive after losing their means for controlling their lives, were often reduced to roaming the streets, mumbling to themselves in fear. Life, as peaceful and friendly as it once was, forcefully and seemingly overnight plunged itself and its participants into unfamiliar, horrifying days of basic survival for those who hadn't observed and acted upon all of the godly warnings regarding the Lord's kind of heart preparation.

The religion of human potential and god-man as the center of all things set the stage for the one great leader who would control everything for the good of mankind. Astoundingly, people who denied, or even cursed, the One, True, Living God, were actually fulfilling His prophecies on His schedule.

With the European economy in place and the United States weak and eroded from within by wars in its own streets and communities, the time had come to truly fulfill the destinies of those who were to come forth and rule for the "betterment of all." As patriotism, once the banner for unifying a land against an enemy, was diluted and yielded to global unity for the sake of peace, laws and the reasons for having them became muddied in the waters of order keeping.

Those who heard the call of the bride, and responded with repentance for their adherence to a self-indulgent gospel, thrived during these times. Never opposing government and never coming against anyone who did not believe as they did, the real church of Jesus Christ was equipped to touch and help many lives, providing basic life needs, even during the hardest of times.

Even though they embraced all, they were labeled as bigots for believing that Jesus was the only way to God as the Bible stated. All real harm - eternal harm - could not touch them as they walked above man's way of doing things and only in the ways of God. Their response to any form of opposition was always to love deeper and forgive more earnestly so that the keeping power of the Holy Spirit would envelop them.

Those who did not respond to God's call to intimacy found themselves unable to grasp real peace in this time of great need. Fear, worry and anger were the constant companions of the children of God who saw fit to do their own thing, maintaining their own agenda when the purifying call went out years before. Now, the spiritual "tools" necessary to walk in love in the worst of situations, as Jesus did, were unavailable to them.  Many died in the subsequent holocaust, cursing those who killed them and losing the opportunity to be a witness of the power of the cross.  Those who embraced the life that had been chosen for them knew that they had been raised up for a time such as this.  Nothing mattered but to love and serve the Lord and others, until their allotted time on this earth ended.

As the purifying fire intensified, it strengthened those who saw their lives as God's property.  They understood the plans of God because they knew Him intimately.  It did not matter whether their God would miraculously intervene in any given situation or whether death by the violence of others' actions would take place to those who were given the faith that Jesus had - faith that caused them to lay their lives in the hands of their loving Father, trusting that He would deliver them should He choose to.  If not, it meant in the truest sense "to live is Christ; to die is gain."

"It's not about us - it's about Jesus" was the watchword on the lips of those who alone cherished intimacy with their loving God and had only His interests - the souls of those who had not as yet accepted Jesus Christ as their Savior and Lord - in their hearts.  They had been shown, in those intimate times with their Lord, the true purposes of God – that none should perish.  No matter what the outward appearances were, God loved even those who hated Him and was using those who loved Him to present the opportunity of salvation to even the most decadent.  His children joyfully submitted to His will for His glory, honor and praise.

************************************

Mob rule reigned on the street and the only real place of safety was to be hidden deep in Christ.  It had become unwise to live independently; so the Brackens, along with many other members of their church, joined together for mutual support, prayer, praise and outreach. Each had in his heart the very soon return of Jesus, so in the midst of tremendous poverty, affliction and even terrorism, there was great peace and rejoicing. Everyone sensed that a common base of living in union would be the most effective way to move in God's Spirit to reach the hurting and see to their true needs. The pooling of resources would help everyone to become more effective.

**************************************

"We're supposed to take only what we need, right, Tom?" Sally said from a small bedroom in their modest apartment. Sally Bracken had spent most of her day communing with the Lord. The fellowship was sweeter than usual that day and Sally knew that sometime very soon she would see her loving Savior face to face. "Tom," Sally began again, turning toward the door. "Tom, are you listening to ..."

"Oh, Jesus," was all that she could manage as her eyes beheld the unimaginable sight before her.

Tom, bloodied from an initial beating intended to quiet him, was thrown at Sally's feet. "Don't pick him up," commanded the meaner of the two hate-filled men. "We're anxious for him to see what's next," he continued, as they moved toward Sally.

Both Tom and Sally went home to be with their beloved Lord that afternoon. To the human eye, it would appear that they suffered immensely before they died, but that was not the case. The heavenly hosts were ordered to hold their positions. As demonic forces unleashed a fury of pent up hatred upon the two who had for so long destroyed Satan's strongholds, much was being accomplished for the kingdom of God.

Long before the beating and torture of Tom, and the rape and stabbing of Sally, the beloved servants of God were face to face with the One they had grown to love most. As with

Stephen in the Book of Acts and many since, Tom and Sally saw the heavens open before them and they beheld the glory of God and Jesus, standing at the right hand of the Father. As it had happened countless times since His defeat at Calvary, Satan again inflicted his fury on the empty shells of what once had been. One more time, things were not what they appeared to be. What looked like hopeless defeat would prove to be glorious victory.

Tom and Sally, through the power of a deeply involved Holy Spirit during their assault, were able to maintain love, forgiveness and mercy in their hearts toward their assailants - one more reminder, in a long list of reminders, of the overwhelming power of the blood shed two thousand years ago. Death had lost its sting and its victory and only served to mark the impending fate of the defeated one.

**********************************

Red Carlson picked up Becky Bracken and gave her a ride home from school. "It's getting pretty rough out there," he said to Becky, as they approached her home. "I'm sure school won't be open much longer."

"We sure need to be close to Jesus, don't we, Red?" Becky said, looking up from her book. "But He showed me that He's faithful and we don't need to be afraid if we trust Him."

"What an incredibly wise, little kid," thought Red of his young passenger as they turned the corner to her home.

The sudden stop of the bus made Becky drop all of the papers on her lap. "What's going on here!?" Red exclaimed, as they both stared at the scene about fifty feet in front of them.

"It's Mic and Steely," Becky shouted gleefully. "They're out again," she continued, looking at Red, who had a knowing, and somewhat apprehensive expression on his face.

"I wonder who those guys sitting on the curb are, though? It looks like they've been crying. Let's go slowly," Red continued, putting the bus in gear and moving forward with foreboding. As they drove closer, Steely, who had been praying with Mic, moved toward the bus. "What do you say, Steely?" Red asked hesitantly as Steely climbed aboard.

Becky simply wrapped her arms around her friend. Before Mic and Steely had gone to prison, Becky would sit enraptured at their feet as they would testify of the glories of God and their love for Him. "Becky, let's sit over here," Steely said, motioning for Red to close the door and for Becky to sit on his lap. Holding her close, Steely related the incidents of the last hour.

Mic and Steely had been called by the Lord from their cells and arrived at the front door of the Bracken's building just as the two murderers were descending the stairs leading to the first floor. As Mic and Steely approached the bottom of the stairs, the fleeing men were dropped to the ground in mid-stride by supernatural forces, and ended up in a pile at their feet, immobile. Just as Saul of Tarsus was supernaturally dropped to the ground by the power of God and shown his life, his murders and the plumb line of the Word of God, these men were also, in an instant, given the option to choose life or death.

The immense contrast between their lives and their most recent actions, and the perfection of Jesus the Christ, the Son of God, left them vacant of any argument. They had only two options: to receive the same grace and mercy that Train, Tom, Sally and countless numbers of people through time had received; or to crawl off to some dingy corner and die in their sin, hopelessly lost for eternity.

As the decision was made, God's covenant promise entered their hearts and they were made new. Seething hatred instantly gave way to remorse, repentance and subsequent forgiveness, as both chose to surrender to Jesus. The light of God's love had come to them in one of the darkest moments of their lives, and rivers of weeping were cleansing them at the very moment Red's bus pulled into view.

Becky, Red and Steely sat in silence for some time as the recent events were being sorted in the minds and hearts of each one in that little bus.

"Becky, I know this is hard, especially after losing Tommy," Steely said, looking directly into the tear-stained face of the little girl on his lap, "but you know the times and seasons we have the privilege of living in, and that this will soon all be over. I'm sure your mommy and daddy accomplished all they were supposed to do before they were taken home to be with Jesus. So their work is done.

"But Becky, we still have work to do. God is going to use those of us who are left to bring home those who will hear before it's all over. This life is all about the plans of God and not about ours. We are simply to serve Him and work to bring glory to His Name because He is worthy."

With that, Steely, Red and Becky held each other in the front of the bus for several minutes. Becky, after burying her head in the shoulder of her friend and releasing the tears for the loss of her mommy and daddy and brother, stood and looked through the bus window at the two men sitting on the curb. Then, God's little warrior spoke with the wisdom of ages, seasoned with the grace of heavenly realms.

"If God can forgive them, then I must, too," she said in a weak voice that didn't even begin to show the determination and agape love that were in her heart. "Mommy and Daddy are with Jesus and they would want me to love them as He does." With those words, God's supernatural agape love actually did flood in greater measure into Becky Bracken's heart. She could see the two men as God saw them - helpless before the cross of Christ, needing Him just as she did.

As hosts of heavenly warriors watched, the frail little girl stepped off the bus with Red and Steely and walked toward the men who were still sitting on the curb, their heads bowed. Mic, Red and Steely cried as the two men, wracked with renewed sobs of remorse, listened in awe as God's little girl revealed greater love to them than they had ever known. She extended forgiveness to the seemingly unforgivable.

Demonic forces, who had been forced to stay long enough to hear Becky's words of forgiveness and hope, were scattered with explosive force from their former hosts, having the unenviable task of reporting the double defeat that had taken place that day to their evil superiors.

Since killings were rampant, it wouldn't have done any good to call the already overworked authorities. They probably couldn't or wouldn't come. What was most important was the two men's need to see God's love, so Red and Steely talked to them and made arrangements for them to learn more about their newfound hope and their part in God's plan.

Mic took Becky's hand and started to walk back to Red's bus. Becky, still holding Mic's hand, turned her little head and through eyes flooded with tears, looked up at the window of her former home and weakly mouthed the words: "Good-bye, Mommy and Daddy. I'm gonna see you soon."

Holy ground is important to Me. There is no way for the unclean to enter if I have girded My guardians around My places. However, My back must be turned and My guardians must create breaches when vice is invited into My holy places by My children. Violations of My Word and the spirit of My Word by relaxed attitudes and thoughtless conversation bring forth harm and breach the safety of My protection. Guard your words, guard your relationships, guard your hearts so that I might maintain My presence in your midst.

Because you are My children, there is no place that you are not safe if I have called you there, for I am with you. No one can intrude upon a place I have established for you if My presence is hallowed and welcome. But be assured that I am calling you to be watchmen over your words and your actions that I might join you in all that you do, wherever you are, for your good and My glory.

# CHAPTER THIRTY

*"I know your afflictions and your poverty - yet you are rich! Do not be afraid of what you are about to suffer."*
                                    ***Revelation 2:9a,10a NIV***

*"...upon this rock I will build my church: and the gates of hell shall not prevail against it."*
                                    ***Matthew 16:18b KJV***

Even the youngest of the prospering church had lost all fear of the nighttime. In the midst of chaos, violence and intense persecution, the children of God once again became the true church of Jesus Christ. With the absence of all material distractions, dreams or hopes of a future other than what the heavenly Father directly provided, men and women were free to function in true honor and glory.

Safety was not found in locked doors, weapons, or in physical or mental prowess, but only in Jesus Himself. The only place for a restful spirit was in helpless dependence upon Him for each move. Being one with Him allowed even the most frail to function with a freedom that overcame the mightiest foe. Death, torture, and famine, even though commonplace, could no longer hold the saints of God in bondage to fear. "To live is Christ, to die is gain" was the cherished scripture of those truly alive to their Lord.

Far from being a fearful, huddling mass, the heart of the church pulsated with the life of Jesus Christ as its source. Activated only by His command, anointed by His very breath, stimulated only by the desire for His will to be accomplished, purposed for service to Him only - men, women and even the very young defied all logic to walk in the miracle-holding power of their Lord.

The hospital that the Lord established through Carlyle Henderson was determined to be the most efficient command center from which they could continue to serve the needy. Prayer proved to be the most effective, and more often than not, the only medicine for the physical and spiritual ills of those who walked in, were carried through or were left abandoned outside the unlocked front doors.

Teams of believers of all ages, when led by the Lord, would walk through literal battle zones, by-passing checkpoints using "heavenly language" to non-English speaking troops, or even drive on "miracle" gas to destinations known only by Him, to accomplish His ordained purposes for His glory alone. Sometimes, these believers seemed to be invisible when it was needed. Other times, invisible shields thwarted any aggressive action, whether it was stray bullets, traveling mobs, or crazed individuals roaming the streets to kill or be killed.

What proved most interesting was the amount of grace shown by God as He was given charge of every emotion. Freedom replaced feelings of loss. Enemies and tormentors - once they repented and came to Jesus - were loved as family for God's sake. The vilest of sinners was held closest in prayer for his best interest - the salvation of his soul. Like the first century church facing the lions in the arena, God's true children rejoiced amidst horrors as they anticipated the joy they would experience when they went home to be with the Father, which replaced the mourning of personal loss. Death in any form could not affect those who had bought gold refined in the fires of affliction and tribulation.

The unstoppable forces of love, praise and selflessness pierced the hearts of all but the most hardened. Children were often used by God to enter the deepest, darkest areas of the vile hovels of humanity. In one such instance, Tammy Casper - a frail, little five year old girl with naturally curly, blonde ringlets that hung to her waist, rosy cheeks and an infectious smile - was awakened at 1:15 a.m. by two heavenly warriors and told to get dressed in something warm. Accompanied by her two friends, she held their hands and talked of wondrous things as they walked twelve blocks from the hospital to The Warehouse, a converted shipping storage facility which served as a haven for only the most decadent. The small, lone, seemingly helpless figure standing at the head of the stairs on the rim of the dance floor, brought silence to the hundreds of startled patrons.

Standing in the calm presence of God Himself, Tammy waited quietly until total silence fell, then finally spoke: "The judgments of God are about to fall on those who are here tonight. He is, at this moment, giving you the opportunity to choose the love of Jesus Christ the Lord, or to be lost for eternity. Choose you this day whom you will serve."

With that, Tammy waited for the Holy Spirit to move. Out of the hundreds gathered there, only five women knelt and tearfully surrendered. Tides of jeers, laughter and cursing followed Tammy as she took the hands of her tall invisible friends and moved through the leering throng toward the door.

As the three crossed the intersection of Walker Street and 13th Avenue, a loud explosion and accompanying blazing inferno occurred behind them. Moments after Tammy left the warehouse, multiple bombs planted by a rejected lover of many in the building detonated simultaneously, taking all inside to their eternal fate. The next morning, Tammy was found sleeping peacefully on a corner mat in the hospital lobby.

I have called you to a Holy Place, a place that cannot be touched by those who would come against you. And still you take deep concern at the seeming power demonstrated by those who oppose My Word.

If you would only receive what I have for you. If you would only look to Me, know Me and listen to what I have said, and am saying; you would never fear again. How could you be afraid after you have seen Me? How could you be afraid once you have beheld My power?

I have called you to an intimate relationship with Me so that you may know Me. But you do not come. I wait and you do not come. I prepare a feast and you eat from the streets. If only you could see. If only you would learn that I have not called you to a place of fear and need. I have called you to a Holy Place. A place filled with Me, where all your needs are met. A place that cannot be affected by the world around you.

Come. Come now and learn of Me. Come to My Holy Place.

# CHAPTER THIRTY-ONE

*"You prepare a table before me in the presence of my enemies."*                              *Psalm 23:5a NIV*

*"...Blessed are they which are called unto the marriage supper of the Lamb."*
*Revelation 19:9a KJV*

"Train, I've looked around and there doesn't seem to be any food," Merry said more quizzically than fearfully or in a complaining manner.

Food was just one of the Lord's marvelous blessings since world havoc had become more heated. The multiplication of what little anyone was able to present as an offering to the Lord became an everyday occurrence - just like the loaves and the fishes of long ago. Some of the most unusual, and sometimes even comical meals allowed the family of believers to see not only the magnitude of their Provider, but also His sense of humor in the midst of chaos. Mealtime was always fascinating, but also typified daily the life of total trust and absolute dependence that each member of Christ's bride embraced.

Sometimes, in somewhat easier times, when the Brackens and others would assist the survival units at a crisis site, they would arrive with next to nothing. Unbelievers became more than interested observers, as the simple meals never seemed to run out. It was a great way to tell of God's keeping power.

People even waited for God to tell them when to eat, which was sometimes in the late evening or early morning hours. Each meal began with absolute faith as its main ingredient. The "family" would prepare the table with whatever was available, no matter how meager or odd. Then, they joined

261

together to humbly wait on the Lord after they had blessed the items and broke or divided them, whenever possible, as a remembrance of the Lord. Conversation, prayer, praise, loving interaction and deep-seated joy ensued.

In the midst of communing with the Lord, someone would be led to start the meal. As they took their portion, or fed it to a young baby or child, they would simply pass it on. There was always enough so that everyone came away satisfied; and rarely was there anything, not even crumbs, left over. If there were any leftovers, however, they were stored and more often than not, some hungry individual would come in off the street and once more the Lord's provision for sustenance – and more importantly, for eternal life - was gloriously manifested.

One day, the only offering that could be found was part of a Hershey's chocolate almond bar, which Tyler Smathers had found in one of his storage boxes. All sat in the large hospital cafeteria and looked at the small portion sitting in the middle of the vast U-shaped main meal table that had been built early on to accommodate the continually growing numbers of people served.

After the candy bar was broken in two during the blessing, Tom Landerfold felt that he should break those two pieces into even smaller ones. Then, he took some and passed the small bowl to the next person. Joy and praise filled the hearts and lips of everyone present as the contents of the bowl satisfied the hunger of whoever requested it.

The most glorious part of this provision was that the almonds took on a very fresh-roasted taste and became much larger and more plentiful as the "meal" continued; and the chocolate took on a heavenly consistency, somewhat like one would imagine manna would look, feel and taste. As an additional testimony, no one experienced hunger until the next meal "arrived," which proclaimed resoundingly, to the glory of

God, the nutritional properties He could provide in one small portion of one candy bar to feed almost five hundred people.

Other interesting meals consisted of a small bowl of "never-ending" mashed potatoes and one grape that became bowls of grapes and juice; or a single head of lettuce that multiplied progressively into a bountiful salad with ripe fruit and fresh vegetables as it was passed from one thankful believer to another.

One Saturday, a truck stalled in front of the hospital, with its angry, fearful driver complaining that all of his steaks, which were on their way to city officials, would be ruined because of the heat.  Then, he said they might as well be thrown away here as anywhere else, which provided a scrumptious steak dinner for the children of God.

The steaks seemed almost incidental, considering the main reason for the truck's motor trouble.  The driver, upon seeing the joy in those whose lifestyle he did not understand and somehow knowing it was no accident that he stopped in front of the hospital, gave his life to the One they served.  Everyone rejoiced and praised the Most High God for yet another miracle.

"Something's different," Train said to Crystal, who was holding a baby whose mother and father had just been reported missing.  "I think that our Father has something new in mind for us this evening," he continued, as he moved toward the ever-enlarging crowd that had been "called" to eat, even though there appeared to be no food.  "Merry, are you sure that there is nothing anywhere available for the offering?"

"I've asked everyone and looked everywhere," Merry stated with a glint in her eye, also feeling that they might be on the threshold of something supernatural.

"O.K., have everyone sit down and we'll begin to rejoice," Train said,  "This could be fun."

Tremendous displays of love, hugs and joyous sounds erupted as pockets of people surrounded Mic and Steely when they arrived. The same happened for Pastor Wickham and many others who had been individually led to come to the "meal" this evening from all parts of the city - even the world! Carlyle Henderson had gone to Australia to avoid those who relentlessly pursued him; but now he had "supernaturally arrived" at Mercy General Hospital to be with his old friends, just as Mic and Steely did. Waco brought many former gang members, some who had joined the army to fight for their country in various humanitarian roles.

It was a wondrous time of fellowship and praise as some families were reunited; and God's family, in unison, sensed that something marvelous was about to happen. After the initial greetings had subsided somewhat, people gravitated to the tables until all had been seated. Train stood to speak.

"Our lives are blessed far beyond what any one of us deserves because we've seen God intervene in our lives time and time again," he began, as those present unanimously agreed in a variety of expressions. Each, at that moment, was given a supernatural revelation of his or her life matched up against the plumb line of God; and if it hadn't been for the accompanying grace of God and for Train breaking the moment as he continued, many would have found a very familiar place under the table or alone elsewhere to meet with their Lord because of His great mercy towards them.

"So each of us has learned to anticipate only God's goodness, no matter what the circumstances appear to be. Tonight is no exception," he continued, looking at Crystal, Becky, Mic, Steely, Morgan Wickham, Mark Deider, Carlyle Henderson and many more who were family and were seated in the room. "It seems that the Lord has chosen to provide for us directly from His hand in a way that no one at present knows, for there is no food to be found anywhere to offer Him."

Spontaneous applause erupted, for the group anticipated something momentous about to happen. Spirit-led excitement was evident in everyone as trusting believers looked and smiled at one another.

"It is especially exciting in view of our friends here," he continued after things calmed down, and motioned toward those who would not normally have been anywhere near the hospital. "Our friends seem to have all been drawn here for this precise moment. Let's pray."

As each closed his eyes and bowed his head to pray, Train continued, "Father, we thank You for what you are about to perform before us and we simply wait..." Train stopped in mid-sentence as aromas he had not smelled for many, many months, or years - some were even unrecognizable - filled the air. Without opening his eyes, he could tell that others could smell them too, as quiet expressions of amazement began to surface as they prayed.

Suddenly, little Margie Whitney exclaimed excitedly, "O, Mommy, look!" And with that, all who were present opened their eyes. Cries of praise and astounding gratitude filled the room as the gathering beheld the sumptuous feast their Father in heaven had laid before them.

The finest catering service in the best of times could not have matched the array of delicacies that were presented on the heavenly plates set before each individual. Meals with each person's favorite foods were perfectly prepared for them to enjoy. To further enhance that wonder, the tables had been adorned with the finest of linen and silver and candles - something no one thought about much in these times of scarcity. Altogether, it was a wonder almost too incredible to behold.

The miracles of God were continually declared as the guests of the Lord's feast ate and shared and sampled each other's foods; and as they praised and sang in small groups or as one large group, led by the Holy Spirit. At times, prayer lasted for hours as people moved to wherever the Lord directed them.

When they returned to their seats, a new meal, on clean plates, would be available to them. If they chose to eat little or nothing, it didn't matter; for everything remained fresh or hot, and accessible whenever and in whatever quantities needed. As the evening progressed into the next two days and evenings, the gathering slept, worshiped, prayed and delighted in fellowship with their God and with each other.

Camille Thurston was more than likely most accurate when she bubbled to Train and Crystal, "This is probably what the Marriage Supper of the Lamb will be like!"

*********************************

"The troops seem to have dispersed, Colonel," Captain Patterson of the Peace Keeping Forces reported as he stood before his superior officer at the command post that had been established on the corner of 34th and Wilson.

"All right, let's move in and finish this foolishness once and for all," Colonel Lassiter demanded. "Remember, no survivors," he added as almost an afterthought, while strapping his sidearm to his waist. "I can't wait until all of these b_____ are annihilated," he muttered under his breath.

Throughout the land, similar orders had been given to capture or kill anyone not openly embracing a one-world concept and all it entailed. After all, human potential and all the new, innovative peace programs provided the answer for all of man's needs. That left no room for these ignorant fools.

266

For three days and nights, several thousand troops and all the associated weaponry needed for a major battle had been positioned around the hospital, which was the known "hideout" for the remnant of Christians who freely roamed the city doing "who knows what" to supposedly hinder the plans of the government. The Christians' army - troops that came in unsuspected and out of nowhere - held the peacekeeping forces at bay. These troops, with the most sophisticated equipment, (some pieces had never even been seen before,) were so organized, so large in number; and so intimidating that the Colonel dared not move against them.

These "standoffs" were taking place in all parts of the world. This created a great deal of worldwide interest as these events were covered by the media day and night with "instant updates." Now it seemed to be over, for the morning light revealed that the massive, protective line around Mercy General, and around all of the other such "fortresses" had, for some inexplicable reason, silently dispersed during the night. The "army" seemed to have disappeared. In reality, heavenly hosts simply resumed their positions in another dimension and went back to observing everything, unseen by those operating in the flesh.

"Take no prisoners" was the direct order as tanks, jeeps and troops advanced toward the hospital entrances. Assault troops, positioned on the roof, had eagerly awaited this moment; and in uniform efficiency, swept through every window or hatch they could find.

After several minutes of silence, Colonel Lassiter yelled into his telephone, "It's too quiet in there. Somebody tell me what's going on!"

After a few more seemingly interminable, quiet moments, the small hand-held telephone came to life. "You're not going to believe this Colonel, but...but..." There was a hesitation, almost fear, in the voice on the other end. "There's no one here, Sir. I mean, no one. It looks like they evacuated in the middle of their meal. The food is still warm and boy, were they eating good!"

Obviously stunned by his surroundings, the voice on the telephone trailed off into nothingness.

**********************************

From their hiding place, Pastor Walter Fairchild, who had taken over His Holiness Christian Fellowship, Stephen MacDougal, the president of God's People for the Restoration of Morality, and several of its other members had watched the television coverage of the sieges with great scrutiny. They knew that the outcome of the local siege would give them good direction for their next confrontation as underground warriors against the state. Excited whispers turned to eerie silence, however, when it was reported that there was no one inside the hospital. Not ones to let anything stop what they believed they must do, speculation as to the Christians' method of escape and debate on the next plan of action followed in short order.

"Wait, wait, listen. Here's another update...quiet!" Stephen said, drawing everyone's attention to the television reporter.

Gloria Manly, world news correspondent and vicious opponent of anything that resembled Christianity and anyone who didn't believe as she did, had taken great delight in being selected for this special assignment. She, and so many others involved in the worldwide peace societies and their affiliates, had long been praying for the removal of those unwanted elements of society that were holding back the beginning of a pure and rational society designed for the betterment of all personkind.

"We have late-breaking reports of the disappearance of Christians all over the world. It seems..." she hesitated, "that our prayers have been answered. Could this be..." she hesitated again, almost too excited to speak, visibly struggling to contain her joy. "Could this be our quantum leap into the next phase of personkind?" Then, regaining her composure, she said, "Stay tuned. We'll have another update, plus global news and weather at 10:00."


Epilogue Follows

# EPILOGUE

The previous story attempts to relate the difference between those who have a relationship with the God of the universe and live their lives His way, for His purposes; and those who don't. Its purpose was to stimulate you to examine your life to see where you fit in God's scheme of things. Now, it is up to you to decide what to do with the comparisons you may have encountered. You have a choice: to examine God's Word (The Bible) to find the answer to your questions and determine to live your life by that answer no matter what it takes, or push the questioning in your heart aside and remain the same. The choice you make will have an eternal impact on you.

As you read the Bible, you'll see that God never intended true Christianity to be a religion. It is not even a belief system. God, in essence, said: "You'll never make it doing it your way, but you will make it if you do it My way. Just accept what Jesus did for you on the cross. You can't change yourself; but because of what Jesus did, I'll covenant with you to change your very nature." If you accept His offer, He will change you on the inside, so that you not only reflect those changes on the outside, but you'll be prepared to live with Him forever.

*"But without faith it is impossible to please and be satisfactory to Him. For whoever would come near to God must [necessarily] believe that God exists and that He is the rewarder of those who earnestly and diligently seek Him [out]."* Hebrews 11:6

To those of you who have always wondered about God, maybe even questioned if there really is a God, I would like to present the following scenario to you.

Suppose that there really is a God. I don't mean one of many gods created by the imaginations of man, but a Ruler and Creator of all things seen and unseen. A one and only

271

Supreme Being who set unchangeable laws into motion, which govern His creations.

What if this Creator decided that one of His creations would be a man and woman upon whom He could lavish His unlimited resources and eternal love. They would take part in all the workings of His future creations and have the privilege of interacting with Him for all eternity. However, one of the stipulations of the laws established for His creation was that man and woman were to continually look to and receive from the Creator everything they needed to exist. The Creator would continually give from His unlimited bounty - with a Creator's knowledge of what is always best for His creation.

Suppose that after man and woman were created, they chose not to receive only from their Creator; but decided to do some things for themselves. In essence, they were turning their backs on the pure ways of the Creator, and thus violating His unchangeable laws that had been set in motion. In doing so, they became a mutation of the pure creation (because of the violation of established laws,) unable to function in the atmosphere and surroundings of their Creator any longer. In other words, the nature of the creation was altered completely and they were unable to function as originally intended.

A somewhat simplistic example of this might be a computer that has been impregnated with a virus. The computer looks and functions somewhat the same; but its nature has, in essence, been altered. It cannot be relied upon to perform as it was intended to until the virus is removed, because it is no longer pure. Any program generated from that computer, because of its impure state, will also be impure and incapable of functioning in a pure atmosphere, as it did before the virus was introduced.

Let's say, however, that the Creator (God) loved His creation (man and woman) and chose to provide a single means by which they could choose to enter back into the state of

272

perfection that God required in order that they might live in union with Him. In other words, they had the opportunity to be made pure again, as they had been originally. As in the example of the computer, an outside influence that had the power to recognize and totally destroy the virus would be introduced into the impure computer, changing its nature back to one that is pure and able to function as before.

Well, in very simple terms, that is what really happened long before you and I were born. The rebellion in our original ancestors (Adam and Eve) has been transmitted from generation to generation to the present time. That rebellion destroyed the ability for man to remain part of God's design as He had originally planned. Man's pure nature had to be re-established before he could function freely, in God's purposes, in the realms in which God functioned.

God provided a way - the only way - the man, Jesus. This man was like no other man. The pure Spirit of God was in Him. He lived a life of perfection to the end, fulfilling the requirements of the established laws. Three days after He was killed, God raised Him from the dead. Anyone who acknowledges his or her need for new life by accepting this act as God's provision of reconciliation invokes all of the covenants, laws and promises of God in his or her own life; and is made pure in the eyes of God. You are literally changed on the inside. The virus, as it were, is totally removed and the original pure life is re-established by God, His way.

*"Therefore if any person is [ingrafted] in Christ (the Messiah) he is a new creation (a new creature altogether); the old [previous moral and spiritual condition] has passed away. Behold, the fresh and new has come!"*     *II Cor. 5:17*

In other words, the real issue has nothing to do with religion, doing good works or individual beliefs, as you may have been taught. It has to do with the impure nature of man being made pure again on God's terms.

273

No one is going to be separated from God for eternity (will spend eternity in hell) because they lived a bad life or did bad things. By the same token, no one will spend eternity with God because they have lived a good life or did good things. It is not about being good or bad, right or wrong. It's about accepting God's provision to have your inherited nature changed, so that you are capable of living in God's places and functioning on His terms. It is that simple, and that wonderful.

All men and women have a choice to make: they can either accept the single way that God has provided for them to be changed so that they may live in the presence of God after they die; or they can simply do nothing about the way they are at present, and remain separated from God for eternity. Which do you choose?

Now you can say, "I don't believe any of this - it's too ridiculous." Well, in doing so, you have made a choice to remain as you are in the state of rebellion. In fact, your statement confirms your rebellious nature. You decide once more as Adam and Eve decided; to do it in your own way and rely on your own understanding.

However, if you see clearly that you need to be changed and are willing to submit totally to God, He will do a wonderful work in you. The Bible says in Romans 10:9, *"If you acknowledge and confess with your lips that Jesus is Lord and in your heart believe (adhere to, trust in and rely on the truth) that God raised Him from the dead, you will be saved."*

If you openly acknowledge to God that Jesus Christ is the single provision of God to reconcile man to Himself and you surrender yourself to Him, you will be saved. In other words, you admit that you have need of a Savior, and that Jesus is that Savior; and then trust that as God physically raised Jesus from the dead, He will remove your dead nature and also make you alive inside.

God will set in motion His covenant promises for He said: "*A new heart will I give you and a new spirit will I put within you, and I will take away the stony heart out of your flesh and give you a heart of flesh. And I will put my Spirit within you and cause you to walk in My statutes, and you shall heed My ordinances and do them.*" *Ezekiel 36:26-27* You will be transformed from your old nature, which separates you from God, to a new nature which lines up with God's ways and makes you able to fellowship with God forever.

If that is your desire - your real heart's desire - pray something like this. (Remember you are, in essence, saying: "From this moment, God, I lay down my way of doing things and will learn and submit to all of Your ways.")

Dear God - I realize that I have inherited a nature that is in rebellion (sin) and that it needs to be changed.

I believe that You sent Jesus Christ to die for my sin, and that You have raised Him from the dead.

I choose to give You my old, rebellious nature (die) and I ask You to give me Your new life (raise me to live for You.)

Forgive me of my sin (rebellion,) my desire to do things my way; and give me a desire to do things Your way from now on. Jesus, be the Lord of my life.

Thank You!

Signed,

_____

Tell someone who will understand - a Bible-believing pastor or a Christian friend.

To the remnant Christians who desires to live
the passionate life of Christ

To those who really hear
what the Lord is saying in these times

Walk in Christ's kind of love. Love the church and love people - not some mealy-mouthed, worldly kind of love, but love as Jesus did. Give your lives for the good of others even if you look foolish doing it. God is with you and it is the way to absolute freedom.

Those who have set aside what most of the church and the world call important are labeled misfits of some sort. Walking and listening to the Lord as your priority in life is a road that few believers choose to take. Seeking after God's anointing and choosing to move only when His presence is with you rarely enters the mind of most Christians. To some of you, however, it is the only gospel that makes sense. Your life is not your own and you know it.

Throughout the Word of God, you are in good company, even if you feel very much alone in some of today's fellowships. Find good counsel - people who believe in your calling - and go for it, no matter what the cost. Listen to what Paul says in I Corinthians 4 from The Message Bible:

*"It seems to me that God has put us who bear this message on a stage in a theater in which no one wants to buy a ticket. We're something everyone stands around and stares at, like an accident in the street. We're the Messiah's misfits. You might be sure of yourselves, but we live in the midst of frailties and uncertainties. You might be well-thought-of by others, but we're mostly kicked around. Much of the time we don't have enough to eat, we wear patched and threadbare clothes, we get doors slammed in our faces, and we pick up odd jobs anywhere we can to eke out a living. When they call us names, we say,*

'God bless you.' When they spread rumors about us, we put in a good word for them. We're treated like garbage, potato peelings from the culture's kitchen. And it's not getting any better.

"I'm not writing all this as a neighborhood scold just to make you feel rotten. I'm writing as a father to you, my children. I love you and want you to grow up well, not spoiled. There are a lot of people around who can't wait to tell you what you've done wrong, but there aren't many fathers willing to take the time and effort to help you grow up. It was as Jesus helped me proclaim God's Message to you that I became your father. I'm not, you know, asking you to do anything I'm not already doing myself."

As far as some members of the church of that day were concerned, Paul's life was a failure. He was in prison; how could that be God's hand? The fact is, however, that he was in the very center of God's will. Most felt that he had not really heard from God for his directions, but he had. They could only see his life with their reasoning minds, not from God's perspective.

If you are following hard after God, you will feel the sting of people who have not heard the heralding call to holiness. Your life will make little sense, especially to those in leadership who have been chosen for their business aplomb rather than their spiritual "selling out." Be encouraged! You are a forerunner, and called as a scout to mark the path of "freedom in Christ" when the world - and most of the church - will walk around wide-eyed, drooling at the mouth from fear as times change. Good business sense will be a pale companion when lives will depend on counsel from the heart of God to make it through perilous times.

If your heart breaks when you see people falling back into the world because they have fallen through the cracks in some congregation when no one was there for them in their need, you are in the company of Jesus Himself. If you see the foolishness of pastors needing to become "cheerleaders" to motivate their people to good works, and good words from the pulpit never reaching the "inner being" of the people in the pews so that real heart change is evident, then God is showing you a church that has chosen to try to maintain status quo when He is calling for more. Because you see the heralding and are responding by repenting of your lack of love for God's ways, you are in training to care as He does. Until the church in general catches up with His heart, you will be branded as somewhat unusual. Get used to it. The anointing of God to deeply impact lives and hold them for as long as needed never came cheap; in these times it will cost you everything.

Forgive those who would attempt to stop your calling, pray for God's mercy toward them; and by all means, continue to minister. Don't attempt to change those who don't yet see God's season or those who choose to remain cold. Find a fellowship that is moving in God's direction and become involved, even if you have to change locations. Time is too short and the harvest is too ready. It is important that you do not become involved in religious games.

God was motivating Jeremiah to sell out and learn His kind of strength for the race he was to run when he was told: *"If you have raced with men on foot and they have tired you out, then how can you compete with horses? And if [you take to flight] in a land of peace where you feel secure, then what will you do [when you tread the tangled maze of jungle haunted by lions] in the swelling and flooding of the Jordan?"* Jer. 12:5 Amp

The "race" that our Lord is calling for in preparation for what lies ahead is a non-compromising, your-life-is-not-your-own, everything for Jesus kind of commitment. That's the way it was for Jesus Himself. That's the way it was for the first century church. That's the call now - to walk a passionate, Christ-like life. It is the crucified life.

279

The embracing of a crucified life has always been God's way for His true believers to find and move in accordance with His heart. He is calling things back to that standard. Be encouraged if you are responding. Do not let anyone put out the fire of that kind of love, no matter how reasonable the words sound or how foolish you may feel. You are not alone even though it may seem like it. Make sure that you are heading toward loving as Jesus did and submit to the training. Embrace all of the challenges you are going through for the love of your Lord and for the good of others who will need you. You are learning to "compete with the horses" and in training for what lies ahead on God's timetable.

Visit our Web site, www.awhitestone.com, for additional tools to be able to live Christ's passionate life in your world.

### To those of you who have said you will serve God, but find that your life is relatively ineffective

I ask you this. How does your Christian life compare to the Christian life of the first century church? Better still, how does your life compare to the life that Jesus exhibited to a world that was perishing in its sin? I John 2:6 in the Amplified version states: *"Whoever says that he abides in Him ought [as a personal debt] to walk and conduct himself in the same way in which He walked and conducted Himself."*

A study of the Word of God as it is written - not as it is interpreted by twentieth-century Christians who haven't beheld the glory of God in their own lives - rings with the truth that the life of a true follower of Jesus Christ is to be lived in the same way He lived - totally dead to self, and living only for the Lord. Stop and truly ponder that concept. As you read it, let the Word of God overcome the teachings of man's self-centered gospel. Don't let the words themselves be nullified in their impact because of the loose usage and weak understanding that have been applied to them. Let the Holy Spirit quicken to you the truth of what is required of you if you claim to be a follower of Jesus Christ.

The time has come to put an end to the self-centered, self-serving attitude that has permeated and nullified the Gospel of Jesus Christ in this land. There is no power to overcome because we do not have the presence - the real Shekinah glory - of God in our lives. We lack this glory because His presence will not reside in dirty vessels. The dirt of self, of the world, of pride, and much, much more is all that is exhibited to the perishing; and none of that will bring people to reconciliation with God.

II Corinthians 5:14-21 in the Amplified version says:

*"For the love of Christ controls and urges and impels us, because we are of the opinion and conviction that [if] One died for all, then all died;*

*"And He died for all, so that all those who live might live no longer to and for themselves, but to and for Him Who died and was raised again for their sake.*

*"Consequently, from now on we estimate and regard no one from a [purely] human point of view [in terms of natural standards of value]. [No] even though we once did estimate Christ from a human viewpoint and as a man, yet now [we have such knowledge of Him that] we know Him no longer [in terms of the flesh].*

*"Therefore if any person is [ingrafted] in Christ (the Messiah) he is a new creation (a new creature altogether); the old [previous moral and spiritual condition] has passed away. Behold, the fresh and new has come!*

*"But all things are from God, Who through Jesus Christ reconciled us to Himself [received us into favor, brought us into harmony with Himself] and gave to us the ministry of*

*reconciliation [that by word and deed we might aim to bring others into harmony with Him].*

*"It was God [personally present] in Christ, reconciling and restoring the world to favor with Himself, not counting up and holding against [men] their trespasses [but cancelling them], and committing to us the message of reconciliation (of the restoration to favor).*

*"So we are Christ's ambassadors, God making His appeal as it were through us. We [as Christ's personal representatives] beg you for His sake to lay hold of the divine favor [now offered you] and be reconciled to God.*

*"For our sake He made Christ [virtually] to be sin Who knew no sin, so that in and through Him we might become [endued with, viewed as being in, and examples of] the righteousness of God [what we ought to be, approved and acceptable and in right relationship with Him, by His goodness]."*

The above verses leave little room for discussion as to what our purpose on this earth is after we have received salvation through Jesus Christ. Once we have received Christ and made Him Lord, our purpose is to lay down our lives, to become like Him in thought, word and deed, to see others as He saw them; and then, to exhibit that life of love before them so that they might see Jesus in us and be reconciled to the Father. In other words, we must allow Him to live His life through us. Any other Gospel is the distorted gospel of man. The other gospel of good works leads to a life of salt that has lost its saltness, to be trampled underfoot by men. It will not and cannot change men's hearts because the life-changing Spirit of God is not in it.

Where do you stand? Who do people see when they see your life daily? Do they see the Jesus of the Bible? They should, or else you are not really following Christ, as you say you are.

How do you perceive those who have not met Jesus Christ as Lord of their lives? Are they enemies? Is the salvation of their souls your deepest care, your only reason for being alive? It was for Jesus. He mingled with, and then He died for, the worst of sinners. His love for those who cursed Him, rejected Him and then crucified Him was so great, that He even pleaded with His Father for them as He hung on the cross.

That's the passionate kind of love that has been given to you and me. Do we have any choice but to give that same love to our neighbor, the abortionist, the pornographer, the homosexual? If you want to become emotional over an issue, ask God to show you the reality of hell and the eternal fate of those going there. If you want to become militant about anything, get militant in prayer for a church body that would rather talk about God, than *meet with God* to become like Jesus.

If you realize that you are not really living the life that God desires you to live - one that is totally dead to your own desires, needs, and way of doing things and alive only to Jesus, so that others might see Him in your life - then you need to repent, recommit every area of your life to the Lordship of Jesus Christ; and start to receive His life, His ways, His thoughts, and His desires. Do it now, for time is very short and many need to see Jesus in your life. That's where we are seeking the Lord to take us. We all may be the only opportunity someone will have to recognize Him.

What Savior will others see - the Jesus of the Bible or angry, sin-laden, condescending hypocrites with no compassion for them or for others? Lord, help us! And He will!

*"Choose you this day whom you will serve..."*
                              *Joshua 24:15*

## What now?

First of all, how many of your friends need to read this book, and what can you do to help them accomplish that? Then, what about you and your representation of Jesus to the world in which you live? How does your life line up with the lives of the characters you have just read about, or the wonderful saints who have gone before you? How does it compare to the pattern of living that Jesus gave us?

You have just completed step one in the series that is designed to help you live your life with the kind of passion that Jesus had. You have experienced the manner in which you are called to live and respond to situations and challenges that present themselves. How would you fare if given the same kinds of challenges or the very real perils that lie ahead?

Step two, our Living Christ's Passionate Life guidebook, will walk you through the heart positions that the Lord desires for you, so that you can personally experience an exciting and thrilling life full of freedom and power that:

1) Is the only proper and fitting response to the life, death, and resurrection of Jesus Christ

2) Is the proper representation of Jesus and a display of responsible citizenship to a world that is dying and out of answers

3) Is the highest form of praise that can be given to the Lord as you live an honorable life and emulate Him

4) Is the proper response to the call of the Holy Spirit to prepare your heart as a waiting bride for the return of Jesus

5) Is the only way to overcome the perilous times and seasons in which we are living, so that you can fulfill your purpose in life.

For copies of A White Stone, the Living Christ's Passionate Life guidebook, and other ministry tools, visit our website: www.awhitestone.com.